"What's your name?"

Roman asked, and saw a different kind of fear move across her face.

"I don't know."

"What do you mean, you don't know?"

She reached toward the knot beneath her scalp. "Somehow I hurt my head. When I came to, I couldn't remember who I was or where I'd been going."

Roman almost sneered. "Amnesia is a lame excuse, lady. Try again."

She turned toward him. "I'm almost afraid to ask, but are you a cop?"

"I'm no cop. I'm a private detective."

She sighed. "I wish I knew if I could afford you. I'd hire you to figure out who I am."

Dear Reader,

It's month two of our special fifteenth anniversary celebration, and that means more great reading for you. Just look what's in store.

Amnesia! It's one of the most popular plot twists around, and well it should be. All of us have probably wished, just for a minute, that we could start over again, be somebody else...fall in love all over again as if it were the first time. For three of our heroines this month, whether they want it or not, the chance is theirs. Start with Sharon Sala's *Roman's Heart,* the latest in her fabulous trilogy, THE JUSTICE WAY. Then check out *The Mercenary and the Marriage Vow* by Doreen Roberts. This book carries our new TRY TO REMEMBER flash—just so you won't forget about it! And then, sporting our MEN IN BLUE flash (because the hero's the kind of cop we could all fall in love with), there's *While She Was Sleeping* by Diane Pershing.

Of course, we have three other great books this month, too. Be sure to pick up Beverly Barton's *Emily and the Stranger,* and don't worry. Though this book isn't one of them, Beverly's extremely popular heroes, THE PROTECTORS, will be coming your way again soon. Kylie Brant is back with *Friday's Child,* a FAMILIES ARE FOREVER title. Not only will the hero and heroine win your heart, wait 'til you meet little Chloe. Finally, welcome new author Sharon Mignerey, who makes her debut with *Cassidy's Courtship.*

And, of course, don't forget to come back next month for more of the best and most excitingly romantic reading around, right here in Silhouette Intimate Moments.

Leslie Wainger
Senior Editor and Editorial Coordinator

Please address questions and book requests to:
Silhouette Reader Service
U.S.: 3010 Walden Ave., P.O. Box 1325, Buffalo, NY 14269
Canadian: P.O. Box 609, Fort Erie, Ont. L2A 5X3

Sharon Sala

ROMAN'S HEART

Published by Silhouette Books
America's Publisher of Contemporary Romance

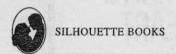

SILHOUETTE BOOKS

RECYCLED PAPER · RECYCLED PAPER

ISBN 0-373-07859-5

ROMAN'S HEART

SHARON SALA

is a child of the country. As a farmer's daughter, her vivid imagination made solitude a thing to cherish. During her adult life, she learned to survive by taking things one day at a time. An inveterate dreamer, she yearned to share the stories her imagination created. For Sharon, her dreams have come true, and she claims one of her greatest joys is when her stories become tools for healing.

This book is about survivors.

No matter how difficult we try to make it, life is simple. It's just a matter of identifying our weaknesses and surviving the trials and tribulations that come with them. Some of us persevere. Some of us fail.

During my lifetime, I have met many people whom I admire. People who've endured and overcome great odds to become the person God meant them to be.

I have been blessed in knowing a man like that.

To a man who has faced true and deep despair—a man who knows better than most what it takes to survive.

To Bobby.

This book is for you.

Chapter 1

It was the sensation of needles poking into the skin on her face that brought the woman to, and when she opened her eyes, the scream that came out of her mouth made a nearby hawk take flight. Framed by the panorama of majestic mountains clothed in the new green of spring, the view was breathtaking. But it wasn't the view that had caused her reaction. It was the binding sensation of the parachute strapped to her body, as well as the fact that she was caught in the highest branches of a towering pine and dangling far above the ground.

In terror, she grabbed for the straps. The sudden movement sent her swaying in the breeze like a flapping shirt on a clothesline. And the weight of her body, coupled with the abruptness of the motion, made the fabric of the parachute rip even more, sending her slipping through the branches to the ground below. She looked down in horror, knowing that if she fell now, it would more than likely kill her.

God help me.

At that moment the fabric snagged and then held on another

great branch, stopping her dangerous descent. With her heart thundering in her eardrums, she closed her eyes in a silent prayer of thanksgiving. In the blessed quiet that followed, a terrifying realization hit. Yes, she was stranded in a tree and dangling from a parachute, and as soon as she'd opened her eyes, a small part of her had accepted that fact without wondering why or how it had happened. But just now, when she'd been about to give thanks to the Almighty for still breathing, a great gap in her memory became fact.

"No! Oh, no!"

She reached for her face, testing the shape and texture of each feature, as if touching it for the first time. She wished for a mirror...or anything that would give back a reflection, because right now she didn't remember who she was.

Stifling a quick shaft of fear, she reminded herself that it wasn't a name she needed right now. What she needed was a way to get down.

She reached toward a nearby branch, and again the movement sent her into motion. Twisting and spinning like a yo-yo on a tangled string, she grabbed onto the straps, willing herself not to panic.

When she could think without wanting to shriek, she began another approach. Maybe she should consider her injuries. The ones she already had were miserable but minor. Adding more could be the difference between being able to walk away from this and dying.

Okay, where does it hurt the worst?

And then she almost laughed. As best she could tell, the answer was *everywhere*. The question shouldn't have been where does it hurt, but how much?

One thing was for certain. Her lower lip was throbbing, and there was a coppery taste in her mouth that made her stomach roll. She reached toward the ache with the tip of her finger, wincing when it came in contact with what felt like a cut.

She closed her eyes and groaned, then leaned to one side and spit, unwilling to swallow her own blood. And while her skin stung as if it had been flailed, the throbbing pain in her head was far worse. It was no surprise to discover a large knot just above the hairline. But when her hand came away bloody, as well, she jerked back in shock. Again, the motion sent her swaying precariously within the branches.

"Easy, easy," she muttered, deliberately taking deep breaths and exhaling slowly after each one. When the movement had ceased without her having fallen any farther, she relaxed.

As she continued to dangle helplessly above the ground, a stiff breeze came up, blasting its way through the pines and blowing her hair into her eyes. When she ventured another look at the sun sinking into the western horizon, panic returned. It would be dark soon. Time was running out.

And while she feared the act would be hopeless, she began to shout, knowing full well that there probably wasn't a human being within miles who could hear.

"Help!" she called, shouting over and over until the word was a scream and her throat was burning from the strain.

An eerie echo bounced back with each shout, and she felt helpless against the fear she heard in her voice.

A startled deer bolted from a nearby thicket. She groaned, envious of its mobility. Off to her left, a squirrel scolded, and something fell through the branches from above, hitting the side of her cheek as it passed.

"Ouch!" she cried, cupping her face.

Blinking through tears, she looked down, watching as a large pine cone ricocheted from branch to branch before hitting the ground. The sight sent a fresh wave of nausea rolling in the pit of her stomach. Quickly closing her eyes to reorient herself within the space in which she was hanging, she kept reminding herself that she hadn't been what was falling. It was only a pine cone that had taken the plunge.

Again, the squirrel's strident chatter broke the silence of her thoughts, and when she opened her eyes, she found herself at eye level and within feet of the bushy-tailed rodent. The little animal's aggressive behavior was unnerving.

"Get!" she said shortly, and the squirrel's pivot on the branch was as neat and swift as a square dancer's step.

With a flick of its tail, it scampered back the way it had come, and as she watched, truth dawned! The squirrel had just shown her the way down. All she needed to do was straddle a branch and then inch her way backward toward the trunk of the tree. After that, she could use the branches like steps on a ladder. In theory, it was simple. But there were the parachute straps to dispense with, and she reminded herself, she was *not* a squirrel. She had to find branches strong enough to hold her weight.

A few minutes later, she had maneuvered herself into position. Straddling a branch, she ignored the rough bark and sticky pine needles as she locked her legs around its circumference. And while she felt comfortable with the fact that the branch would hold her weight, the true test of her faith came as she unbuckled the parachute and let go of the straps. As they slipped through her fingers to dangle down through the branches, she saw that even they were pointing the way down. She began her descent.

The pale green pants and sweater she was wearing were no protection to her body. By the time she reached the last limb, her clothes looked as if she'd been carrying a panicked cat through a room full of barking dogs. There were snags, pulls and tears everywhere it mattered. And if that wasn't enough of an insult, she had run out of limbs a good ten feet from the ground.

Her hands were raw and the skin all over her body felt as if it were on fire. The throb in her head was making her sick, and she knew that the jolt of her landing would only make things worse. But there was no other way to get down. With one last look below, she let go of the limb with her legs, letting them dangle over the floor of the forest.

And then she let go.

The smell of rotting vegetation was suddenly strong in her nostrils as she hit feet first, and then pitched forward, falling onto her hands and knees and plowing through the mat of leaves on the forest floor. But she was down, and from what she could tell, still healthy enough to move.

She started to pull herself up when a bit of color off to one side caught her eye. It was a navy blue duffel bag that she'd seen.

Jump, girl! Take the bag and jump...and don't look back!

She spun, expecting to see...

But the moment she thought it, the name and face disappeared, and to her dismay, she was still alone. Curious, she reached for the bag, and as she did, the skin on the back of her neck suddenly crawled. She fell backward, as if she'd just seen a snake.

"Oh, God, what's happening to me?" she groaned, and sat back up, cradling her head against her knees until the feeling had passed.

But time was at a premium. There was a cool bite to the air that hadn't been there before. This time when she looked at the bag, she ignored her feelings and grabbed it. She pulled at the zipper, then rocked back in shock.

Money! It was full of money! Bundle upon bundle of one-hundred-dollar bills.

How could you? I trusted you, and this is the way you repay me?

Like before, the words came out of nowhere, and even though she knew there was no one there, she couldn't help looking over her shoulder. Without giving herself time to think, she zipped the bag and then stood, pulling the straps over her shoulders and carefully balancing the weight against her pain-racked body.

"Now to find shelter."

Ignoring her misery, she shifted the bag to a more comfortable position and began to walk, following the lay of the land down the side of the mountain. Somewhere below she would find help. She had to. Her endurance was just about gone.

Just as the last rays of sun were sliding behind the tallest of trees, she spied the rooftop of what appeared to be a cabin.

"Thank you, God."

Blinking furiously against tears of relief, she began walking faster, desperate for shelter before the impending darkness caught her out here alone.

Her legs were trembling from exertion. And although the rooftop was no longer visible, she'd gotten a pretty good fix on the direction. If she kept walking, she kept telling herself, she was bound to find it again.

The oncoming night was turning the deep green of the forest into a waning black. The ordinary became frightening; the unfamiliar brought terror. The night wind was still blowing, and a chill was seeping into her bones. Just as she feared another step would be impossible, she walked into a clearing and it was there. The cabin that she'd seen. But it, too, was quickly disappearing within the oncoming shadows. She began to move faster, frantically circling the building and searching for a door to gain entry.

By normal standards, the cabin seemed ordinary. An A-line roof. Log walls. A door and two windows in the front. But to her, it was magnificent. Within seconds, she was running, the bag bouncing against her aching body with every step. And when her fingers closed around the doorknob, it never occurred to her to wonder why it was unlocked. Staggering out of the night and into another sort of darkness, she slammed the door behind her and then stood without moving, absorbing the quiet—and the blessed sensation of safety.

There were shadows inside the room that appeared to be furniture, and just to her right, a light switch on the wall. Across the room was a narrow staircase leading to what appeared to be a loft. It was desolate and dark, and she wondered if she'd ever appreciated anything as much as she did this place.

Overwhelmed with a great weariness, she allowed the bag to slide from her shoulder. She realized, even as she was dropping to her knees and then stretching out on the floor, that there was bound to be a more comfortable place somewhere inside the cabin to rest, but right now she was too exhausted to search. Trembling in every fiber of her being, and hurting in places she couldn't even name, she cradled her head on her arm and closed her eyes.

"Just for a minute. I'll rest just for a minute."

It was her last conscious thought until morning.

Royal Justice had been mad at his youngest brother, Roman, plenty of times in his life. In their younger days, there had even been a couple of times when their arguments came to blows. But that was then and this was now, and Royal wasn't about to trade punches with the man his little brother had become. All he could do was state his position and hope that Roman saw the sense in it all. Unfortunately, Royal had a tendency to lose his cool under pressure, and yelling, which was what he was doing now, was getting him nowhere.

"Damn it, Roman! You are not indispensable. You aren't the only private investigator in the city. The citizens of Dallas will not suffer if you take some time off. God knows you can afford it. You are not a robot, and contrary to what you may think, you are not immortal." He took a deep breath and pointed a shaking finger in Roman's face. "If you don't take a vacation, you...little brother...are going to burn out! And I don't have time to pick up the pieces of what's left of you."

Roman folded his arms and leaned against the wall, listening to Royal's demands with an inscrutable expression on his face.

Royal continued without missing a beat. "So, here's the deal. Yesterday I called and had the utilities turned on in the fishing cabin. I even had some basic supplies delivered, although I suggest you take plenty of anything else you might want. All you have to do is get in your car and drive till you get there."

Having said what had to be said, Royal Justice stood in the doorway, determined not to move from the only exit out of the men's room at the Quesadilla Queen until Roman admitted he was right.

Roman considered his options. One, he could choose to ignore his brother's less-than-subtle suggestion to go to the family cabin in Colorado. If he was going to take a vacation, the least Royal could do was let him pick the place. But then he'd never hear the end of it, and there was a slight truth to some of what Royal just said. He was tired. In fact, he was so tired of the whole damned rat race that for two cents he'd quit.

At that point, a thoughtful frown creased his forehead. But what would he do then? Inactivity was his hell. It brought back too many memories he'd spent years trying to forget.

Then he remembered the couple waiting for them at the table outside and shifted mental gears.

"Damn it, Royal, don't you think it's more than a little rude to invite Ryder and Casey out to dinner and then leave them alone while you pitch this fit?"

Royal didn't flinch. The fact that their brother and his wife were in town visiting from out of state was not as important as getting what he wanted from Roman. And the fact that he'd left them alone at the table to follow Roman into the bathroom was moot. He was on a mission to take care of his family, whether they liked it or not. But Roman was not cooperating as he'd planned. And the cool, absent tone in Roman's voice was adding to his frustration.

Royal glared.

"Ryder is fully capable of entertaining his wife for a few minutes without our presence," he muttered. "And you haven't answered my question. Did you hear a thing I said?"

Roman's composure slipped—but only a little. "Hell, yes, I heard you...and so did everyone else within a city block."

Royal flushed. He knew he'd been yelling, but he didn't have it in him to quiet down when he was on a roll.

"And," Roman continued, "you didn't ask a question. You made a statement. One, I might add, that is shot full of flaws. I never claimed I was indispensable to anyone except your daughter. I can claim to being Maddie's favorite uncle, and we both know it."

Royal almost grinned. "That's because you never tell her no."

Roman arched an eyebrow, but never cracked a smile. "She's only four. There will be plenty of people telling her no for the rest of her life. I see no reason why one of them has to be me."

The door opened behind Royal, and he spun, glaring intently at the man who just entered.

"We're full up in here right now, buddy," Royal drawled, and the glitter in his eyes sent the fellow scurrying back to his table.

Roman rolled his eyes in disbelief. "This is a public bathroom in a public restaurant. You can't commandeer the whole place just because you get an urge to play big brother. What if he was in a hurry?"

Royal's chin jutted dangerously. "When it comes to my family, I can do anything I damned well please if it means keeping them whole. Ryder is finally back on track. I don't intend to have you pull a similar stunt and disappear on me some day just because you let the pressure get to you."

Roman straightened. He'd let Royal blow off steam, partly because he *was* the oldest Justice, and partly because in a small, quiet corner of his mind, he knew Royal was right. But enough was enough. He took a step forward.

"Look, you bullheaded fool. Get out of the doorway before you get us both arrested. Let's go back to the table and enjoy the evening. Ryder and Casey will be leaving for Ruban Crossing tomorrow."

But Royal wouldn't budge, and as hard as Roman had let himself become, he knew he couldn't hold a candle to Royal Justice when it came to bullheadedness.

"Okay, I'll make a deal with you," Roman said. "I'll go to the damned cabin, but only after Ryder and Casey leave."

Royal started to frown. "You have to promise."

Roman threw up his hands. "I promise. Now are you happy?"

Royal gave him a long hard stare. "You swear."

Roman sighed. "Swear."

Royal relented. Roman was hard, but he didn't lie, and he didn't go back on his word. He grinned and held out his hand.

"Shake on it, buddy, and it will be a deal."

Given the fact that he might never get to order his food if he didn't comply, Roman cursed beneath his breath as he extended his hand. Royal's grip was as firm as the smile on his face. Moments later, they walked out of the men's room, sidestepping the line of men who'd been waiting to get in.

"Gentlemen, it's all yours," Royal said, waving his arm magnanimously.

"Big brother, you are a real charmer," Roman said, and knew that he'd been had.

A small sports car swerved into the passing lane behind Roman and sped past him as if he were sitting still.

"Crazy damn fool," he muttered, his eyes narrowing as he kept his four-wheel-drive vehicle to the inside lane of the narrow highway. There was a steep drop-off to his left that went straight down the side of the mountain. Speeding was not an option he was willing to consider, no matter how badly he wanted to reach his destination.

Not for the first time, he wished that he hadn't let Royal talk him into this trip. Hell, he didn't even like to fish, and from the looks of the sky, a storm was moving in. It would be just his luck to come all this way and then wind up stuck in the cabin with nothing to do.

He glanced at his watch and then shrugged. If he did get caught in the rain, it would be his own fault. He shouldn't have waited so long to start the trip. But Ryder and Casey had stayed and stayed, and by the time they'd left the ranch, it had been after 10:00 a.m. And then it had taken nearly thirty minutes more before Roman had been able to tear himself away from Maddie. For a four-year-old, she was a demanding little wench.

He glanced at the sky again. It was unusually dark for this time of day, even in the mountains. Normally it would be light for a couple more hours, but not this evening. The storm would take care of that. He shifted wearily in the seat and thought of his niece again.

Damn, but he loved that kid. It never ceased to amaze him how he'd let one small little girl twist him into knots. Thinking of one female only led to thoughts of another. And it was only in rare times like this that they came. An old pain tried to raise its ugly head, but he shoved the memories back into the past where they belonged. Twelve years had come and gone since he'd watched her die. Part of him had died that day, too, and he knew it. He'd buried what was left behind an impenetrable wall, and that's where he stayed. It was lonely, but safer.

A sound of distant thunder rumbled across the peaks. He looked back up at the sky. If he didn't hurry, he wasn't going to beat the rain. And that would mean unloading his vehicle in a downpour, or sleeping in a bed with no sheets.

As soon as he thought it, he snorted. Maybe Royal was right. Maybe he had needed to get away. He must be getting soft, worrying about where he was going to sleep. There had been plenty of times in his life when he would have settled...and quite happily...for a safe place to close his eyes, never mind whether or not there was a bed.

He'd taken far too many risks during his military career, although he rarely dwelled on the past. These days, he focused his energies on his job and the fact that he *was* still alive. Then he amended that thought. At least he was still alive, but that could change at any moment if he didn't start paying closer attention to this damnable road.

A few moments later, he began negotiating a nasty turn in the road, and out of habit, glanced up at the rearview mirror. Startled by the expression on his own face, he looked away.

Returning his focus to driving, he took the curve with cool skill, refusing to admit, even for a moment, that Royal could have been right. Roman knew himself. He wasn't about to break. It would take more than a few late nights on the job to wear him down.

Within a half hour, he had reached the cabin. The storm hit as he was carrying the last load inside. The rain began peppering against the windows as he kicked the door shut behind him.

He glanced around the room, trying to remember the last time he'd been here, and couldn't. The overhead light cast a dim yellow glow onto the brown leather furniture. He looked toward the loft, thinking of the king-size bed that was there.

And at that moment, the power went off, casting everything into darkness. With a muttered curse, he headed for the kitchen, trying to remember where he'd packed the flashlight and candles.

Yanked from a deep, dreamless sleep, she sat straight up in bed, her eyes wide and filled with fear. With a pounding heart, she listened, trying to discern what she'd heard. A nearby roll of thunder rattled the loft window behind the bed on which she'd been sleeping, and she wrapped her arms around herself and shuddered.

Thank God I'm not out in that.

A door suddenly slammed downstairs and she rolled from the bed, wincing as the movement sent fresh waves of pain shooting through her battered body. Shaking in every fiber of her being, she crept to the edge of the loft and gazed down through the railing, trying to pierce the darkness below. All she could see were more shadows, and yet she knew.

The owner! He's come!

Her first instinct was to believe she'd been saved. But then she remembered the duffel bag and panicked. She had visions of revealing her presence, only to find herself on the small end of someone's hunting rifle. People had been killed for far less than the money she was carrying. It would be very easy to hide a body in woods as dense as these, and whoever was down there could, quite literally, get away with murder. The instinct for survival that had gotten her this far kicked in again. She dropped to her knees and crawled across the floor, then shoved the bag beneath the bed and went in after it.

The floor was cold and hard against her belly, and the dust motes she'd unwittingly disturbed were tickling her nose. The duffel bag was against the wall at the head of the bed. Every time she flinched, the bulk of it pushed against her feet. Outside, raindrops were ricocheting off the roof like bullets against rocks. A cold draft was beginning to circulate around her legs and feet, while outside the thunder rumbled like a runaway wagon on a downhill ride.

She kept telling herself that maybe it would be okay. Surely God wouldn't let her survive all of this, only to let her perish at a stranger's hands. But she was too frightened to take a chance. And it would seem that the proper time for making oneself known had come and gone. In the midst of it all, she heard a sound that sent her into a panic. Someone was coming up the stairs!

Holding her nose to keep from sneezing, she scooted as far back as she could get and watched the landing, anxious to see his face.

The rain was coming down now in sheets. Roman could hear it running off the roof and down onto the hard-packed ground below. Out of habit, he flipped the light switch a couple of times and then shrugged. He wasn't the kind of man to waste time on things that were out of his control. At least there was dry wood by the fireplace. He'd build a fire. That would provide light and warm the place up, too.

Satisfied that he had something to accomplish, he began laying the kindling. A short while later, he stood before the fireplace, watching in satisfaction as tiny orange tongues of flame began eating their way into the dry wood.

His belly growled, but he ignored the complaint. Without power, he would have to cook over the fireplace and he wasn't in a Daniel Boone frame of mind. A gust of air rattled the door on its hinges. He thought of his apartment and of the well-stocked refrigerator he'd left behind.

"Damn Royal's meddling butt, anyway," he muttered, and laid one last log on the fire before moving the fire screen into place.

Chilled from the weather and weary from the drive, he was immediately drawn to the loft. He reached for his suitcase and then changed his mind. To hell with sheets. All he wanted to do was lie down. He'd make the bed tomorrow in the bright light of day. With one last look behind him, Roman started up to the loft, taking care not to miss a step in the darkness.

Halfway up, he froze. He could feel the hair rise on the backs of his arms. Something wasn't right! Long ago, he'd learned not to ignore his instincts. He turned, gazing down at the scene below, and wondered what it was that he'd heard. Nothing seemed out of place. Everything was just as it had been when he'd come inside. A hard gust of wind hit the side of the house, rattling the windows, as well as the door.

Frowning, he retraced his steps to the door and turned the lock, relaxing only after the distinct click had sounded. Then he dug his handgun from a bag and started back up the stairs, satisfied that he'd done all he could. If someone wanted to try him, he was more than ready.

Heat was rising from the fire below as he dropped to the side of the bed and set the handgun on a nearby table. He looked down at his feet and then back at the bed. The mattress smelled a little bit dusty, but he was too tired to care.

In the back of his mind, he could almost hear his mother admonishing him to get his shoes off the furniture. With a rare smile, he bent down and pulled off his boots before dropping them onto the floor. With a weary groan, he lay down, folding his arms beneath his head and sighing as he looked up at the ceiling.

The rafters had taken on a warm, amber tinge from the glow of the fireplace below. His stomach rumbled again, but it was a small complaint he willingly ignored. He closed his eyes, inhaled slowly and never knew when he fell asleep.

Hours later, he awakened suddenly to hear the indistinct sound of fabric rubbing against wood. Without taking a breath, he reached for his gun.

Chapter 2

He's asleep.

For her, that fact had been too long in coming. The floor was cold and she hurt—hurt all over. If she didn't get out from under this bed and soon, she would never be able to move again. What's more, she needed to go to the bathroom.

Inch by painful inch, and using the duffel bag at her feet as a launch, she began to scoot forward. As she did, the stiff nylon fabric suddenly rasped against the hardwood floor. Although it was still raining, the sound seemed magnified by the quiet within the room. She froze, relaxing only after the soft, even sounds of his breathing could still be heard.

Easy does it, she told herself, and once again, began to pull herself out from under the bed.

The stairwell was only feet away when something—call it instinct—made her look back over her shoulder. Through the glimmer from the firelight below, she saw him, raised up on one elbow, the gun pointed straight at her head. A calm settled over her as she rolled over on her back, and for the first time since she'd regained consciousness in the tree, came face-to-face with the fact that she might not live through this after all.

"Don't shoot," she said quietly. "I'm not armed."

"But I am."

The words were harsh, the warning tone of his voice deep and angry, like the storm still raging outside. She took a slow breath and started to sit when his voice cut through the quiet again, this time in a manner she couldn't mistake.

"I didn't say you could move."

"Please," she said. "I need to go to the bathroom."

The request was so unexpected he laughed, and the short, angry bark brought goose bumps to the backs of her arms. She swallowed past a knot of cold fear.

"I never meant to deceive you," she said quietly. "I just needed shelter. I was asleep when you came. Your arrival startled me so that I hid before I thought. After that, it seemed anticlimactic to announce myself."

The bed squeaked as he stood, and when she looked up, fought back an urge to scream. He was so big...and so menacing.

"Get up."

His order was brief. As she rolled to her feet, it occurred to her that this man didn't waste energy on words.

Her movements seemed slow and measured, and once Roman believed he heard her groan. The thought crossed his mind to offer her help, and then he remembered that while she'd been hiding under that blasted bed, he'd been asleep on it. He rejected the notion. She got down on the floor; she could get herself up.

The muscles in his belly knotted at the thought of someone under the bed. It was a kid's worst nightmare come to life—a monster under the everlasting bed. It remained to be seen if she was really a monster after all.

"Downstairs," he ordered, waving the gun in her direction. "And take it slow."

"That I can do," she said briefly, unaware that her answer

deepened the frown on his forehead. With aching muscles protesting her every step, she bit her lip and began to move.

The floorboards creaked beneath his weight as he moved in behind her. At that point, the phrase *breathing down her neck* took on new meaning. A short while later, they were standing before the remnants of the fire, and staring into the bits of dying embers rather than at each other.

Roman pulled back the fire screen and then pointed toward a nearby stack of logs with his gun.

"You. Toss one on the fire."

The very idea of gripping anything with her hands was impossible to consider. She turned to him, holding out her hands in supplication.

"I don't think I—"

"Do what I said, lady, or we're right back where we started."

She turned toward the stack, gritting her teeth against the pain as her fingers curled around the rough, dry bark.

This time, her groan was loud and clear. Halfway to the fireplace, she lost her grip. The log fell to the floor with a loud, abrupt thump, rolling to one side as she dropped to her knees, cradling her hands against her chest.

"What the hell—?"

"My hands are hurt."

This time, he was forced to listen. He grabbed her hands and turned them toward the fire. In the light of the dying embers, he could see dark slashes and bloody stains. Guilt hit him belly high. He cursed beneath his breath and finished what she'd started.

Then without excuse or apology, he took her by the arm and pulled her to her feet. Within minutes, the room was aglow. And although they were still in shadows, they were finally able to see one another's face.

Even though she knew it was rude to stare, she couldn't help it. And, she reminded herself, so far he'd been anything but a gentleman himself. He was very good-looking, but the fact was lost in the fear rolling in her mind. In her entire life, she couldn't remember ever seeing such a cold, flat expression on a living man's face. And then she reminded herself that she was hardly in a position to be judging character. She couldn't even remember her own name.

Roman's gaze was hard and fixed. He had already schooled himself not to react to her condition until he had some answers he could live with. Yes, she was cut and bruised, and her clothing was bloody and all but in rags. And the dried blood matting parts of her hair to her scalp was further proof of her injuries. So at least part of her story had to be true. Problem was, he didn't trust pretty women. In fact, he didn't trust women at all.

"What's your name?" Roman asked, and saw a different kind of fear move across her face.

"I don't know."

That wasn't what he'd expected to hear. "What do you mean, you don't know?"

She reached toward the knot beneath her scalp. "Somehow I hurt my head. When I came to, I couldn't remember who I was or where I'd been going."

He almost sneered. "Amnesia is a lame excuse, lady. Try again."

Her gaze never wavered, nor did the tone of her voice. "Frankly, I don't care whether you believe me or not."

Reluctantly, he gave her points for attitude. Score one for you, he thought to himself. He shifted his stance. "You look like hell. What happened?"

There was no mistaking the anger in her eyes and it came through with the bitterness of her question.

"You're not married, are you?"

Roman was taken aback and found himself answering before he thought.

"No."

This time, she was the one who almost sneered. "Now, why am I not surprised? Your bedside manner leaves a lot to be desired."

His glare deepened. He didn't give a damn about her opinions of his manners or of anything else. In typical Justice fashion, he disposed of the subject by ignoring it.

"Lady, I don't waste my time on congeniality. In my line of work, it rarely gets the job done."

She stared pointedly at the gun. "I'm almost afraid to ask, but are you some sort of cop?"

"I'm no cop," he said shortly.

"Wonderful," he heard her mutter. "And where does that leave me...conversing with a hit man?"

A rare grin tilted the corner of his mouth. "I'm not a hit man, either. I'm a private investigator."

She sighed. "I wish I knew if I could afford you. I'd hire you to find out who I am."

The grin disappeared. She seemed bent on sticking to her story, and in spite of his better judgment, he was starting to believe her. He lowered the gun without comment, then pointed to her injuries.

"Did you have a wreck? I didn't see any signs of one on the road when I came up."

"I wasn't in a car. I think I was in a plane."

His eyes widened. "Are you saying your plane went down?"

She fought an urge to scream. The man was infuriating. But, she reminded herself, he was the one with the gun.

"No...maybe. Oh, I don't know. All I know is, I jumped out before it went down."

"Jumped?"

The room was beginning to tilt, and she reached out to steady herself, all but swaying on her feet.

"I regained consciousness in a pine tree. The parachute I was wearing was caught in the branches. Now, please. The bathroom. I need to go to the bathroom."

Roman hadn't missed a nuance of her expression. He had to admit she was good. But parachuting out of a plane and landing in a tree? The story was too far-fetched. He hated to let her out of his sight, even for a minute, but he could hardly ignore the request. Besides that, where the hell could she go? He finally relented.

"Down the hall, first door on your left."

"I know. I've been here since last night."

While he was absorbing the shock of that news, the power came back on, flooding the room in a sudden burst of light that left them both blinking...and in an odd, uncomfortable sort of way, slightly embarrassed.

"Thank goodness," she said. "At least now I won't bump into anything else." Her hand brushed across the surface of her belly as she turned away. "I don't have room left for another bruise."

There was no way Roman could ignore the truth of her condition now. In the light, the evidence of her injuries was overwhelming. He caught himself wincing in sympathy as she walked away. And as he stared at her backside, another, but far less serious, fact of her life began to emerge. She was missing a pocket on the seat of her pants. He grinned. Her choice of underwear was remarkable, to say the least. Daisies. Her panties had daisies on them—small white blossoms with bright yellow centers.

On a rare, mischievous impulse, he called out to her. "Hey, Daisy."

Startled by the unexpected and unfamiliar name, she pivoted. There was a tremor in her voice that hadn't been there before, but she couldn't help it. Did he know something about her that she didn't?

"Why did you call me that?" she asked sharply.

He shrugged. "Got to call you something. It's as good a name as any."

She frowned, waiting for him to continue.

"Wait a minute," he said, and stepped into the kitchen. Moments later, he came out and handed her a roll of toilet paper.

She blushed, but took what he offered with her head held high.

"Thank you," she said shortly, more focused on gaining relief than worrying about some fool name that he fancied.

Yet when she stepped inside the bathroom, the fact that she was still at his mercy hit her again, and she locked the door behind her. Considering his size and the fact that he was armed, it was a futile act of defiance, but it made her feel better, just the same.

Easing her aching fingers around the zipper, she pulled, breathing a sigh of relief as her pants dropped down around her ankles without fuss. But when she reached for her underwear, she stopped, staring intently at the fabric, and then down at the obvious hole in the back of her pants.

Daisy... It's as good a name as any.

A bright red flush crept up her face and into her neckline. He had some nerve. And then she thought of the look in his eyes and amended. An overdose of nerve wasn't the only thing he had. A complete lack of fear was more like it.

She caught sight of herself in the mirror and rolled her eyes in disbelief. He was right. She did look like hell.

Daisy. She said the name aloud, testing the sound on the tip of her tongue. "Daisy."

The name didn't ring any bells, but it didn't set off any alarms, either. She shrugged. He was right. For now, it was as good a name as any.

A short while later, she came out of the bathroom. Water was dripping from her hands and face, but the worst of the bloodstains were gone. To her surprise, the man was nowhere in sight. The urge to run was strong, but where could she go? She wrapped her arms around herself, shivering as she headed for the fire. The room seemed colder now than it had been a short while ago, and she was tired...so tired. The old sofa beckoned. It was four cushions in length, with just enough dignity to make a good bed.

Crawling onto it, she rolled herself into a ball, facing the fire. The heat emanating from the blaze seemed heaven-sent. In the next room, something hit the floor with a thump, but she didn't flinch. In a way, the sound was almost reassuring. It was sort of like belling a cat. At least now she knew where he'd gone. She sighed and closed her eyes, only planning to rest. But moments later, exhaustion claimed her and she slept.

That was where Roman found her, curled up on the old leather sofa with one hand beneath her cheek and the other dangling over the edge of the cushion. Her vulnerability caught him by surprise. He found himself studying her in a way he would never have done had she been awake. He looked past his doubts to the woman beneath, realizing that he was more than intrigued. But he kept telling himself it was the mystery around her and not the woman herself that had caught his interest. And as he stood, he wondered how often he would have to remind himself of that to finally believe.

She was tiny, both in build and height. The top of her head was just below his chin, and she was a brunette. He preferred tall, leggy blondes. The cut on her lip broke the symmetry of her mouth in a way that made him ache. He winced, thinking about the blow it would take to split such a tender spot. There was a bruise on her right cheek and scratches down the side of her face and neck. Remnants of the tree, he supposed, and at that moment, realized that he'd bought into her story. It was far-fetched, but he knew crazier things had happened.

His gaze moved to her hands. They were ringless. So she wasn't married. He didn't ask himself if it mattered. He was simply following procedure—finding out all there was to know about a subject before he took him or her apart at the seams.

When she shivered in her sleep, his frown deepened. Her clothes were in rags, and even if they hadn't been, they weren't suited for this type of climate.

Well, hell.

A few moments later, he came out of the kitchen carrying a blanket. When he bent down to cover her up, a wave of emotion hit him that had nothing to do with the suspicion he'd had earlier.

She was so damned small and helpless looking. He pulled the blanket up over her shoulders, making certain that her back was covered. He watched as she grabbed the edge of the blanket, pulling it tight beneath the curve of her chin. It was an unconscious gesture, but an endearing one, as well. It reminded him of his niece, Maddie. Maddie was afraid of the dark and slept under covers, no matter what time of year. He wondered if Daisy was afraid of the dark, and then laid another log on the fire.

Outside, the wind continued to blow, although the rain must have passed. He hadn't heard it against the roof for some time now. Curious, he went to the front door to look out and was greeted by a blast of cold air. In spite of the darkness, the swirling snow eddying in the wind currents was impossible to miss.

"Son of a..."

He slammed the door shut and then turned, staring around the cabin and then at the woman asleep before the fire. At that moment, he made himself a promise. When he got home, he was going to punch Royal Justice in the nose. Not only had he let himself be bullied into taking a vacation he hadn't wanted, but if the weather didn't change, he was about to be snowed in, and with a woman he still didn't trust. He walked to the sofa and looked down, whispering more to himself than to her.

"Well now, Miss Daisy, we've got ourselves in one fine mess."

But Daisy didn't hear him, and if she had, at that moment she wouldn't have cared. Even though she was unaware of the snowstorm, she already knew there were worse things than being stranded inside this cabin. She could still be dangling from the limbs of that tree.

"Look, Holly-berry, look! See the bubbles. Now blow. Pucker up your mouth and blow!"

Daisy's mouth pursed slightly as she went with the dream, watching from inside the little girl's eyes as the bubbles flew from the wand and out into the air.

Laughter spilled from the child's lips as she gave chase, waving her hands toward the bits of sunlight captured on the surfaces of the bubbles.

"More," she cried. *"Blow me some more!"*

And they came, swirling through the air, dancing on wind currents, sailing too high to catch and far out of sight.

Still drifting with the pleasure of the dream, Daisy opened her eyes to a reality far removed. The log walls of the cabin were an abrupt reminder of the past two days of her life. And then she looked toward the window and amended that thought. The past *three* days of her life. It was morning.

The scent of coffee was strong, as was the ever present smell of the wood fire. She rolled over onto her back, contemplating the idea of moving farther, then abandoned the thought for the comfort of the cover and the fire.

Cover!

She reached down, fingering the softness of the blanket. A frown creased her forehead. Sometime between last night and this morning, her reluctant host had tossed her a crumb of kindness.

Humph. I didn't think he had it in him.

Guilt shafted as she reminded herself that, technically, *he'd* been the one who'd been wronged. She'd infringed upon his property and hospitality, and without notice or warning. She sighed, trying to put herself in his place. What would she have done had she awakened to find someone crawling out from under her bed?

At that moment, a picture flashed into her mind—of a large room done in shades of blue, with touches of white, and of a great four-poster bed. The image came and went so quickly she could have let herself believe it was still part of her dream, but something told her it was not. Somewhere inside her mind, she was waking up, and the room she'd just seen did exist.

When tears spiked, she jutted her chin and gritted her teeth. Crying would get her nowhere. If that memory had come, then others would follow. For now, she needed to be concerned with getting down from this mountain and getting to the authorities. Then she remembered the bag full of money she'd left under the bed.

So maybe I don't go straight to the authorities. Maybe I do a little checking on my own before I announce myself to the world. I don't want to appear in public, only to find I'm on the FBI's most-wanted list.

With a reluctant grunt, she tossed back the blanket and rolled, first to a sitting position, then standing, looking down at her stained clothes with distaste.

"Oh, for a steed and a pot of gold," she muttered.

"And where would you go if you had them?"

Daisy spun. That man. How long had he been standing there?

"You startled me," she accused.

"Sorry," he said, but she knew he was not.

"You didn't answer my question," Roman said. "If you had that horse and money, where would a woman named Daisy go?"

"I'm sure you would agree, but for starters, out of your hair. You've been kind to put me up, but I think I've outstayed my welcome."

Her reference to the fact that he'd kept a gun trained on her most of the evening was not lost on Roman, nor was the fact that she was keeping her distance. He didn't know whether she was still afraid of him, or if she was standing where she was because it was close to the door. And because he was the man that he was, he chose not to comment on either of her remarks.

Her eyes narrowed in anger. The man was inscrutable, as well as insufferable. She pitied the woman who—

"I just realized," she said. "I don't know your name."

"Justice. Roman Justice."

Justice...as in my way or no way at all? But she refrained from voicing her thoughts.

"Mr. Justice, I'd like to say it's been a pleasure, but we'd both know I'd be lying, so I'll stick to the facts. I don't know where we are, but I assume you had transportation up here, and I would appreciate a lift down to the nearest city. I can take it from there."

Roman shook his head. "Afraid I can't do that just yet."

Her heart skipped a beat. "And why not?"

"Take a look outside."

She headed for the door. Even before she turned the knob, she felt the cold. Oh, no, this isn't going to be good. She looked outside. As far as the eye could see was a heavy layer of snow—cold and white, pristine in color and deadly in depth—and it was still falling.

She slammed the door and spun around. Her shock was evident.

"It's just a late-spring blizzard. They don't usually last all that long, but travel is out for the duration."

Daisy shuddered, partly from the cold and partly from nerves. Being trapped in this cabin, with this man—

She refused to think past being trapped. The possible consequences of the rest of it were too appalling to consider.

"Look at me," she muttered. "My clothes...my hair...I'm a mess...and I'm freezing."

He frowned. "Yeah, I figured when you felt better you'd start worrying about all of that stuff, so I dug around and found a few things you might be able to wear. They're on the bed upstairs."

Daisy had the grace to flush. Here she stood, worrying about the demise of her moral character, when for all she knew, she was an out-and-out thief.

"Thank you," she said shortly. "Is there a problem with the power?"

He shook his head.

"Then, if you don't mind, I would really like to take a bath and wash my hair." She shrugged by way of explaining. "The blood, you know. It's all dried in my hair."

Roman nodded, and when she started toward the bathroom, he felt obligated to add, "There's a clean towel on the back of the door, and you're welcome to use my shampoo. After you've dressed and had breakfast, I brought a first-aid kit. If you want, I'd be glad to look at your hands and that cut on your head."

Daisy started to smile, but there was an expression on his face that stopped her intent.

"Thank you," she said. "I won't be long."

"Coming from a female, that would be a first," Roman muttered as he turned away.

"I heard that," Daisy said, and then shut the bathroom door behind her with a solid thump.

Roman looked back at the door and thought of the woman beyond, then reached for his coat and gloves. They'd be needing more wood and he needed to put some distance between himself and that woman.

Certain things about her were beginning to catch his eye. When she stood a certain way, he knew she was nervous. Something about the way she held her head at a dare-to-mess-with-me angle. And there was the way her eyes seemed to change color according to her moods. Sometimes they seemed dark, and more than once he'd seen them glittering with unshed tears.

He stomped out into the snow, kicking his way through the drifts to the woodpile and reminding himself that women were nothing but trouble. Oh, they had their place in his life, but nothing permanent. He'd learned the hard way about counting on women to stay the course. Granted, the ones he'd loved hadn't left of their own accord, but he was past trusting in fate, or in God, to give him one he could keep. He picked up the logs one by one, and when his arms were full, headed back to the cabin.

Chapter 3

The assortment of clothing he had laid out for her was, to say the least, eclectic. There were odds and ends that didn't match, and all of them smelled a bit like the cedar chest they'd been in, but Daisy didn't care. They were clean and, except for having to roll up the waistband of the gray wool pants she had on, almost a fit. The old red flannel shirt was soft and comfortable, and a welcome respite against her scrapes and bruises. And when she sat down to put on her shoes, she saw that he'd left her a pair of socks, as well. She pulled them on, savoring the warmth against her skin. They made her shoes a bit too tight, but she wasn't going to sacrifice warmth for comfort.

When she bent down to straighten her pants, a lock of her hair slid forward. Still wet from her shampoo, it felt cold against her cheek. Shivering, she headed for the stairs and the fire that was blazing below.

Roman looked up as he heard her coming, thinking he was prepared for the sight of a stranger in his mother's old clothes. She was shorter than Barbara Justice had been, but there was that same unmistakable air of fragility in their build. Just for a moment, he felt as if he were seeing a ghost. He stared at her, unaware he was frowning.

Daisy paused in midstep, with her hand still on the banister. If she was honest with herself, she would have to admit Roman Justice scared her to death. He was so big and his expression so cold. It was as if his very presence sucked the life out of a room. But there was something inside of her that refused to let him know how she felt. Instead of cowering, she lifted her chin and met his gaze straight on.

"Thank you for the clothes," she said quietly. "They feel warm and wonderful."

He nodded.

"Your sister's?" she asked, trying to make conversation.

He shook his head. "Don't have one."

"Oh."

Silence lengthened between them. Finally, it was Daisy who broke it.

"Do I smell coffee?"

Her question made him remember she hadn't eaten. "Yes. I left you a few strips of bacon on the back of the stove, and there's bread in the box. You better make yourself a sandwich to go with the coffee. I won't cook again until evening."

"Thank you."

Green. Her eyes are green. For some reason, he felt satisfied with having answered that question. A few moments passed before he realized that she'd spoken.

"What did you say?"

"Thank you," Daisy repeated. "I said thank you."

He shrugged. "You're welcome." Then he remembered her hands and the injuries she'd suffered.

He caught her by the arm as she started into the kitchen, then grabbed her hands, turning them palms up. They didn't look much better than they had before her bath. He knew they must be painful.

"I'll get your food. You dry your hair. It's bad enough that we're stuck here together. The last thing I need is for you to get sick."

Daisy didn't know whether to thank him or kick him in the shins. His offer of help could be taken several ways, and none of them was particularly complimentary.

"Yes...well, I..." Daisy said, and then gave up conversation as a lost cause when he walked away.

With a shrug, she turned toward the fireplace. No use talking to herself. And the fire did feel good.

When he came back in the room, Daisy was still running her fingers through her hair, using them in lieu of a comb to separate the strands so they would dry. He set the coffee and sandwich on the table at the end of the sofa and then took a tube of ointment from his pocket.

"After you eat, I'll doctor your cuts. You don't want to get an infection."

Again, Daisy was forced into accepting his reluctant offers of help. She nodded, wondering what she'd done to deserve such a plight as she was experiencing now. If she *was* a crook, her justice was being meted out in a more effective manner than any the criminal system could have accomplished.

There is the money, she reminded herself. But until she knew where it came from, she wasn't the least bit comfortable about considering it as any sort of backup.

Uncomfortable at Roman's nearness, Daisy picked up her sandwich and then looked away as she took the first bite. But the wonderful flavor of crisp smoked bacon and sliced tomato, coupled with soft, fresh bread and some sort of sandwich spread came as a great surprise. She hadn't been expecting the garnishes he'd added, and made no effort to hide her appreciation.

"Mmm, this is good!" she said, and then leaned back on the sofa and proceeded to down the rest of it like a starving pup.

Roman turned away, refusing to acknowledge her appreciation.

"Just a sandwich," he said shortly. "Let me know when you're through. I'll see to your cuts."

She looked up. "It's much warmer by the fire. You don't have to leave on my account."

Roman stood for a moment, staring intently down at the woman in his mother's clothes, and wondered what Barbara Justice would have had to say about her. Her hair was almost dry. The same length all over, the chocolate brown strands fell just short of her shoulders. A single strand of hair was stuck to her cheek near the corner of her eye. It startled him to know he'd thought of brushing it back.

"Oh, but I think I do," he said, and left her to make what she chose of the ambiguous remark. Besides that, he was still trying to get through to Royal, although none of his calls would go through. He supposed it was because of the storm.

So Daisy ate, alternating bites with slow sips of coffee as Roman finished unpacking. A short while later, he went upstairs with an armload of linens. When she heard him walking from one side of the bed to the other, she realized he must be making it up. A quick wave of panic came and went as she thought of the money hidden beneath it. What would he do if he found it? While he didn't seem like the type of man who would kill for money, she already knew that he *was* the type of man who, if he had to, wouldn't hesitate to kill. She set her cup aside and then leaned forward with her elbows on her knees, staring down at the floor and praying for insight that would help her get through this.

There was no sudden revelation—no bright burst of light holding badly needed answers—only the realization that she was on her own. Despair settled heavily on her shoulders as she buried her face in her hands.

And that was how Roman found her.

She looked so lost. He wondered if she was crying and was angry with himself for caring. He didn't want to be embroiled in anything personal, especially with a woman. When you got personal with a woman, emotions became involved, and Roman had learned long ago to keep his emotions in check. Life had aged him far beyond his thirty years. He didn't want to care. People who cared were people who set themselves up for a fall.

"Are you sick?"

Daisy jerked. She hadn't heard his approach, and that deep, angry voice startled her.

"No."

She refused to look up at his face. She was an unwelcome presence in his life, and she knew it.

Roman's conscience pulled. For a woman, she was being a trouper. Not once had she relied on tears or hysterics. His admiration for her lifted a notch.

"Let's take a look at those cuts," he said.

Daisy looked up, and although there were tears glittering in her eyes, she would have choked on them before she let one fall.

"Please do," she said. "I'd hate to be a larger burden than I already am."

Her sarcasm was impossible to miss, and Roman's guilt deepened.

"I never said you were a burden," he muttered, and reached for the ointment he'd laid on the table.

"Should I sit or stand?"

He glanced at her face. It was void of any expression, save that of waiting.

"Stay where you are," Roman said. "I'll come to you."

It was a poor choice of words. The moment he said them, they both knew there was another connotation that could have been taken.

She shifted farther back onto the sofa cushions and looked into the fire, telling herself that the flush on her face was from the heat and nothing else.

Roman stood behind her, waiting until she settled, then bent forward, carefully moving aside a lock of her hair above her eyebrow, then searching for the injury that had been the source of all that blood. Moments later, he felt a great lump beneath her scalp and frowned at the size of the cut on top of it. No wonder she didn't remember her name. Hell, it was a wonder she'd had enough sense left in her to walk.

"This might hurt," he said, squeezing a bit of ointment onto his finger before applying it to the cut.

She didn't flinch, but as he leaned closer, he heard the rapid and shallow breaths she was taking, and knew she was hiding her pain. Wishing there were a way to do this without hurting her, he touched her shoulder, feeling the rapid beat of her pulse pounding through her body.

"I'm sorry."

It was the quiet in his voice that calmed Daisy as nothing else could have done. At last, he said something she could believe.

She closed her eyes, taking a deep breath before she trusted herself to speak. But when she looked up, she found herself locked into a clear blue stare. She shuddered.

I don't know this man and yet I'm letting him call every shot about me, including my physical well-being.

The urge to bolt was strong, but there was something in his gaze—something strong and solid—that told her to stay, that it would be okay.

"It had to be done," she said, and held out her hands.

Roman circled the sofa, then sat on the cushion next to her. Again, the unexpected contact of her skin against his made him antsy, and he forced himself to focus on her injuries.

"You need a number on these," he said, turning them palms up, then palms down before applying ointment to both sides.

"If I'd been able to fly, it would have been easier to get out of the tree."

The unexpected bit of humor made him laugh before he thought, and a small smile played at the corner of his mouth as he finished the first aid.

But something had happened to Daisy she hadn't been prepared to withstand. In the short space of time between his laughter and his smile, she'd seen the man beneath the mask. In that moment, he'd become more than her captor, more than an unwilling host. He'd become human. For Daisy, that was a danger she couldn't afford. There were too many unanswered questions about her life to risk trusting anyone, especially a man who had her at his mercy.

"I think that's enough. Thank you very much," she said quickly. Before he could argue, she reached for her plate and cup and headed for the kitchen.

The smile died on his face as he watched her walk away. Everything in him was on alert. A woman with a past was always a complication. A woman with no past spelled trouble with a capital *T*.

He tossed the antibiotic aside and strode to the door, yanking it open with a jerk and then standing in the doorway, breathing in deep, cleansing drafts of the cold, sharp air. Tiny flurries of snow blistered his cheeks and burned his eyes, but he didn't budge. He stood, letting the wind and snow cleanse his mind in a way he could not.

By the time he stepped back, his focus was clear. All they had to do was coexist for a few more days. The weather would clear. He'd take her down off the mountain, and she'd be out of his life. The plan was a good one. It should have made him happy. It did not.

The scent of their supper was still in the air. Although Daisy's memory was as blank on food as it was on her personal past, she was pretty sure that she'd never had anything as good as the wieners he'd grilled over the fireplace and the beans he'd poured out of a can. For dessert, he'd opened a package of chocolate cookies filled with double helpings of white cream filling. When she saw them, she smiled in anticipation.

"Ooh, those are my favorites," she said, and then the smile froze on her face. "How did I know that?"

From his seat on the floor near the fireplace, he handed her a couple of cookies, then took one for himself.

"People with amnesia rarely forget everything about their lives," he said, twisting the cookie apart and then licking at the filling in a studied manner. "They will remember inconsequential facts. It's the big things that usually take time."

"Oh." It was all she could manage to say. Her gaze fell on the slow, steady lick of his tongue as it swirled around the cookie. There was something sensuous about the act that made her stomach pull. She swallowed nervously.

Look away. Look away. Don't let him see you watching.

Something crunched in her hand and she looked down. The cookie she'd been holding was in bits.

"I, uh—"

"Give it to me," he said, and held out his hand.

Embarrassed, she dumped the broken pieces into his palm and watched as he turned and tossed them in the fire.

"Here you go," he said, handing her another one. "Easy does it this time, Daisy Mae. You're supposed to put it *in* your mouth before you crunch."

There was a glimmer of jest in his eyes that she fought to ignore. Daisy Mae, indeed! She couldn't believe he was actually comfortable enough with her to tease, and she kept telling herself to lighten up.

Just eat your cookie, woman, before you do something you will regret.

Pretending great interest in which side to bite first, she turned the cookie around and around before she put it in her mouth. When the rich, familiar flavor of chocolate hit her tongue, she closed her eyes with pleasure and chewed slowly, savoring every bite. Then she proceeded to eat the two that he'd given her, and three others besides. When he offered her another, she shook her head.

"I couldn't possibly, but thanks," she said, daintily wiping at the edges of her mouth with the tips of her fingers.

Roman hid another grin. She'd be irked to know there was still a bit of cookie on her chin, but he wasn't going to tell her. With all her fussing and wiping, she was bound to come across it soon enough.

"Want a beer?" he asked as he got to his feet.

Daisy looked startled. "Uh, no. I don't drink. At least, I don't think I—"

Roman shook his head. "Don't apologize, and don't second-guess yourself. First instincts are always the best. How about some coffee, or maybe a pop?"

Daisy's interest returned. She'd seen the six-packs on the cabinet earlier.

"Too late for coffee, but I would like a pop. However, you don't need to wait on me. I can get it for myself."

Roman folded himself back up and sat down on the floor without arguing. "Fine. Bring me a beer when you come."

Her eyebrows rose, but she refrained from making a remark as she went into the kitchen. *He's been waiting on me all day. It's the least I can do,* she reminded herself. But she knew there was something inbred in her that resented like hell taking orders from a man. It made her wonder what her life had been like before.

As she was reaching into the refrigerator, the wind suddenly rattled the window over the sink and she looked up in fright. There was nothing beyond the glass but darkness. In a quick burst of panic, she grabbed the drinks and bolted for the living room, sliding to a halt as she reached the fire.

"Here's your beer," she said, still breathless from her sprint.

He'd heard her coming, her footsteps short and quick...all but running out of the kitchen. He took the can without comment as she settled onto the sofa. She was still fidgeting, even as he was taking the first drink. He stared at her without making any apology for doing so.

She stood up to him in ways that would have made his brothers laugh. She wasn't prone to hysterics and seemed to have a high tolerance for pain. Yet she ran from the night like a child afraid of the dark. Taking another drink, he tilted his head as the fluid slid down his throat, savoring the smooth tang.

"Tell me, Daisy, what *do* you remember?"

The question took her aback. But the images were quick to come to mind.

"Waking up in a tree—and hurting." She looked away for a moment.

Roman sensed she wasn't trying to hide her thoughts, but rather to gather them. He waited. It was her tale to tell.

She set the can of pop aside and then held out her hands.

"The blood. There was so much blood. I remember wondering if I was going to die."

Roman's gut knotted. He knew what that felt like.

She shuddered. "Each time I tried to move, the parachute ripped. I thought I would fall, you know." Then she looked at him. "The tree was very tall."

And you are very small.

Again, Roman was startled by the empathy he was feeling for her. It wasn't like him to be soft, not about anybody or anything— except Maddie. Where she was concerned, he was putty.

"But you got down," he said.

She nodded. "Yes. I got down." She thought of the bag and the money and looked away.

Her hesitation was obvious to a man of his profession. There was something she wasn't saying, yet he refrained from pressing the issue.

"Then what did you do?"

She looked back at him. "I started walking."

"How did you know where to go?"

"I didn't. I just followed the down slope of the mountain."

Smart girl. But he only nodded.

Her tone deepened as she continued, and he could hear the stress in her voice.

"It was almost dark before I saw the cabin." Caught up in the telling, she leaned forward. "You don't know how glad I was to see that roof. It was getting cold, and I'm afraid of the dark."

Again, saying that came as a surprise to her. She tried to laugh.

"This feels so weird. You know what I mean? It's the not knowing those little things about myself until they've snuck up on me that's driving me crazy."

Roman emptied the last of his beer and then set the can against the wall, giving her time to settle before he spoke.

"It's human nature to be in a state of constant change. I don't think it's unusual to not know everything there is to know about oneself."

Daisy leaned back, eyeing the big man with hard intent, trying to picture him in an unsettled situation.

"Somehow, I can't see you losing focus."

Roman had never felt as out of sync as he did right now. He tried to look away, but couldn't.

"Oh, I don't know. I think we all wear blinders from time to time. It's nature's way of protecting us from something we're not ready to face."

Daisy folded her hands in her lap.

"Roman?"

He hesitated to answer, wishing he was anywhere except pinned beneath that clear green gaze. Finally, he was forced to respond.

"What?"

"Are you running away from something, too?"

Only myself. But he chose not to answer her.

The wind subsided sometime during the night. Roman woke suddenly from a deep, dreamless sleep. He lay in the bed, listening for a sound from below, wondering if it was Daisy he'd heard.

But there was nothing but silence. He relaxed, telling himself to go back to sleep. Sleep wouldn't come. It took a few seconds longer before he realized that the quiet wasn't only inside the cabin; it was outside, as well.

The storm is over!

He rolled out of bed and reached for his jeans, telling himself he probably needed to put wood on the fire and knowing all the way down the stairs that he just wanted to see Daisy's face. He needed to know she was right where he'd left her—safe and warm by the fire.

He thought of trying the phone again. Maybe now that the winds had died down he would be able to get through to the ranch. Then he glanced at his watch. It was a quarter to three, which meant it was a quarter to four back home. No use waking everyone up now. There would be plenty of time in the morning to try the call.

He leaned over the sofa. Daisy was still there and rolled up in her blankets. Her hair was tousled and falling down on her forehead, as well as all over the pillow. Again, the urge to brush it out of her eyes was strong, but he stayed his ground, reminding himself not to get too close.

The fire was sputtering on a weak, dying flame, and he added some wood, taking comfort in the blaze that came forth. Then he stood, quietly moving the screen back in place and dusting off his hands, satisfied that they would be warm until morning.

He turned, glancing down at Daisy once more and making sure she was covered. Several seconds passed before he realized she was watching him. It startled him. He was the private investigator. He was the one used to doing the observations. He didn't much like being on the other end of the spectrum.

"Sorry," he said briefly. "I didn't mean to wake you."

She didn't speak, but her gaze moved over his body in a way that made him nervous. She stared, from the waistband of his jeans to the thrust of his chin and then down again. At this point, he clenched his teeth as a muscle in his jaw began to jerk.

Damn this impossible situation. "Are you warm enough?"

Her gaze locked on to his. "What's happening?"

Her voice was soft and sleepy, and the sound did a number on his heart. The barriers that he so prudently kept up were in serious trouble of shattering.

"The storm has passed...at least for the time being. I came down to add some wood to the fire."

"Oh."

Another lengthy silence ensued. The heat from the fire was warming his backside quite nicely, but it was the heat in his belly that was starting to burn.

"Go back to sleep, Daisy."

Like a child, she obeyed, and when she shut her eyes, he thought he heard her sigh.

He headed for the stairs without looking back, dropping into bed and closing his eyes, willing himself to sleep. But it took a very long time for nature to overtake nerves. It was almost dawn before it happened, and it was after nine when the smell of cooking food drifted into the loft and brought him into an upright position.

The knowledge that he'd overslept was only half as startling to him as the fact that Daisy had rummaged around downstairs long enough to cook. It was disconcerting to know he'd accepted her presence enough to sleep through the noise.

He swung his legs over the side of the bed and grimaced as he looked down at his jeans. They looked slept in, which figured, since he hadn't pulled them off after he'd gotten up last night. Then he shrugged and reached for his boots. The leather was cold and stiff as he pulled them on, and he wished he'd left them downstairs by the fire.

He grabbed a black sweatshirt from the back of the chair and pulled it over his head as he started down the stairs. By the time he came out of the bathroom, his hair was damp, as was the day-old growth of black whiskers still glistening from the water he'd sloshed on his face.

He entered the kitchen just as Daisy was taking a pan from the oven. The smell of fresh-baked bread hit him right where it mattered. His belly grumbled, but it wasn't all hunger that drew him into the room. Part of it had to do with the woman at the stove. There was a smudge of flour on the breast of her red plaid shirt, and a smaller one on the side of her cheek. Her hair was piled high on her head, but there were long, curling tendrils that had escaped from the knot, teasing the sides of her cheeks, as well as the back of her neck.

"I made biscuits." She held up the pan as if it were a seven-layer cake frosted with gold.

All he could manage was a smile and a nod.

Her eyes were alight with a joy he envied. "I wasn't sure I knew how," she continued as she set the pan on the old wooden table with a thump. "But you know, it was like you said. When I don't think about it too hard, I find I do things on instinct."

He took a deep breath and finally found the guts to speak.

"You didn't have to cook."

"I know, but you've been so good to take care of me. It was the least I could do."

"Your hands..."

Still smiling, she held them up. "They're still a bit stiff, but that ointment you used worked wonders. Most of the soreness is gone." She turned and reached for the coffeepot. "Time's a great healer, you know."

The phrase had come to her from nowhere, but the moment she said it, the image of a short, gray-haired man flashed through her mind. She held her breath, certain that at any moment she would hear his voice and then know who he was. But the notion disappeared as quickly as it had come, and when she turned back around, some of the delight in her morning had faded.

Roman saw her shoulders tense and suspected she'd had another one of her "moments." When he saw her face, he knew he'd been right.

"It will get better."

Daisy blinked back tears of frustration as she poured out the coffee.

"Let's hope you don't have to say the same of those biscuits."

Again, her humor in the face of a serious situation caught Roman unaware, and he chuckled.

The transformation of his expression was startling—from cold to devastatingly handsome. Daisy busied herself with flatware and plates, and by the time the table was set, she had her emotions firmly in check.

They shared the food, but little else, each lost in troublesome thoughts. A short while later, their elation fell even further. Yes, the storm was over, but from the looks of the sky, another was impending. Twice Roman tried to use his cellular phone to call out, and each time, all he got for his trouble was static.

He kept thinking that if what Daisy remembered was true, there could be other people who'd gone down in the plane she'd been on. The authorities needed to be notified of the crash, and of her whereabouts, as well. But the snow was up over his knees, and the road he'd come up on was obliterated. Without the use of his phone, there was nothing they could do but wait for the weather to break.

Chapter 4

Davis Benton was standing on the roof of the Denver hospital when the medi-flight helicopter landed. He'd been waiting for this moment ever since he'd been notified of Gordon Mallory's plane going down. The terror of knowing his only daughter had been on the flight had been exacerbated by the snowstorm that had followed the crash. For a day and a half, search had been impossible. It was one of the few times in Davis's life when being rich didn't count. He could have bought this hospital and a dozen like it more than ten times over and never noticed a dent in his holdings. But he hadn't been able to beg, order or coerce even one pilot to take a chance on searching for the downed plane.

He'd been in Denver since the day before yesterday, waiting for a search to begin. Holly was his only daughter, in fact, his only child. They'd been close, but not unnecessarily so, and even though she was a grown woman, he was still dealing with the fact that she'd planned a trip with Mallory without telling him first.

He squinted, shielding his eyes and pulling the collar of his coat closer around his throat as the helicopter began to descend. All he'd been told was that they were coming in with three victims. Two were in serious condition. One of them was dead. His heart was in his throat as he watched the chopper descend. He kept thinking of death and how final it was.

Davis Benton had firsthand knowledge of such things. One day he'd been a happy, expectant father awaiting the birth of his first child, and before the day was out, his wife had gone into labor, delivered their baby and then died. Marsha had been taken from him without warning, yet he'd managed to survive. But if Holly was taken from him, there wasn't enough money in the world to make up for her loss.

The wind from the blades of the descending helicopter burned at his eyes as he tried desperately to focus.

Please, God, don't let Holly be dead.

When the chopper landed, his first instincts were to run toward it. But then the rescue team emerged and began unloading gurneys out of the helicopter's belly, and he found himself unable to move.

One group of hospital personnel raced past him, their expressions fixed with a purpose he didn't dare impede. His stare was blank, frozen with the horror only a parent could know as he gazed at the shape, then the face, of the first patient they pushed by him.

When he realized it was a man, his heart sank. That left only one other survivor. The odds in Holly's favor had just dropped.

"Please, please, please," Davis heard himself muttering, and blinked furiously to clear the thick film of tears from his eyes.

When the second gurney came out, even from here, he knew it wasn't his girl. The body was too long and the hair too light. They came closer, and he recognized the bloody but familiar face of Gordon Mallory.

At that point, his legs went weak. It was all he could do to stand upright as the last gurney was pulled out. When they began moving the covered body toward the rooftop entrance to the hospital, he became faint.

Hang in there, he told himself. You owe it to Holly.

"Wait!" he begged as they started to move past him.

The rescuers paused, their faces grim from the exhaustion and cold.

"Please," Davis said, reaching toward the body. "My baby...I need to see my girl."

"I'm sorry, sir," the nearest rescuer said. "But this isn't a woman. It's a man."

Davis's hand began to shake. "But Holly...where's Holly?"

The rescuer shook his head. "I'm sorry, sir, but there was no woman at the crash site. Only the three men we pulled out of the plane."

Davis was forced to step aside as they moved past him, but his mind was in a panic.

My God! They came back without her! How could they do that? Why didn't they stay to look for her?

He thought of her bleeding and disoriented, of wandering off from the crash site and then lying somewhere buried beneath the snow. Although it had been a long time since he'd bothered to pray for anything, he closed his eyes.

"Help her, Lord, because I fear right now she cannot help herself."

His mind was in a whirl. He had to get the rescue team back out there! But where to start? They'd obviously known there was a woman on board. He knew enough to realize they had probably searched as much as possible, but whatever clues would have been left had most likely been obliterated by the snow. A knot formed in his belly as the impossibility of the situation became real. What on earth were they going to do?

Then it hit him. Mallory was alive! And he would have answers. With resolve in his heart, Davis Benton bolted into the hospital.

* * *

It had been snowing since noon. As Roman had feared, the storm wasn't over. Being shut inside had made the day endless for both of them. They had done nothing but sidestep each other's presence, and now with the onset of the second wave of the storm, the cabin was closing in.

They spent the afternoon in near silence. Daisy tried to nap, and Roman pretended to read a book. He turned forty-four pages before it dawned on him that not only did he not remember what he'd been reading, but he didn't even know the title of the book. He gave it up as a lost cause and played solitaire until dark.

Then, while Roman was gathering in wood for the night, Daisy disappeared. When he heard water running in the tub, he knew where she'd gone. But an hour later, she had yet to emerge, and he was beginning to wonder if she was all right. Twice, he walked to the door with full intentions of calling to her, and for lack of a good reason, changed his mind each time.

He was in the kitchen when he heard her footsteps in the hall. A skitter of nerves danced their way down his back, but he made himself stay where he was. Instead, he reached for another potato and began to scrub it beneath the water running in the sink.

"Need any help?" Daisy asked.

"Nope."

"I took a bath and washed out a few things."

That made sense. Their choices of clothing were limited.

"I heard," he said, and scrubbed even harder on the hapless vegetable.

"It felt good to soak. Worked a lot of the soreness out in my muscles."

Soak? She was soaking. The hair stood on the backs of his arms as the image enveloped him.

"I changed clothes, too. I hope you don't mind, but you know how it is. Don't you just hate to put the same clothes back on once you've bathed?"

He turned, and the potato he'd been scrubbing fell out of his hands and into the sink while the water continued to flow.

"Uh..."

"It doesn't really fit, but it's so much warmer than the other shirt you loaned me. I know you have several, or I wouldn't have assumed."

"Fit?"

He wasn't making much sense, but Daisy thought nothing of it. The man was hardly a conversationalist. She pushed the rolled-up sleeves back up toward her elbows.

"I know it's way too long, but the cabin gets cold at night and I thought it would be warmer to sleep in."

"Sleep?"

"Yes. Your sweatshirt will be so much warmer to sleep in. You don't mind...do you?"

He shook his head, unable to tear his gaze away from what she held in her hands.

She turned away, her voice becoming fainter as she walked out of the kitchen, but he heard enough to know it was going to be a long night.

"I'm going to lay my underwear by the fireplace to dry, then I'll help you fix dinner."

Underwear. Those were the "few things" that she'd laundered. Every time he went to add wood to the fire, he'd be dodging lingerie. Well, hunky-damn-dory. Those blasted daisy panties and that bit-of-nothing bra were going to be the evening's entertainment.

He spun, turning off the water with a vicious twist of his wrist, then poking a couple of holes in the potato before tossing it into the oven with the other one he'd just cleaned.

Frustration mounted as he yanked a cast-iron skillet out of the cabinet and slammed it on the stove while considering the possibility of never speaking to Royal again.

She came back into the kitchen with that smile in her eyes, and Roman's temper fizzled like a wet match. If he hadn't come, what would have happened to her? Guilt hit him. She would probably have frozen to death, that's what. So what was a little inconve-

nience, compared to her life? It wasn't going to kill him to dodge
a couple of unmentionables. And he was a very grown male, not
some sex-starved teenager with a full set of raging hormones. So
she didn't have a stitch on under his sweatshirt except those jeans,
and they were so old and faded they clung to her skin like silk.
So what? Now, if she'd been some tall, leggy blonde, this might
have been a different story. He reminded himself again that she
just wasn't his type. Daisy...or whatever her name was...was
more than safe. Then she handed him a can of corn and the can
opener and smiled. Yes, she was safe, but was he?

Daisy whimpered in her sleep, but the sound went unheard.
High in the loft above, Roman tossed restlessly, trying to find
ease, both in his mind and his bed, unaware that her dreams had
taken her back into hell.

*Heat waves danced just above the surface of the runway as
Holly Benton got out of the cab. The private plane was there,
right where Gordon said it would be. She glanced at her watch.
She was early. But that was all right. It wouldn't take long to tell
him she'd decided not to go. This was a step in their relationship
she wasn't ready to take. In fact, she wasn't certain the day would
ever come when she'd be ready to take a step like this with him.
He was nice, and he treated her wonderfully, wining and dining
her all over Las Vegas, but he didn't make her heart skip beats.
All her life, she'd heard her father talking about how much he'd
loved her mother and that the mere sound of her voice had made
his heart skip a beat. She wanted that kind of relationship—that
kind of love. But it wasn't going to happen with Gordon.*

*She turned to the cab driver. "Wait for me. This won't take
long."*

He settled back in the seat as she started across the tarmac.

*She could hear Gordon's voice inside the plane as she started
up the steps. The tone was loud and threatening, and she wondered what on earth had angered him. Not once in the three*

months she'd known him had she ever heard him raise his voice, and because it was so out of character, she hesitated, thereby forever changing her fate.

"Damn it, Billy, it's too late to chicken out on me now."

"I don't care. I never signed on for murder."

Gordon Mallory sneered. "And it wouldn't have happened if you'd done what you were told to do."

"But I did what you said."

Gordon slapped his brother up the side of his head in frustration.

"Yeah, after the fact. This would have been an easy heist. Carl Julian had been skimming from the daily take at the casino for over six months. He had a million dollars of his boss's money in his safe. The last thing he would have done was report a robbery. What would he have said? 'Oh...by the way, the money I stole has been stolen from me.'" *He hit Billy again, only harder.* "If you'd done your job, Julian wouldn't have surprised us in the act."

"He wasn't gonna talk. You had no business killing him," *Billy mumbled.*

"I don't leave witnesses."

Holly froze. Her heart was in her throat. All she could think was that she had to get to the police. In her haste, the strap of her purse caught on the portable stairway. She gave it a yank, and everything inside went flying down the steps. Horrified, she looked up at the open doorway.

It was just as she'd feared. Gordon appeared in the doorway with his brother, Billy, right behind him.

Gordon took one look at her face and knew that she'd heard. When she began to run, he started down the steps after her, catching her by the arm before she'd reached the ground.

"Sweetheart, where do you think you're going?"

Play it cool, she kept telling herself, but her mind had gone blank. Where was a good lie when you needed one? Then she remembered the cab and tried a smile.

"I didn't have change for the cab," she said. "Then as I started up the steps, my purse caught on this stupid old railing and look what happened."

Gordon frowned. She was good. He'd give her that. But he could feel her pulse racing through her system and wasn't buying a word of what she'd just said. Spilling the contents of one's purse did not cause this kind of reaction.

Gordon pointed toward the cab. "Billy, pay the man while I get my sweet Holly out of this sun."

Oh, God, now what do I do? She took a deep breath and then pressed a hand to her forehead.

"No, Billy, wait," she said, trying to regain some control. "I was coming to tell Gordon that I'd changed my mind. I'm not really in the mood for Nassau after all."

A dark smile broke the scowl on Gordon's face as he began dragging her back up the steps. "Oh, but Holly, I'll put you in the mood."

"But my things," she said, pointing back toward her scattered belongings.

"Where you're going, you won't be needing them," he whispered.

"What are you going to do with her?" Billy asked.

The smile on Gordon's face darkened even more. "She doesn't want to go. I thought I'd give her about an hour to change her mind. Then—" he tightened his grip on Holly's arm "—if she still wants out...why, far be it from me to force a woman into anything she doesn't want to do. If she wants out, then out she goes."

Holly's heart dropped.

"But, Gordon, in an hour, we'll be in the air," Billy argued.

"Exactly," Gordon said, and then shoved Holly into the plane before she could scream for help.

Daisy's head rolled from side to side on her pillow as she struggled to breathe. Now she was caught in the darkness behind a dirty blindfold and the rubberlike scent of duct tape beneath her nose.

They'd been in the air for forty-five minutes, and in that time, Billy Mallory had hardly taken his eyes off of the woman Gordon had dumped on the floor between them.

"Damn it, Gordon, I still don't like this. Why can't we just drug her or something? It would be hours before she came to and we could be out of the country."

"You know me," Gordon said. "I don't leave witnesses."

But Billy stood his ground, desperately pleading his case. "Think what you're doing. Think who she is. Her old man has more money than Midas. If something happens to her, he'll tear up heaven and earth to find out who hurt her. If she dies, we'll never stop running."

Billy wasn't prepared for the blow, or the anger that came with it. When the fist connected with his jaw, he fell backward onto Holly's legs before dragging himself upright.

"You're going to be sorry," he said, wiping the blood from his lip.

Gordon cursed beneath his breath. "I already am. I should have known better than to let you get involved in something this big."

Billy spit blood as Gordon entered the cockpit, closing the door behind him. He could hear Holly Benton crying. If he hadn't looked down at her, he might have chosen a different path. But he did, and when he saw twin tracks of tears flowing out from beneath the blindfold, he snapped. Without giving himself time to rethink his actions, he yanked off her blindfold and tore off the tape before dragging her upright. He clapped his hand over her mouth and whispered near her ear.

"Keep quiet or we're both dead."

Her eyes were round with fear, but she did as she was told, watching in growing panic as he pulled a parachute from a nearby cupboard. The realization of what he intended seemed impossible to consider.

"What are you going to—?"

"You ready to die?"

She swallowed harshly, then shook her head.

"That's what I thought," he muttered, strapping her into the chute and giving her a quick, thumbnail sketch of what to do.

"After you jump, count to ten and then pull this."

Jump? She looked nervously over her shoulder and then ran her hands across the front of the straps, feeling for the handle he'd just mentioned.

Billy glanced over his shoulder as the enormity of his betrayal sank in. His hands were shaking as he grabbed a nearby duffel bag and hung it around her neck.

"There, now," he said, adjusting the straps so the bag wouldn't interfere with the deploying chute when she jumped.

"What's in this?" she asked.

"The reason we're in this mess. I have no more stomach for crime. You can tell the authorities whatever you want, but when we land, I swear to God I'm going straight. I've pulled my last con, and that's a fact."

The roar of rage that came from behind startled them both. Gordon had come back, and God help them, she was still in the plane.

Billy threw his weight against the door, anxiously twisting the lever. The door popped, like a cork out of a bottle. Instantly, the cabin was engulfed in a blast of chilling cold. In the wild rush of wind that followed, the inside of the cabin became a maelstrom of everything that wasn't tied down.

A piece of newspaper hit Holly in the face as the pressure inside the cabin dropped. Between the weight of the parachute and the bag Billy had hung around her neck, she was helpless to stop the inevitable from happening. Along with everything else that wasn't tied down, she tumbled out of the plane and into the sky, falling head over heels like a broken doll. Hurtling toward earth, the bag around her neck was alternately choking her or pulling her down. Once as she rolled on her back, she looked up at where she'd just been. Things were flying out of the plane right behind her, fluttering like so much confetti that had been tossed to follow her down.

And then the rush of wind in her ears and the sight of the earth coming up to meet her brought her to her senses. She closed her eyes, counted to ten, and then pulled the handle on the chute just as that damnable bag hit the side of her face. Blood was filling her mouth as the parachute deployed.

Daisy rolled off the sofa and onto the floor just as the parachute ballooned, stopping the woman's descent with a jerk. The memory was gone the moment she opened eyes, but the instinct to run was still with her. Without knowing why, she crawled to her feet and ran out of the door and into the storm.

The brutal cold was like a slap in the face. Reality surfaced just as she fell off the porch and into a snowdrift that was over her head. She opened her mouth to scream and got a mouth full of snow instead. Choking and gasping for air, she inadvertently sucked snow up her nose, as well. The harder she struggled, the deeper she fell into the drift. Further disoriented by the engulfing darkness, she tried to dig her way out, unaware that she was upside down and digging the wrong way. When her hands hit solid earth, she panicked. Something was wrong! Fear cut deep, like the blistering cold surrounding her. There was nothing before her but blackness, and nothing to hear but the muffled sound of the wind.

The scream came at him in stereo, echoing within the cabin and then up into the loft. He came off of the bed within seconds, and was halfway down the stairs when she ran out the door. Even though he saw it happening, he couldn't believe his eyes. She'd gone out into that blizzard in her bare feet, wearing nothing but a sweatshirt that barely covered her knees.

"Daisy! No!" he shouted, but she kept on going and, moments later, disappeared from his sight.

In the seconds it took him to get down the stairs and across the room to the door, his heart had stopped and started twice over. If she got lost out there, she'd be dead before he could find her.

He paused in the doorway, shouting her name aloud. But the wind threw it back down his throat. He reached back inside the house and hit the light switch, instantly flooding the porch with a weak but welcome glow.

And then he saw it, a dark indentation in the snow just off the porch. His heart dropped. She'd fallen into the drift! Without thinking of his own bare belly and feet, he stepped off the porch, only to find himself chest high in snow, and with more still falling.

With great effort, he began to move. Moments later, he stumbled upon something solid. To the best of his knowledge, there'd been nothing in this area but grass. What he was feeling had to be Daisy.

Thrusting deep, he began digging wildly, desperate to find her. The wind made the falling snow into a natural weapon, cutting his cheeks and stinging his eyes from the blast. And he was cold…so cold. Instinct told him to go back after some clothes, but he stayed. It was all he could do to keep digging.

When he felt fabric, then flesh, his heart skipped a beat. God help me, he thought, and went in after her, head first. When a hand suddenly closed around his wrist, he knew a moment of relief. At least she was conscious. In one motion, he scooped. When he stood, she was in his arms.

Staggering out of the snow and back onto the porch, he stumbled into the house. Clutching her close to his chest, he moved toward the sofa and the fire still burning in the fireplace.

"Daisy, can you hear me?"

When she didn't answer, his heart sank. Although her body was trembling, her eyes were closed. Snow clung to her skin, and her hair, and her clothing.

His hands were shaking as he laid her down. There was a panic in his voice that was relayed to his legs as they finally gave way. He knelt, and for a heartbeat, closed his eyes and leaned forward, resting his forehead on the sofa cushion and thanking God that she hadn't gone too far.

Daisy felt the heat first, then a pressure against her arm. When she opened her eyes, she saw him kneeling at her side.

Everything was mixed up in her mind. The dream that had sent her out on the run was gone. There was nothing left but the reality of a bone-chilling cold and the man at her side.

"What happened?"

Roman inhaled slowly, then looked up. "You went out for a little midnight stroll."

Her eyes widened. Only then did she notice the fact that they were both soaked to the skin.

"Dear God." She wiped a shaking hand across her face. "I must be going out of my mind."

She looked so small, so bedraggled, his heart went out to her.

"I know what you mean. For a moment there, I thought I was going to lose mine."

Daisy reached for him, touching the wet black hair plastered to his forehead and then grasping his wrist. His pulse was rock steady, just like the look in his eyes.

"I owe you my life."

He shook his head. "I don't believe in those kind of debts. Now, let's get into some dry clothes before we both catch pneumonia."

She started to get up.

"Stay by the fire," he ordered. "I'm going to run a hot bath. You need to get warm as quickly as possible."

"But what about you?" she asked, eyeing his bare feet and chest.

"I'll be fine," he said shortly. "I've been worse and survived. I will again."

Shuddering, she watched him walking away and knew how

fortunate she was to have stumbled into his life. There was something about this man that demanded respect.

She rolled over and sat up, leaning toward the heat of the fire as melting snow puddled around her feet. And as she waited for him to come back, she kept thinking of the money hidden upstairs beneath his bed. He was taking good care of her now—but what would he think and how would he behave if he knew?

Leaning forward, she rested her elbows on her knees and covered her face with her hands as an old saying kept circling through her mind. "Oh, what a tangled web we weave, when first we practice to deceive." All she'd done since they'd met was hide. And she was still hiding something from him—the truth as she knew it.

The fire was blazing. Daisy's underwear was dry and had been moved to make room for the wet clothes steaming on the hearth. By morning, the clothes would be dry. But to Daisy, the incident would never truly be over. She would never forget the panic of feeling buried alive, and then the overwhelming relief of his hand upon her thigh.

Cradling her cup of coffee between her hands, she stared into the fire, mesmerized by the flames slowing eating their way into the wood. It was thirty minutes past four in the morning. Sleep was over for her. The last thing she wanted to do was relive whatever it was that had driven her out into the storm.

Something banged in the hallway behind her. She didn't have to look over her shoulder to know it would be Roman, and not the wind. His voice cut through the silence in which she'd been sitting, sending her pulse into a swifter rhythm.

"Are you still cold?"

She shook her head, watching as he circled the sofa and then sat at the end, near her feet. She had a swift image of him stretching out beside her instead, and looked away before he could see it in her eyes. When he tucked at a loose edge of her covers, she took a quick sip of coffee, so as not to give herself away. The more she was around him, the more she wanted to be with him...in the true sense of the word.

Three days ago, she hadn't known he existed. And now, he'd become the most important thing in her life. She tried to tell herself it was all due to the predicament in which she'd landed. She didn't know who or where she was and she needed him for shelter and sustenance. And when the snow melted, she would need him to get her down off the mountain.

More than once, she'd seen the hard, unyielding side of him. But it was his gentleness and consideration that kept coming through, time and time again. That, and that slow, devastating smile. When she left, would he forget her? The thought hurt. She would never forget him.

Roman wanted to hold her. The feeling had been in the back of his mind for some time now. At least a day, maybe longer. Maybe as far back as the moment he'd seen daisies shining through the seat of her pants.

There was a knot in his throat that had nowhere to go. He'd done the unthinkable and let himself care for a woman he didn't even know. He tried not to think of the stupidity of the act, but it was almost pointless. There was nowhere he could go to escape her presence. Even when she wasn't in the room, the scent of her seemed to linger, like a fresh breath of the spring.

He kept reminding himself that she could be someone's wife— someone's mother. She could have a lover who was desperate to know of her fate. There was a selfish part of him that almost wished she would never remember—that her life would begin from the moment they met. At that point, his thoughts kept fading. What comes afterward? What happens when the snow melts? What do I do when the time comes for her to walk away? In his mind, he knew it was imminent. In his heart, the notion was abhorrent.

When Daisy stirred, he looked up. Their gazes met, then locked. A silence grew between them.

He kept looking at her eyes, then her mouth and the healing cut at the edge of her lip.

There was a muscle jerking at the side of his jaw. Daisy wondered if his belly was in knots. Hers certainly was. He inhaled slowly. When his gaze drifted down toward her mouth, she saw his nostrils flare. It wasn't much of a signal, but it was enough to let her know something of his mood. Unaware she was holding her breath, she waited for him to make the next move.

Roman's gut clenched. There was an unmistakable look in her eyes, and he knew why it was there. More than once during the past couple of days, she'd come close to dying. When that happened to people, quite often they would turn to something to remind them how precious life really was. And what better way to do that than to lie in someone's arms, to feel the thunder of your own heartbeat rolling through your ears, to savor the feel of body-to-body contact in a never-ending embrace. With the right person, it could be heaven. But with the wrong person, it could be the biggest mistake of your life. He gritted his teeth and tried to shift the mood.

"Don't you want to try and get some more sleep?"

Her eyes never left his face. "I'm afraid to sleep."

He swallowed and tried to look away, but there was an energy between them he couldn't ignore.

"If you're afraid of a repeat performance, we could trade beds," he offered.

She shook her head, and there was a tone in her voice he'd never heard before.

"I don't need sleep."

He leaned forward. "Then what is it you need?"

Her breath caught. Say it. Tell him now. It's only three little words. I need you. That's what I need. I need you.

But the words wouldn't come, and although he could see her struggling, she remained silent.

He leaned back, only then aware he'd been holding his breath. Daisy shuddered and then drew her knees up toward her chest, as if she'd come too close to a flame. She had to say something, do something, anything to break the tension between them.

"Then talk to me," she said softly. "Tell me all there is to know about Roman Justice."

He almost smiled. "Not much to tell."

"Then tell me the little bit."

He sighed. She was persistent. He'd give her that. T..en he remembered. She'd fallen out of a plane, been up a tree and up to her eyeballs in snow, and he had yet to see her come unglued. Hell, yes, she was persistent, even tenacious, and talking should be safe.

"I'm the youngest of three brothers, and my parents are dead."

Daisy sighed, wishing she knew enough to reciprocate.

"Why did you become a private investigator?"

"I wanted to be my own boss and I needed a job that would utilize the skills Uncle Sam taught me."

Daisy frowned, a bit lost to the connection. "And that would be?"

"How to hide in plain sight."

"Can you teach me how?"

His eyes narrowed sharply. "Why would you want to hide?"

She thought of the money and then looked back at his face. If ever there was a time to trust him, it was now.

Chapter 5

"Roman?"

"What?"

"There's something I haven't told you."

His emotions went into shutdown. I knew this would happen. I let myself get too close to a stranger.

"So talk," he said shortly.

Daisy's heart dropped. The wariness was back in his voice, but it was too late to stop now. She got up from the sofa.

"Where are you going?" he asked.

She sighed. "Just wait here. You'll know soon enough."

When she started up the stairs, he stood.

She looked back just as she reached the landing, and he would have sworn there was true regret on her face. When she dropped to her knees beside his bed and then lay down on her belly and crawled under it, a knot began forming in the pit of his stomach.

Daisy came down the steps with the bag in her hand and dropped it at Roman's feet. Then she stepped back, waiting for him to make the next move.

"What's in that?" he growled.

"See for yourself. But don't ask me where it came from. All I know is, when I finally got down from the tree, it was lying nearby. I have a vague memory of falling out of the plane with it hanging around my neck."

"What's the big secret? If it's so all-fired important to you, why didn't you tell me about it sooner?"

She took a deep breath, gauging his reaction to what she was about to say.

"Men have killed for less. I didn't know you. I was afraid for my life."

"You aren't making sense," he said shortly, then knelt and unzipped the bag. The sides parted like an overripe tomato, revealing the contents all too clearly.

Roman's heart sank. Oh, hell. There was never a good or honest reason for someone to be in possession of so much cash. And she was right about one thing. Men had certainly killed for less reason.

Daisy held her breath. He was too calm. Then he looked up, and the blaze in his eyes seared her soul. All the doubt and mistrust that he'd had before was back—and a thousand times over.

"Is this yours, or did you steal it?"

The tone of his voice cut straight to her heart. Tears blurred her vision, but she wouldn't look away.

"I don't know." Her chin quivered. "I wish to God I knew, but I don't."

"There must be close to a million dollars in here."

She shrugged. "I didn't bother to count it."

He pulled the zipper and then kicked the bag toward her as he stood.

"Maybe I should have named you Bonnie, 'cause you can bet your little daisy behind that there's a Clyde out there somewhere who's wondering where you've gone."

She started to cry. Not sobs, but slow, silent tears that slid right down her face. She looked down at the bag and then back up at him and felt as if her heart were breaking.

"I don't want it. Put it somewhere, anywhere. Toss it out in the storm for all I care. I've had nothing but a bad feeling ever since I saw it."

Roman glared as she walked back to the sofa and lay down, pulling the covers up over her head.

"Hiding won't make it go away," he said shortly.

She didn't answer.

He looked back at the bag and cursed. He didn't want to be mad. He didn't want to distrust. But what the hell did she think he would do?

"I'll put it here in the downstairs closet."

She yanked the covers down long enough to get her message across. "You can throw it in the fireplace. Use it to start your next fire. Take it to the bathroom and use it for toilet paper. Just get it out of my sight."

He tossed it in the closet and then stuffed his hands in his pockets.

"Daisy."

There was a muffled answer from beneath the covers.

"Damn it, woman. Come out from under the covers and talk to me."

She emerged, her eyes red rimmed and swimming in tears, her lips quivering.

"You don't want to talk, you want to accuse. I may deserve everything you're thinking about me, but right now it doesn't feel like it, okay? Right now, I feel indignant as hell. Besides, how can I talk about this when I can't remember anything?"

"Look, I'm sorry," Roman said.

"Yes, and I'm..." The answer was right on the tip of her tongue. If she hadn't been listening to herself talk, it would have come out; she just knew it. "Oh, Roman, I almost had it," she said, and laid her arm across her eyes in defeat. "My name—it was right on the tip of my tongue."

He shook his head. If she was lying to him, then she was as good as it gets.

"It will come when it's time," he said.

A log fell off the stack and down into the ashes as sparks flew up the chimney. Daisy shook her head, no longer able to believe in anything or anyone.

"Roman."

"What?"

"Why do I feel like I'm running out of time?"

"I don't know. Maybe your subconscious is trying to tell you something."

"Then I wish it would talk a little louder. I think I'm going crazy."

She turned over on the sofa with her back to the fire and closed her eyes.

He felt her rejection, both of him and the entire situation, and knew she was justified in feeling this way. The investigator in him kept trying to think of legal reasons as to why she could be in possession of so much money, but there were far too many illegal scenarios that kept coming to mind.

Frustrated, he shoved his hand through his hair, combing the short, dark strands in an absent fashion as he headed for the kitchen. He needed a drink. He would settle for caffeine instead.

A short while later, the rich aroma of freshly brewed coffee filled the room as he poured himself a cup. In the past few minutes, one thing had become patently clear. If Daisy hadn't trusted him enough to take him into her confidence, he would never have known the money was there. And what's more, she'd been right to hesitate in revealing the bag's presence. If the situation had been reversed, he would have reacted the same way.

Something blew against the outside of the kitchen door. He glanced toward it and then out the window. There was a faint glow to the east. Morning wasn't far away. There was another, less distinct sound behind him. He turned. Daisy was standing in the doorway.

"Roman."

"Yes."

"How much do you charge for your services?"

Although the corner of his mouth twitched, he responded with a straight face.

"Are you referring to personal or professional?"

"Do shut up," she muttered. "I'm serious."

"Enough," he said. "Although, from the contents of that bag, I don't think you'll have a problem with your bills. Why?"

"Because I want to hire you. I want you to help me find out who I am and why I have all this money."

He shrugged. "We'll see," he said shortly. "There's a real good chance that you'll remember everything on your own, you know."

But she wouldn't give up. "And there's a good chance that I won't. I have to know. Will you or won't you?"

He sighed. She reminded him of Royal, tenacious to a fault.

"I will."

"Then that's that," she said, and walked out of the room.

No, Daisy, that wasn't that, Roman thought. It was only the beginning.

Davis Benton prowled the hospital halls like a man possessed. While Gordon Mallory had yet to wake up, another stormfront had moved in right behind the first one, making further search of the crash site impossible. He kept thinking of his daughter. Holly hated the cold. And he kept mentally replaying the message she had left on his machine.

Daddy, Gordon and I are flying to Nassau for a few days. You know, a fun-in-the-sun sort of thing. I'll call you as soon as we get there so you'll have my number. Take care and I love you.

He stuffed a handful of coins into a vending machine and then wearily rested his forehead against it while waiting for the coffee he so badly needed. Although he hadn't completely given up hope, there was a part of him that had already begun making concessions with God. If he couldn't find her alive, he still needed to find her. He didn't think he could go through the rest of his life without at least laying her body to rest.

"Davis Benton?"

He turned, the hot coffee sloshing over the rim of the foam cup and onto his fingers.

"Yes, I'm Davis Benton."

"You're to come with me," the orderly said. "The patient you've been waiting to see just woke up."

"Thank you, God," Davis muttered, tossing the coffee in the trash as he went past.

A doctor emerged from Gordon's room just as they reached the door.

"Mr. Benton?"

Again, Davis nodded.

"You can't stay long," he said. "He's only just awakened, and he'll be groggy, so don't expect miracles."

Davis nodded again and started to push past him when the doctor took him by the arm, momentarily stopping him.

"If it weren't for the circumstances surrounding your missing daughter, I wouldn't be allowing this," he said.

Davis swallowed nervously. "I know, Doctor, and I appreciate your cooperation, more than you will ever know."

The doctor shrugged. "Ultimately, it's not my cooperation you need. It's Mr. Mallory's. Now, remember, don't stay long."

"I won't," Davis said, and then went inside.

Gordon Mallory's first thought upon awakening was that it felt good to hurt. After Billy had popped the door to the plane, all hell had broken loose. His fight with Billy had been put aside when the plane had suddenly gone into a nosedive.

Seeing the pilot slumped over the controls was the second-worst moment of his life. Seeing Holly sucked out of the door with his money was the worst. At that moment, he was certain they were going to die. And then Billy astonished him by climb-

ing into the copilot's seat and taking control. The anger between
them vanished, and it was anyone's guess as to whether they
would make it or not.

The pilot continued to groan and clutch at his chest as the plane
kept losing altitude. Even Gordon said a few prayers. Twice they
just missed going into the side of a mountain, and each time,
Billy managed to keep them in the air. But when they began
skimming the treetops, they prepared for the worst.

They went down in a tree-covered valley between two peaks,
taking out a swath of trees and bushes with the underbelly of the
plane before going nose first into the earth.

And when it was over, the silence was almost as frightening
as the moments before had been. Where there had been screams
and shouts, there was quiet. Great trees had snapped like tooth-
picks, and the fuselage of the jet was crumpled like used tin foil.
Now there was nothing but the hissing sound of escaping steam
and the frightening stench of spilled fuel.

He remembered trying to run and being unable to feel his legs.
It was the next morning before he realized he wasn't paralyzed,
only pinned down by the wreckage.

Billy was pinned in the cockpit, still alive, but from the sound
of his voice, badly hurt. He answered Gordon's intermittent que-
ries for several hours, but by morning, he became as silent as the
woods in which they'd crashed. Gordon held out hope for a rescue
up until the time it started to snow. After that, he lost all track of
time.

When the rescue team broke into the cabin, Gordon thought he
was dreaming. It was only when they freed him from the wreckage and he began to feel pain that he knew he was going to live.
Then all his energies were focused on getting well and finding
Holly, because where she was, his money would be also. He had
a pretty good fix on where she'd gone down. With a little luck,
he should be able to find her body.

And he was certain it would be her body they'd find. Billy had
all but sealed her fate when he'd strapped a parachute to her back

and then hung that duffel bag around her neck. Gordon was convinced that the duffel bag would have interfered with the opening of the chute. And even if the chute had managed to open, the straps on the bag would have certainly strangled her. Either way, it was just a small setback. The snow couldn't last forever. All he had to do was get well and then recover what was rightfully his.

Then Davis Benton walked in the door. Gordon's first instinct was to panic, but he reminded himself there was no way Benton could know anything. There was no one left alive who could tell.

"Gordon, thank God you survived."

Gordon took a deep breath and then groaned with the pain of the motion.

"Don't move," Davis said. "Let me do most of the talking, okay?"

Gordon blinked that he understood. It wouldn't hurt to let Davis think he was worse off than he really was.

"They didn't find Holly. Do you know what happened to her?"

Gordon groaned. Hell, yes, he knew. She jumped out of the plane with his money.

"Don't know," he muttered.

Davis's hopes fell. The two small words were like a knife in the heart.

"Can you tell me what happened? Why did you crash?"

Gordon's mind was racing. Here's where he covered his tracks—just in case.

"We lost cabin pressure and I blacked out. I don't know what happened to Holly, or to the plane."

Davis wanted to cry. "Ah, God," he groaned, and covered his face with his hands.

If nothing else, Gordon Mallory was a realist. There *was* the possibility he'd never see his money again. And Davis Benton had just bought the entire story. It wouldn't hurt to add a bit to the scenario for good luck. He took a deep breath, aware that it would cause enough pain to bring tears to his eyes, and right now, he needed some tears in his eyes to say what he had to say.

The groan that came out of Gordon's mouth was not faked. The pain was real, as were the tears that followed.

Davis looked up. "Don't move," he said quickly. "I'll get a nurse."

"Don't want a nurse," Gordon mumbled. "Want Holly...my Holly."

Davis wanted to scream. "I know, son. I want her, too."

"You don't understand," Gordon continued, playing his role to the hilt. "We were eloping. She was going to be my wife and now she's gone." He closed his eyes and turned his face to the wall. "Without Holly, I don't want to live."

Davis rocked back on his heels, stunned by what Mallory had to say. Elope? He knew they'd dated. But he'd had no idea their relationship had gotten to this.

"Look, son, we need to think positive," Davis said. "I don't believe in giving up until someone else tells me it's over. And right now, I will have to see Holly's body before I quit hoping."

Gordon shook his head slowly from side to side. "It's hard to hold out for hope when you're the only survivor," he whispered.

Davis's eyes brightened as he suddenly clutched at Gordon's arm.

"They didn't tell you!"

"Tell me what?" Gordon mumbled.

"You aren't the only survivor. Your brother, Billy. He's still alive!"

The morning dawned bright and clear. Snow was anywhere from knee to chest high, but it had stopped accumulating. Roman stepped out of the cabin and took a slow, cleansing breath. Last night had, quite possibly, been the longest night of his life.

The money was still in the downstairs closet where he'd tossed it, and his accusations still hung in the air between them, although a semi-truce had been reached. When he thought about it, it was almost laughable. If he wasn't mistaken, Daisy had just hired him to solve the mystery surrounding her, and she was going to pay him with someone else's money. What was worse, he'd all but agreed to do it. If the legal system had a mind to pick nits, that probably made him an accessory after the fact to a possible crime.

He looked out into the clearing. The only thing visible of his vehicle was the roof of the cab and the upper portion of the windows. He shoved his hands in his pockets and frowned. Even if it started thawing right now, it would be two or three days before the roads would be passable.

He thought of Royal and went back inside for the phone. The air was clear, the wind almost nonexistent. Maybe now a call would go through. Knowing Royal, he'd be waiting.

Daisy was coming out of the bathroom when he came down from upstairs.

"What are you doing?" she asked, eyeing the cellular phone he was carrying.

"Going to try and contact my brother again. I just want to let him know I'm okay."

A nervous look came on her face. "Are you going to tell him about me?"

Roman frowned. "I'm going to tell him that there's a possibility a plane went down up here. Didn't you ever stop to think that there could be other survivors?"

The blood suddenly drained from her face. She could almost hear the urgency in the man's voice. *After you jump, count to ten and then pull this.*

"There *was* someone. I keep remembering a voice telling me to jump, then count to ten and pull." Her fingers fluttered around the middle of her chest, where the handle had been. "You know...the rip cord."

Another chink in the armor around Roman's heart just gave way. Every time he heard that frightened tone in her voice, he wanted to hold her.

"You did good, didn't you, Daisy?"

"What do you mean?"

"You're alive, aren't you?"

She shuddered and then sighed. "Yes, there's that." The tone of her voice grew firmer. "Of course the authorities must know. Make the call. Do it now while I'm here."

"Then put on your shoes," he ordered. "I'm going outside. The reception should be clearer."

"Wait for me. I won't be a minute."

Roman stood for a moment, watching as she ran to get her shoes. She had put the old gray pants and the red flannel shirt back on, and even though she was dressed warm enough for indoors, the cold outside was quite bitter.

"I'm ready, Roman. Let's make the call."

He took his parka out of the closet and held it out. "Put this on first. It's cold as blazes outside. You'll freeze."

She was enveloped by its weight and warmth, as well as the scent of the man who wore it. Her heart told her that this was a little bit of what it would be like to be held within his arms.

There was laughter in Roman's voice as he leaned down to zip it up. "You're lost in there, but at least you won't freeze."

His head was close to her mouth. If she leaned just the least bit forward, she would have been able to feel the dark, springy strands of his hair on her face. She took a slow, deep breath, telling herself not to move.

Then he looked up.

The smile froze on his face as his gaze locked on to hers, and Daisy knew without words that he could see what she was thinking.

"Roman."

The sound of his name on her lips was little more than a whisper, and yet he would have heard it if she'd never voiced the word. His gaze drifted across her face, from those deep, expressive green eyes, past the natural pout of her mouth to the tremble he could see in her chin. His belly clenched with a longing that shocked him. He inhaled slowly, watching every nuance of her expression for a warning to back off. It didn't come.

"You know," he said softly. "You're not my type."

Her eyelids fluttered. "I don't like you much, either," she said softly.

"Liar."

She leaned forward and felt his breath upon her face. "I'm not."

Roman cupped the back of her neck. "Then prove it."

Daisy sighed as he came closer still. She couldn't stand it any longer. Their lips met. Someone groaned. Daisy broke their connection long enough to whisper, "Take that."

Then she kissed him again. "And that." She clung to his shoulders as he wrapped his arms around her and lifted her off of her feet. Once again, there wasn't enough room between them for a thought to pass through. "And that, too."

Roman groaned. He had more than he could take and still have good sense.

"Stop now, woman, while there's something left of me to recycle. You're right. You win. You don't like me one bit."

Roman nuzzled the side of her neck near the collar of his coat. She was the first woman he'd ever met who smelled sweeter than any perfume.

Daisy closed her eyes as her knees went weak. "I guess you'd better try that call."

Roman groaned. He didn't want to talk on a phone; he wanted to take her to bed.

"Yes, I guess you're right," he said, and reluctantly turned her loose.

"Still coming with me?" he asked.

"You couldn't lose me if you tried."

A rare smile broke the somberness of his face. "It scares the hell out of me to admit it, but I think I'm counting on that."

For the first time since Daisy's trauma had begun, she had a good feeling about tomorrow. No matter what happened now, she had Roman Justice on her side.

Roman pulled her beneath his arm as he punched in the numbers. Then he counted the rings. If Royal didn't answer before the fifth ring, the answering machine would come on. He didn't want to talk to a machine. He wanted to talk to—

"Hello! It's your nickel, start talkin'."

Roman grinned. As usual, Royal sounded annoyed. He hoped Maddie wasn't at the bottom of the problem.

"Royal, it's me, Roman."

Royal almost shouted. "Boy! It's about time you called."

"If you were so worried, you could have done the calling," Roman said.

Royal muttered a slight curse beneath his breath. "I lost the damned number to your cell phone. Maddie, I told you to take that mangy-ass cat out of this house and back to the barn."

Roman grinned. Unfortunately, his guess about Royal's mood had been right on the money. Maddie *was* the root of her father's ire. And he could hear the bell-clear tone of her little-girl voice in the background, still arguing her case.

"You heard me, girl," Royal roared. "And for Pete's sake, quit kissin' the damned thing. It's got fleas and God knows what else."

"Royal."

Royal paused in his tirade, as if he'd forgotten that Roman was even on the phone.

"Oh...yeah...sorry."

"You're going to be even sorrier if you don't clean up your vocabulary around her. Just listen to yourself. 'Mangy-ass.' 'Damned.' And who knows what else. You're going to be highly sorry when she goes to kindergarten this fall with those words on her lips."

Royal sighed. "I know. I know. Hell's fire, I need a keeper." Then he shifted gears. "Back to you. Are you snowed in?"

"Up to my chest."

Royal whistled. "You're kidding."

"No, brother, I'm not. And I have only myself to blame. Had I not given in to you in a weak moment, I could be home right now, enjoying a warm spring day, not shoveling wood into this fireplace like there was no tomorrow."

Royal chuckled. "Well, at least you 'got away from it all'."

Roman glanced down at Daisy. "Umm, not exactly."

"What does that mean?" Royal asked.

Roman changed tactics. There was serious business to discuss.

"Hey, Royal. I need you to do something for me."

"Yeah, sure," Royal said.

"I want you to check with the FAA and see if there was a plane that went missing anywhere in this area, then get back to me."

"Why?"

"Because I think one went down somewhere around here, and because we need to notify the authorities, if they don't already know."

"Well, okay. But—"

Roman started to mention Daisy's presence, but he kept thinking of the money in the downstairs closet.

"Just do it," he said. "And if there's one that went down, call me back with whatever information you can get and we'll go from there."

"In the meantime," Royal said, "enjoy the view."

Roman looked down at Daisy. "I am."

Chapter 6

Gordon Mallory was in a panic. Billy was alive! Even if he was a screwup, he was still his brother and, in effect, had saved both their lives. But Gordon hadn't forgotten that Billy had also betrayed him. Not only had he helped Holly escape, but he'd also given away Gordon's money.

His thoughts kept turning in circles, with fear uppermost in his mind. Had Billy talked? He didn't think so, at least not yet. If he had, Gordon would have already experienced the consequences of the revelation. The fact that Gordon was flat on his back in a hospital bed wouldn't matter to the authorities if they knew he'd committed a crime. He'd never known the authorities to be particular about where they found the guilty parties, just as long as they found them.

Gordon also figured if Holly's father had talked to Billy, he would never have set foot in this room. All he could do was hope and pray that Billy had the good sense to keep quiet. If all else failed, there was the fact that Billy could still die.

Out in the hall, he could hear carts rattling. They were bringing the food trays. He shifted on the bed, trying to find ease. Moments later, a nurse came in with a tray.

"Good evening, Mr. Mallory. Your meal is here."

He managed a smile, although how anyone could call this stuff edible was beyond him.

"I don't know why they call this food when everything is liquid."

"Now, Mr. Mallory, you're quite lucky to be alive, and I'm certain Doctor has his reasons for putting you on a liquid diet."

Gordon tried another smile. The last thing he wanted to do was antagonize his source of information. He sighed loud and long.

"I know, but it's just hard to be positive when I'm so worried about my brother. They won't let me see him and—" he let his voice drop an octave for effect "—he's all the family I have, you know."

The nurse's expression softened. "It must be rough," she said.

He nodded. "If only I knew how he was doing. Have you seen him?"

She hesitated. It was against hospital policy for a nurse to give out any sort of patient information other than affirming their condition.

Then Gordon added. "I know his condition is listed as serious."

That much she could say. "Yes, that's correct."

Gordon glanced down at his tray, as if contemplating where to start. He picked up his spoon and took the lid off a small cup to his right.

"Well, now, cherry gelatin. It's Billy's favorite."

The nurse frowned. "I'll be back later for your tray."

Gordon sighed again, hoping for a forlorn expression. When the nurse paused at the door and then turned, he hid his glee.

"Your brother is stable, Mr. Mallory. However, he hasn't regained consciousness, so that's probably why they have discouraged you from visiting. He couldn't talk to you anyway, so there's no need putting any stress on yourself by trying to walk."

Gordon wanted to shout with relief. Instead, he maintained a calm demeanor.

"Nurse, I appreciate what you've told me. Rest assured I will keep the information to myself. And I will say a prayer for Billy's recovery."

She slipped out the door, leaving Gordon with a lighter heart. In fact, he felt so good about the news that he jabbed the spoon in the gelatin and started to eat. He was halfway through before he remembered he didn't even like the stuff.

Davis Benton was in his hotel room and in the process of making a nuisance of himself, but he didn't give a damn. He was on the phone with search and rescue, and until they promised him what he wanted to hear, he wasn't going to go away.

"Look," he said, "if it's a matter of money, I'll pay whatever it takes. The snow has stopped. The sky is clear. For God's sake, please reconsider! The least you can do is go back to the crash site and search the surrounding area. My daughter was on that plane, and even though she wasn't on board when you got there, she couldn't have gone far."

As he listened, the frown on his face began to smooth out. The next argument he'd been planning wasn't necessary. It seemed they were already loading their gear.

"I'll be at this number all day," he said quickly. "You will let me know if—"

Then he nodded as the man on the other end of the line told him what he needed to hear. Moments later, he disconnected, then dropped to the side of the bed with a thump.

The room was quiet. Too quiet. There was too much silence and too much time to contemplate his shortcomings as a father. The only thing left for him to do was pray, so he did.

Roman was shoveling a path to the woodpile. The exercise felt good, even though the air was so cold it hurt to draw a deep breath. More than once, he'd caught Daisy watching him from the window. There was a tension between them that he couldn't deny, and it had nothing to do with the weather. After what had happened between them this morning, the tension had increased. Everything he was about warned him to seize the moment—to go back into that cabin and take her to bed. He'd lived his life on the edge for too long and he knew all too well that for some people, tomorrows never came. The only certainty was the present, and even it could disappear in the space of a heartbeat.

It was the wisdom of getting close to Daisy that he questioned. Her amnesia and that bag full of money were two deterrents he couldn't ignore. He didn't want to fall in love with a criminal...or another man's wife.

He scooped the last bit of snow from the path and tossed it aside before glancing back at the cabin. Daisy wasn't at the window, but he would lay odds she wasn't too far away. He stuck the shovel in the ground and began to gather another load of wood. May as well make the trip back a useful one.

She met him at the door, holding it open as he came inside.

"Thanks," he said.

"I saw you coming," she said quickly.

He stood without moving, staring at the confusion on her face and contemplating the idea of pushing this further. His heart said yes. His instincts for survival said no.

"You're letting in cold air," she said, and slammed the door shut with a thump as Roman moved past her, dumping the wood on the hearth and then dusting the snow off his coat and gloves before hanging them nearby to dry.

She was standing so close that when he turned, he almost bumped into her.

"Sorry."

Her blush deepened. "My fault," she said, and turned away.

Roman hid a frown. They were caught in an emotional seesaw, and unless one of them had the good sense to stop it, something was bound to happen that they couldn't take back. And since his mind was supposedly sound, it was left up to him to be the one to practice good judgment.

She was busying herself at the sofa, brushing at a crumb that wasn't really there, then picking up a book. She looked as awkward as he felt.

"Daisy."

She jerked, and the book she was holding dropped out of her hands onto the sofa as she looked up.

"What?"

"About this morning..."

A faint flush spread up her cheeks.

"What about it?"

"What if you're somebody's wife?"

His meaning was all too clear, but giving up what she felt seemed a worse sin than persisting.

"And what if I'm not?" she countered.

"But you could be, and if it were my wife who was missing, I wouldn't want her in some other man's bed."

She bit her lip to keep from crying. "But I don't feel like I belong to anyone."

Her answer intrigued him. "Then what *do* you feel like?" he asked.

Like making love with you.

The thought stunned her, and she looked away, but not before Roman had seen the want in her eyes.

"Never mind," he said shortly, and headed for the kitchen, mentally cursing the size of the cabin and the snow outside. He needed to get away from her, and there was nowhere else to go but upstairs to bed. Since that was out of the question, then the kitchen it had to be. Only when he turned around, she was standing in the doorway. Her expression was grim, and there was a glint in her eyes he'd never seen before.

"I want you to understand something," she said.

He waited.

"I'm attracted to you, but I'm not stupid, and I can only imagine what you must think of me. Whether I'm married, or have a significant other, is immaterial to the fact that I am, quite possibly, a criminal.'' She drew a deep breath. ''If the situation was reversed, I wouldn't want me, either.''

Then she spun on her heel and stalked out of the kitchen, leaving Roman with the impression that she'd just thrown down the gauntlet. Whatever happened now was up to him.

It was almost midnight. Roman came out of the bathroom, towel drying his hair and glancing at the sofa. Daisy was already in bed. He looked toward the fireplace. There was plenty of wood on the fire, and the screen was in place. She should be fine until morning.

The sweats he was wearing were old, his T-shirt even older. And thanks to the bit of laundry Daisy had done this morning, the socks he was wearing were clean and dry. He tossed the towel on the back of a nearby chair and then used his fingers for a comb as he slipped past the sofa to check the lock on the door. Even though they were miles away from any sort of civilization, he locked it out of habit.

He was halfway up the stairs to the loft when Daisy's soft voice broke the silence.

''Roman.''

He paused in midstep, his heart suddenly hammering against the wall of his chest.

''Yes?''

''Good night.''

Only then did he realize he'd been holding his breath. He exhaled slowly.

''Good night,'' he said, and listened until she'd settled again.

He crawled into bed with an ache on his mind. All he could think was, damn the snow and damn this situation all to hell. He thumped the pillow several times in succession before shoving it to one side. Then he rolled over on his stomach and, using his arms for his pillow, fell fast asleep.

* * *

Locked in a nightmare, Daisy struggled to get free of her tangled covers. In her dream, they'd become the ropes around her wrists, and her sleep had become the blindfold across her eyes. She kept trying to scream, but nothing came out except sobs. God help her, she didn't want to die.

Roman opened his eyes with a jerk, his heart pounding. For a moment, he lay without moving, listening for the sound that had disturbed his sleep. Then he heard it. Daisy!

He kicked back the covers and rolled out of bed, afraid that she was about to pull a repeat performance of the night before. The last thing they needed was to take a midnight dip in another snowdrift.

He was halfway down the stairs before the sounds that he'd heard became distinct. And when he could see that she was still asleep on the sofa, his panic abated. Moving quietly, he circled the sofa to kneel down beside her. In the glow from the fireplace, the tracks of her tears had become thin silver threads stringing down her cheeks. Her forehead was knit in a frown, and she kept fighting the covers under which she lay. He hated to wake her, but watching her torment was worse.

In a voice he would have used with Maddie, he whispered her name.

"Daisy. Daisy. Wake up. You're having a bad dream."

Her eyelids fluttered, then her nostrils flared as she took a deep breath. Her forehead smoothed. The frown she'd been wearing disappeared with the dream, and as she opened her eyes, she swallowed a sob.

There was momentary confusion on her face as she focused on where she was and not where she'd been.

"Roman?"

He wiped at her tears with the balls of his thumbs. "You were having a bad dream."

Her lips were trembling as her gaze raked the contours of his face. Even in the dark, his strength shone through. The contours of his features were highlighted in the faint light from the fire.

The familiarity of them gave her comfort. At last, something she knew. Something she recognized. Roman. Her Roman.

"Dear God," she whispered, and slipped her arms around his neck. "I'm so tired of this. I'm so everlasting tired of this. Ah, Roman, what if I never remember?"

Her gesture was unexpected, but the symbolic meaning was not lost on him. It was trust. Pure and simple. She trusted him, but did he trust himself?

"You will. You will," he said softly, and then pulled her arms from around his neck. "Easy," he urged when she would have fussed. "I'm not leaving you."

Instead, he sat down beside her and then pulled her into his lap before wrapping them both with her covers.

"Are you comfortable?" he asked.

Daisy shuddered on a sigh. Comfortable? The word was more like *content*.

"Yes," she said softly, and settled her head against the strength of his shoulder as he tightened his grip. She was certain that whoever she was, she'd never felt this safe. If the world—and that bag full of money—would just go away, she could be happy for life.

"Try to go back to sleep," he said.

"But you won't be able to rest sitting up."

He looked down at the crown of her head nestled beneath his chin. Considering the weight of the knot in his stomach, she felt surprisingly light in his arms. A slight grin broke the somberness of his face.

"I've been in a lot worse places."

Daisy tried to relax, but there were too many extenuating factors. As hard as she tried, she couldn't forget where she was—in Roman's arms—or where she was lying, next to Roman's heart.

The steady beat next to her ear matched her own pulse. She closed her eyes and tried to think of something else, only to become aware that one of his hands was cupping her bottom.

Afraid to move, and a bit afraid not to, she let her mind go blank. And then she felt the faint but unmistakable stirring of his breath upon her face and looked up. At that point, the inevitability of their circumstance took over.

Roman blinked, but not fast enough to hide what he'd been thinking. The impossible had happened. She'd seen through the wall behind which he lived, all the way to his heart.

"Don't," he warned her.

She pushed herself up until she was sitting in his lap, and facing him. There would be no more hiding.

"Don't what, Roman? Don't care? It's too late for that. I already do."

Her words hit him hard. And in that moment, he knew she was the stronger for having voiced the truth.

"And what happens tomorrow, Daisy? What happens after we make love? After you're embedded in every part of me? How do I give you up?"

Daisy knew what he said could happen, but there was a surge of need within her that told her to seize the moment, that tomorrow was never a guarantee.

"Then don't," she said. "Don't give me up. Ever!"

He took her by the shoulders and rolled, pinning her beneath him on the sofa as the covers slid off their bodies and onto the floor. His voice was a whisper against her cheek.

"This is dangerous, in more ways than one."

She wrapped her arms around his neck. "But, Roman, you forget. I can't remember living any other way."

He groaned and then lowered his head. Their lips met in a frenzy of need that never slowed down. He took the shirt from her body; she pulled his over his head. Piece by piece, their clothing came off until they were lying naked in each other's arms. He shoved a tousled lock of her hair away from her eye and then kissed the spot where it had been.

"Still hate my guts?"

Her eyes were alight with desire. "Clear to the bone," she said softly.

He brushed his mouth across the crest of a breast, before moving on to the other one. When she gasped and arched to his touch, he stopped and pulled back.

"Friendly enemies?"

She nodded and encircled him with her hand. "You know what they say about fine lines between love and—"

He thrust against her hand and when she felt him growing, hardening, pushing toward a promise of ecstasy, she knew this was going to be right after all. Then tears blurred her vision, leaving him slightly out of focus.

"Oh, Roman."

He thrust again, gritting his teeth against the need to hurry.

"What, baby?" he said softly.

"No regrets?"

A swift pain hit him right in the vicinity of his heart, but it was gone as swiftly as it had come. His head bent as he kissed an escaping tear.

"No regrets."

She wrapped both arms around his neck and pulled him down until all of his body weight was resting on her.

"Wait! I'm too heavy for—"

She soothed his concern with a touch of her hand to his cheek. And then so it began.

A log shifted on the fire, sending up a shower of sparks that crackled and popped. Outside, the wind played with the last fall of snow, lifting it up into the air and then letting it go. Like the tides, there was a steady rise and fall, from without, and within.

Roman moved them to the floor. Cushioned by the covers they'd tossed aside, they made love with a frightening passion. Whispers sifted into the silence. There was a quick gasp—a soft sigh. Touch followed touch; kiss followed kiss. Each step of the loving continually moving them toward a certainty they could no longer deny.

And finally, there was a fever in the blood that demanded release. Roman shifted, moving between her legs and then holding himself suspended above her. He looked down into her face—that beautiful, beautiful face—and knew a moment of pure peace. And yet the man he was gave her one last chance to pull back.

"Still sure?"

The need to be with him was making her crazy. It was all she could do to answer.

"Yes, oh yes."

He slid inside.

For one brief, silent moment, neither breathed—neither moved. The suddenness of their joining was replaced by a familiarity that they'd done this together a thousand times before.

For Daisy, the world tilted. She grasped his forearms, needing to hold on to solid substance. Her body was shaking, her voice full of tears.

"Roman...oh, Roman."

He pulled back, but only a little. Just enough to let her feel him once more, and as he did, her eyes closed and her lips parted with a sigh. He thrust again—slower, deeper. When she arched beneath him, his world suddenly focused on the feel of being inside her.

"Ah, baby," he whispered, and the dance began.

Time lost all meaning. It could have been minutes. It could have been hours. They rode the heat, letting it build between them until it began to consume.

For Daisy, it came in a swift and blinding flash, taking her out of herself and then dropping her back into place without warning, leaving her weak and breathless and hopelessly in love.

But Roman was prepared. He'd felt it coming. That need to hurry on the edge of sweet pain. Each stroke bringing him closer and closer. And there was Daisy, beneath him, around him, begging, holding on to him because she'd already taken flight.

It was the heat of her body, and the tiny tremors within her that sent him over the edge. That and the fact he couldn't bring himself to let her go alone.

Muscles corded in his arms, in his neck, in his back. It came over him in a wave, then spilling into her with a groan, shattering the last of the wall behind which he lived.

Their bodies were slick with sweat, their hearts hammering against their chests. But there was a knowing between them that hadn't been there before. He looked into her eyes and thought, So, woman...you may not know your name, but I know you.

"Have mercy," he whispered, and kissed the edge of her lips. Then he rolled onto his side and pulled the covers over them.

Daisy didn't move, couldn't move. She lay within the shelter of Roman's arms, waiting for her heartbeat to settle back into a normal rhythm.

Just before they fell asleep, Roman thought he heard her whisper.

"I take no prisoners."

He fell asleep with a smile on his face.

Chapter 7

It was just after dark when the phone rang in Davis Benton's hotel room. He came out of a deep sleep within seconds of the sound, grabbing for the phone.

"Hello."

"Mr. Benton. This is Lawrey, of search and rescue."

"Yes, Mr. Lawrey. Any news?"

"I'm sorry, sir, but no. In fact, the snow is so deep that any further searching is futile."

Davis's hopes fell. "But—"

"Understand that we will resume the search as soon as the snow melts. I don't know if you're aware, but the snowfall was well over four feet. With the drifts, it's often over six feet deep. She could be anywhere, and we'd be walking right past her...or on top of her. Do you understand?"

Davis groaned. Although the images were sickening, he understood all too well.

"Yes, and thank you for calling," he said.

When the line went dead in his ear, he started to cry. This was hell. If only he could wake up to find it had all been a dream. He thought of Gordon. If Holly had loved him enough to marry him, then he deserved to know the decision search and rescue had made. The last thing he wanted to do was get dressed and go out, but it was something that had to be done.

Gordon Mallory was progressing. It was unfortunate the doctors couldn't say the same for his brother, Billy. Billy Mallory's condition hadn't changed. He was stable but still in a coma. The head injury he'd sustained when the plane had crashed had been severe, and even though the doctors were doing everything possible, he had yet to wake up.

Gordon had made a public show of grief as he'd instructed the doctors not to put Billy on any sort of life support, claiming it would have been what Billy wanted. He didn't know that for certain, but it was definitely what Gordon wanted.

His entire focus was on getting out of the hospital and finding his money. Thanks to Billy, Holly had all the money. In a way, Gordon looked upon this judgment as fair. After all, if Billy had minded his own business, none of this would have happened...so it stood to reason that if someone had to pay, even with a life, Billy was it.

Lost in his own world, Gordon was startled when the door to his room opened, but when he saw who it was, he adopted the proper attitude of grief.

"Mr. Benton! Any news?"

Davis tried for a smile. It never came.

"Some, but it's not good. The search has been called off until after the snow melts."

"Oh, no!" Gordon cried. "Don't they know she could freeze to death?"

Davis's shoulders slumped, and his voice started to shake. "Actually, they didn't come out and say it in so many words, but I believe that's already what they think."

Gordon groaned and covered his face, but to hide his elation, not his grief. He had his own plans for finding the interfering bitch, and they didn't include mixing with a search-and-rescue team. If he had to, he was going to walk the entire area over which they'd been flying, and by damn, he'd find his money if it took the rest of his life.

"I'm so sorry," Davis said.

"I don't know what I'm going to do," Gordon said.

"Come home with me to recuperate," Davis offered. "It's the least I can do."

Gordon wanted to crow with delight. Although he had left a small nest egg in a Las Vegas bank, this was perfect. A free place to rest until he was back to full strength.

"That's very generous of you, Mr. Benton, but I can't leave my brother, Billy. He's going to need around-the-clock care. I'll have to stay here to—"

"We'll move him to Las Vegas, too. There are plenty of care facilities out there, and if he's able, he can stay at the estate. Now don't argue. I won't hear of you having to bear this on your own. In times like this, people need to stick together."

Gordon gathered his sheet around him, pretending to smooth out the wrinkles.

"I don't know how to thank you," he said. And it was true. He didn't know how to say thank-you. It was a skill he'd never learned.

Davis nodded. "I'm going back to the hotel now. If there's anything you need, please call. Meanwhile..."

Gordon smiled. It was a pious bit of playacting that would have made his old daddy proud.

"Meanwhile," Gordon echoed, "I'll be saying prayers for us all."

Davis left, assured that he'd done everything necessary to make things right. When he exited the hospital, it was almost dark. He flagged a cab, and the ride back to the hotel was one of the longest rides he could ever remember. He kept thinking that it wasn't fair, that a parent should not outlive his or her children. It was too much pain for a person to bear.

Roman had been awake for some time when dawn came to the mountains. After making love by the fire, they'd moved upstairs to his bed. Daisy had crawled into it, and into his arms without reservation. The crazy part was, it hadn't seemed strange to him, either. They hadn't known each other a week, and yet they'd made love with a familiar passion. Now here they were, sharing a bed as if they'd done this every night of their lives.

Part of Roman's restlessness was due to the woman in his arms, the other to a large dose of guilt. He kept thinking of what they'd done. Last night, making love to Daisy had seemed so right. Even more, it had *felt* right. She'd matched his emotions with a passion of her own that had surprised him. But in the light of day, there was a truth he couldn't deny. Daisy was a beautiful, loving woman, but she might not be free to give back that love. That was what worried him. That was what hurt. He looked down at her, wondering if, when the time came, he would have the guts to give her up.

She lay spoon fashion within his arms, her back to his chest, her head pillowed upon his arm. He held her close, his hand resting just beneath the softness of her breasts. In repose, she looked so innocent, but what the hell was an innocent woman doing with that bag of money?

She sighed in her sleep and then rolled over, burying her face against his chest. It was a gesture that didn't go unnoticed. He felt the burden of her trust and hoped when the time came he would have the strength to do the right thing.

The contents of the purse went flying, spilling everything that had been inside. Lipstick rolled off the edge of a step and fell to the pavement below. The faint shattering sound of the compact mirror breaking sent the woman into a panic.

Get away, get away! I have to get away.

Her legs felt weak, her body devoid of breath. No matter how hard she tried to move, she seemed frozen to the spot.

He'll find me here. I have to hide!

A shadow fell over her shoulder and onto the steps in front of her. Her mouth went dry. Someone grabbed her by the arm. Before she could scream, a hand clamped around her mouth while she was yanked up and backward. The last thing she saw was a patch of blue sky, and then everything went dark.

Daisy jerked and then gasped, trying to breathe for the woman in her dream. In the midst of her panic, someone caught her, holding her close and whispering words of comfort that set her heart back into a normal rhythm. She opened her eyes and then sighed as she remembered where she was, and who it was who was holding her.

"Roman."

"It's okay, baby," he said softly, smoothing the tangles of her hair away from her face. "I've got you. You're safe."

She shuddered, then slid her arms around him, holding him close.

"Something spilled, I think."

"What?"

"My purse...I think I dropped my purse."

He frowned. In the grand scheme of the mess she was in, that made little sense, but he let her talk, knowing she needed to get it all said.

"Then what?"

"I tried to run, but my legs wouldn't work."

He knew that feeling. It was pure, unadulterated fear. Only someone defensively trained would have been able to bypass that very human reaction. Gentling her in the only way he knew how, he held her close, letting her tell the story at her own pace. She continued.

"They heard me, you know."

"Who heard you, baby?"

Her mind went blank, and as hard as she tried, nothing else would come. She leaned her forehead against his chest in frustration.

"I don't know. Oh, God, I don't know."

Damn. Hiding his own frustration, Roman kissed the side of her face.

"It's okay. Look on the positive side. This is more than you remembered yesterday. Just focus on the fact that things are coming back to you."

She looked at him, and there was such terror in her eyes. "What if—?"

He shook his head. "No ifs. First rule—deal only in known facts."

She tried to smile. "Who's rule is that? The military, or some private-investigative thing?"

"Neither. It's something my father taught me. I guess you might say it's just the Justice way."

The mention of his family made her think of the brother he'd called.

"Do you think your brother will call today?"

Roman tilted her chin with the tip of his finger and centered a hard kiss on the curve of her mouth.

"He'll call when he has something to tell me and not before."

Daisy cupped the side of his face, remembering the way he made love and wishing they could stay like this forever.

"Is he like you? Your brother, I mean."

"No one is like Royal. He's a law unto himself."

A slight frown furrowed her forehead. "Would I like him?"

Roman grinned. "Probably. Most women do."

"What does his wife think about that?"

"His wife is dead. He's been raising his daughter, Maddie, by himself almost from the start. Doing a good job of it, too. But don't tell him I said so."

Daisy's expression grew solemn. "How sad for him. How old is Maddie, anyway?"

"She's four, going on forty. She's definitely a female, just short."

"She's probably resilient, too." Daisy said. "I know I was. My mother died when I was..." She paused in midsentence, a look of wonderment coming over her face.

Roman tensed. When she hadn't been concentrating, a truth had slipped out.

"Oh, Roman. I remembered something." Her voice was shaking. "My mother died when I was born."

"See," he said softly. "Like I said. When you're ready, it will come."

Daisy closed her eyes and turned her head, but Roman wouldn't let her hide, not even from herself.

"Daisy. Look at me."

She sighed, then did as he asked. "What?"

"Why did you do that?"

"Do what?" she said.

"Turn away from me."

Her hesitation was brief, but it was there all the same.

"Daisy...don't you think that last night moved us past the stage of keeping secrets?"

She nodded.

"You should be happy that things are coming back to you. Right now, they don't make much sense, but in time, they will. So what's the problem?"

Her lips were trembling as she looked into his face.

"I think I'm afraid."

He groaned and then hugged her close. "I'm with you on this all the way, remember?"

"But, Roman, what if you were right all along? What if I stole that money?"

"Then we'll give it back and deal with the consequences."

"What if the consequences aren't all I have to deal with?"

"What do you mean?" he asked.

"What if it's like you said? What if there's a man in my life?"

There already is a man in your life. Me. But he couldn't say it, and no matter how hard he tried, he couldn't ignore the fact that when her memory came back, the woman she would become might not like the man he was.

She slid her arms around his neck and pulled him closer. Her voice was soft, her gaze filled with tears.

"Roman?"

"What?"

"It's been a long time since last night."

The longing in her voice matched the one in his heart, but he was too attuned to what was still wrong between them to ignore how right this all felt.

"Have you faced the fact that getting more involved might make things worse?" he asked.

Daisy locked her fingers at the back of his neck.

"Right now, the worst thing I can think of is losing you."

He shook his head and grabbed her wrists. "Damn it, Daisy, you're ignoring the truth. You don't have me." And I damned sure don't have you.

Her voice started to shake as tears welled in her eyes. "Truth? You're my truth. You're my yesterday, and you're my tomorrow. Don't *you* understand? I can't remember anything or anyone but you."

Pain tore at his gut as he pulled her close again. "I understand more than you think. And I know something you aren't willing to face. Whatever you feel for me now is based on fear. You think you love me because I make you feel safe. You get your memory back, and then see how you feel. Until then, I think the less talk of making love, the better off we'll both be."

She tore free from his grasp. Tears were streaming down her face as she stood. Just when he thought she was going to stomp away, she spun, and there was a fervor in her voice he couldn't ignore.

"You speak for yourself, Roman Justice. Maybe you don't have the guts to trust your heart, but I trust mine."

* * *

Gordon was mobile.

He was a man who'd dreamed of traveling in style, and the gaping back of his hospital gown and the IV he was wheeling up and down the hall had never been part of the dream. But he was also not a man to stand in the way of progress, and getting off his back and onto his feet was progress indeed.

The nurse at his side was nothing like the elegantly dressed women he usually cultivated, but she would do until something better came along. At least this nurse had succumbed to his charms and his story. She'd taken him farther up the hall than he'd ever gone before, and that was just where he wanted to be. Up two more doors, and then the next room would be Billy's. It was simple. All he had to do was get there.

"You're doing great, Mr. Mallory, but I think we've gone far enough for today. We need to turn around and—"

Damn, damn, damn. Not yet. Not yet.

Gordon paused, pretending to rest while his mind was racing. And then a nurse burst out of a room up ahead and started toward them. When she drew near and realized it was Gordon she saw, without thinking, she burst out with her news.

"Good news, Mr. Mallory. Your brother is coming to."

The fact that Gordon paled was not lost on the little nurse at his side.

"Here, now," she said quickly. "You've been up too long. You need to get back to your bed."

Gordon shook off her hand. "No. I need to see my brother. That's what I need." And he started up the hall toward the open door.

"Wait, Mr. Mallory. You can't—"

He staggered inside, one hand clutching his broken ribs, the other dragging his IV. His gaze went directly to Billy, and had he not known for certain it was his brother in that bed, he would never have recognized him. Unprepared for the shock, all he could do was stare.

All those tubes. All those machines. And his face! My God.

"He's not as bad as he looks," the nurse said quickly, and grabbed Gordon by the arm, guiding him out of the room and back down the hall. "Most of that is superficial swelling, and the bruises will fade with time."

Gordon's stomach pitched, and it was with great effort that he made it back to his room before he heaved up the contents.

Long after the nurse was gone, the image of his little brother's face kept moving in and out of his mind. He kept remembering the days of their childhood, and hearing his mother reminding him over and over that Billy was his responsibility. That he was the big brother and to make certain that Billy didn't come to harm.

He closed his eyes, hoping sleep would help him escape the reality of the truth, but even then, it was with him. It was all Gordon's fault that Billy was in this mess. He'd needed a lookout at the casino. He'd talked Billy into doing the job, even though he hadn't really wanted to. And he hadn't planned on killing the casino owner. It had just happened. It was no wonder Billy had freaked out in the plane. It was no wonder he'd strapped a chute on Holly Benton and dumped the money out with her when she jumped.

Gordon accepted the guilt for the mess they were in. He hadn't meant to hurt anyone, but he'd gotten caught up in the power of having so much money in his hands. He'd been willing to do anything to keep it. Even murder...twice. If he had it to do over—

Then he cursed beneath his breath. It didn't pay to look back. What was done, was done. All he had to do was focus on getting better and, thanks to Davis Benton's offer, getting Billy out of this hospital and back to Las Vegas. The bottom line was, he didn't want his brother to die.

He tried to roll over, groaning aloud as he shifted position. It was no use. His ribs hurt too much for the effort.

"Well, damn, little brother. We nearly had it made."

There was little rest for Gordon that night. He was forced to lie in the bed, contemplating his sins and praying that whatever

Billy might say in the future, the authorities would attribute to hallucinations, and not the truth.

It was beginning to thaw. From the loft where Roman was standing, he could hear water running off the roof. On the one hand, that was good. The supplies he'd packed were running low. But that also meant they would have to leave. The insular world in which they'd been existing was about to come to an end. Just the possibility of never seeing Daisy again made him sick. But if there was a man on the other side of this snowfall who had a prior claim on her, it could happen.

He leaned over the railing and looked down. She was sweeping up the bits of wood chips and ashes that were scattered on the hearth, oblivious to the fact that she was being watched. He glanced at the closet near the front door. There was a small fortune in that unassuming bag he'd tossed inside. As he looked back at Daisy, he kept asking himself, What's wrong with this picture? Experience told him to be wary until he knew all the facts, even though his heart was already committed. Instinct told him he already knew all he needed to know. She was innocent. She had to be.

He started down the stairs, suddenly needing to be near her, to see that look she got just before he touched her. A board creaked beneath his weight and Daisy turned with an expression of hope upon her face. Before either of them could speak, Roman's cellular phone rang, shattering the quiet with a rude reminder of the civilization they'd left behind.

Daisy froze as an overwhelming urge to hide came over her. Roman saw her fear and understood. It would be Royal. He ran the rest of the way to the phone.

"Hello."

"Little brother, how goes it?"

"It's starting to melt," Roman said. "What did you find out? Were there any reports of missing planes?"

"Yeah."

Roman's gut clenched. "So tell me."

"Some private plane went missing right before the snow. Took off from Las Vegas bound for the Bahamas."

The Bahamas. A good place to launder a whole lot of money.

"Go on," Roman urged, refusing to let his imagination get ahead of the facts.

"They found it before that second snow hit. Three on board. Two survivors, one dead. They are being hospitalized in Denver."

"Anything else?" Roman asked.

"Search and rescue is supposed to go back after the snow melts."

"Why?"

"To look for another body. It seems there was a fourth passenger in the plane, but she wasn't anywhere around when they pulled the others out. They're guessing she wandered off after the crash and probably froze to death. Have to wait until the snow melts to find her body."

The knot in his belly tightened. "She?"

"Yep, and are you ready for this. It was Davis Benton's daughter."

Roman frowned. The name was familiar. Benton? Benton? Where had he heard that name before? And then it hit him.

"Benton, as in the computer magnate?"

"That's what they said. I guess this was one of those times when being rich didn't help."

"What was her name?" Roman asked.

"Uh, Holly, I think the name was Holly."

"And the other passengers. Who were they?" Roman asked.

"Hang on a minute, will you? I have it all written down somewhere. Maybe in my other jacket. Here, talk to Maddie while I go look."

Roman winked at Daisy, trying to ease the tension on her face, and then covered the phone long enough to explain what was going on.

"Royal is looking for something. He's putting Maddie on the phone."

And then a sweet little voice piped in his ear. "Hello, Uncle Roman."

"Hey, Little Bit, what have you been doing?"

She sighed, and he could imagine the look on her face—the one she wore just before she unloaded a list of wants in his ear.

"Jus' nothin'," she said.

He grinned. "Nothing? You haven't done a thing since I left?"

Her voice grew smaller, more pitiful. "No, not a gol-durned thing."

He stifled a laugh. Royal was going to pitch a sweet fit when he heard that come out of her mouth.

"What about that cat you were playing with the other day?"

Her sigh deepened. "I can't play with it no more. It's flea-bit."

He chuckled. "Anymore. You can't play with it anymore."

"That's what I jus' said."

This time he had to laugh, and as he did, wished he could share the moment with Daisy. She looked as upset as Maddie sounded.

"Uncle Roman?"

"What, honey?"

"When you comin' home?"

"As soon as the snow goes away."

The moment it came out of his mouth, a loud clunk sounded in his ear. He could hear Maddie's footsteps as she ran away, and then he heard Royal yelling at her from across the room. Moments later, Royal was back on the phone.

"What the hell did you say to her?" Royal asked.

"Nothing."

"Well, you said something. She lit out of here, yelling at the top of her lungs that she was going to build a snowman before the snow was all gone." He snorted beneath his breath. "It's in the high eighties down here."

Roman laughed. Now he understood. "She asked me when I

was coming home. I told her I'd come as soon as the snow melted. I guess she thinks when it snows, it snows everywhere.''

''Oh, great,'' Royal muttered. ''Now we'll be talking about weather patterns for the next week. I swear, I don't know where all that curiosity comes from.''

''Royal...'' Roman prompted.

''Oh, yeah. The notes. Now, what was it you wanted to know?''

''The other passengers. Do you know who they were?''

''Only names. The deceased was the pilot, Everett Bailey. The two survivors are brothers. Gordon Mallory and his brother, Billy. My source told me they buy and sell real estate.''

Roman frowned. ''Is that all?''

''Yeah, except...''

''Except what?'' Roman asked.

''Well, not that it matters, since she never made it to the altar, but the missing woman was eloping with one of the Mallorys. Don't know which one. Hell of a thing, isn't it, to lose your sweetheart on the eve of a wedding?'' Then he muttered, more to himself than to Roman, ''In fact, it's hell losing her, no matter when it happens.''

Roman's heart sank. Elope? That meant love—love strong enough to marry. Ah, God. Then his mind went back to the matter at hand.

''What about Benton?''

''What about him?'' Royal asked.

''Is he in Denver, too?''

''Oh, yeah. They said he's been hounding search and rescue every day, and can you blame him? I'd be doing the same.''

''Did they say where he was staying?''

Royal glanced down at his notes. ''No, but if I was guessing, I say at the most expensive hotel in the city.''

''Thanks, Royal. I'll be in touch.''

''Take care, Roman. See you when I see you.''

The connection was broken. Roman straightened and then

looked at Daisy, trying to imagine her as someone named Holly. It didn't work.

"What did he say?" Daisy asked. "Am I a criminal?" Then her face crumpled. "Oh, please, Roman, tell me. I can't stand it any longer. Did I murder someone? When you take me back, are they going to put me away?"

He wanted to hold her, but considering what had to be said, keeping his distance seemed the wisest move.

"Does the name Benton mean anything to you?"

Chapter 8

Something nudged at the back of Daisy's mind, but it was too far back to remember. Her gaze was fixed and almost panic-stricken, her expression grim.

"No. Should it?"

Some of the tension Roman had been holding dissipated. He'd prepared himself for a revelation that hadn't happened.

"Maybe," he said, although he knew in his heart the answer should have been yes. The coincidence of her parachuting from a plane other than the one that had crashed would have been ludicrous.

Daisy staggered to the nearest chair and dropped. Her hands were in fists, her body shaking.

"Tell me," she said. "I have to... No, I deserve to know what was said."

Roman sighed. She was right.

"A plane did go down. The timing coincides with your arrival here. It went down the evening before the storm."

She swallowed once, but remained silent, her gaze fixed upon the sternness of his expression. She was afraid—so afraid.

"They didn't find it until after the first snowfall had ended. There were three people on board. The pilot was dead, but there were two brothers on board who survived." Roman shoved a hand through his hair, while watching her every move. "As soon as the snow melts, they're going back out again to look for the woman who was supposed to be on board."

Her heart dropped. *Oh God. It has to be me.*

"Who was she?" Daisy asked.

"Her name was Holly Benton, the daughter of Davis Benton."

Again, something whispered in the back of her mind, but the voice wasn't loud enough to be heard. And then she focused in on the way Roman had spoken his name.

"Is he somebody? Davis Benton, I mean."

Roman nodded. "'Somebody' is hardly the word. The man is a megamillionaire. Controls a huge share of the computer market."

She thought of the money in the bag. Maybe that would explain why she had so much with her. But that didn't really make sense. No one, no matter how rich, carried hundreds of thousands of dollars around in a bag.

"Is that me, Roman? Am I Holly Benton?"

Roman shrugged. "Most probably. Royal indicated that her father was pretty upset about the fact that the search was called off without finding her."

She covered her face with her hands. "Oh, God. Why can't I remember something as important as a parent?"

Roman's belly was in a knot. Once he said it, there would be something worse between them than their earlier suspicions of each other. There would be the guilt. Hers for not remembering she was about to become a bride. His for taking what had been meant for another man.

"Do the names Gordon or Billy Mallory mean anything to you?"

Damn you, Billy! What have you done?

She jerked. The voice had come out of nowhere, and with it,

an inordinate degree of fear. Her voice was trembling and it was all she could do not to cry.

"Why?"

Roman took a deep breath. "Because Holly Benton was on her way to the Bahamas with one of the brothers to get married."

She stood abruptly, her words running into each other like tumbling blocks. "No. That isn't me...wasn't me. I would remember something like that. I would remember loving—"

Roman took her by the shoulders, holding her until she was forced to look at him.

"Don't fight a truth we both knew could be there. We did what we did, and it can't be taken back. But—"

Daisy tore free of his grasp, her eyes huge and filled with tears.

"Don't you understand? I don't want to take it back!" She pressed the flat of her hand over the center of her heart as tears fell down her face. "It's not true!" she cried. "I would know it in here if it were so."

Roman reached out for her, but she spun and ran for the stairs. There was a pain in his chest that kept spreading, threatening to swallow him whole. He wanted to go with her, to run and hide, but there was nowhere to go. Once a truth had been spoken, it became impossible to deny its existence.

When he turned away, there was a stillness on his face that his family would have known, and for which they would have grieved. It was the wall behind which he lived. This woman hadn't died, but he was losing her just the same.

He picked up his phone and walked into the kitchen to hunt for a paper and pen. He had some calls to make. Somewhere in the city of Denver, one man believed he'd lost a daughter, while another believed he'd lost his future wife. Neither deserved to spend an added night living with such sorrow.

Davis Benton was coming up the hall to his room when he heard a phone beginning to ring. His heart began to pound. It was coming from inside his room. He jammed the key in the lock and dashed toward it. Slightly winded, his voice was unusually curt.

"Hello. Benton here."

When Roman heard the man's voice, another knot was added to the others sitting in the pit of his stomach. This was one more step to the distance he was putting between himself and Daisy.

"Mr. Benton, my name is Roman Justice. I'm a private investigator out of Dallas, Texas."

Davis frowned. He'd had a few quack calls already, one from a lawyer offering to sue the dead pilot's family for the loss of his daughter, and another from a psychic who claimed she'd seen his daughter safe and sound and asleep in some cave. The urge to hang up was strong, but something made him hesitate.

"Look, Mr. Justice. I don't know why you're calling, but I can assure you that whatever services you think you can offer, I have more and better ones already at my disposal. So thank you, but no—"

"There is a woman standing beside me who doesn't remember her name. A few days ago, I came up to Colorado for a fishing trip and found her in my cabin. She claims to have parachuted out of a plane."

Davis froze. Please God, don't let this be a scam.

There was a distinct silence, and for a moment, Roman thought the man had hung up.

"Mr. Benton?"

Davis stuttered, trying to regain his composure. "If this is some hellish scheme to extort money from me, I swear I'll have you—"

Roman interrupted before the threat could be made. "Look, Mr. Benton. I don't want your money. I'm trying to help Daisy, not you."

Davis's heart sank. "It can't be my daughter," he said. "Her name is Holly."

If Roman hadn't been hurting so much inside, he would have managed a smile. "I told you, she doesn't remember who she is. I'm the one who gave her that name."

No longer able to stand, Davis dropped to the side of the bed.

"My God, my God," he whispered, and wiped a hand across his face.

"Mr. Benton?"

Davis shook off his shock. "Yes?"

"Will you describe your daughter to me?"

Davis frowned. He hadn't become wealthy by being stupid.

"No, you describe this...this...Daisy person to me."

Roman swallowed past the lump in his throat. "Daisy, honey, come here, okay?"

When Daisy walked into Roman's arms, the fear on her face was almost palpable. Yet when his arms came around her, she knew that for a while, she was safe.

Roman gazed down at her face while talking to Davis Benton on the phone.

"She's not very big. In fact, the top of her head doesn't quite touch my chin, and I'm over six feet. Her hair is dark and shoulder length. Her eyes are green and there is a very small scar beneath her chin. When she laughs, her nose wrinkles just above the bridge and—"

Davis started to cry. "Oh God, oh God, that's my Holly. Please, let me talk to her. Let me hear her voice."

The weight around Roman's heart continued to pull as he looked down into Daisy's face.

"Just understand one thing, Mr. Benton. She doesn't remember her own name, so she's probably not going to remember you, either."

Davis nodded, and then realized they couldn't see. "Yes, yes, I understand," he said quickly. "Just let me hear. I'll know for sure if I hear her voice."

Roman handed Daisy the phone. "He wants to talk to you."

Her hands were shaking, but her voice was calm. As long as Roman was beside her, she could handle anything that came her way.

"Hello?"

Davis choked on another sob. "Holly? Holly? Is that you?"

Daisy sighed. "I don't know, but I wish to God I did. It's very disconcerting to look into a mirror and see a stranger."

Davis's pulse leaped. That voice! That voice! He would have known it anywhere.

"Holly, sweetheart, it *is* you! Dear Lord, how has this happened? Why did you parachute from the plane? Why haven't you called sooner? Why—?"

Daisy paled. There were too many questions for which she had no answers. She thrust the phone back at Roman and hid her face against his chest.

Roman took the phone from her hands as he pulled her close.

"Mr. Benton, this is Roman Justice again. I don't know what you were saying just now, but Daisy is pretty upset. I think she's a little overwhelmed by all of this."

Davis took a deep breath. "I'm sorry. Of course. I don't know what I was thinking. But there are so many things I want to know."

"Yes, sir, and so does she. Unfortunately for her, she remembers nothing before coming to in the tree."

Davis's voice rose an octave. "Tree?"

Roman almost smiled. "Yes, sir. She dropped into a very wooded area, and the parachute got caught in a tree. She'll have to tell you all of that at a later date, but I'll say one thing for her, she's quite a survivor."

Davis could not contain his joy. "You must tell me how to get there. I can't wait to touch her. To hold her." His voice broke. "My God, I've been trying to face planning her funeral."

Roman understood all too well how Davis must have felt, because right now, he was facing a loss of his own.

"I understand, sir. But there's too much snow up here yet to drive down."

"To hell with driving down," Davis shouted. "I'm coming up in a chopper. Just tell me where you are from the nearest city. We'll find you."

Roman gave him directions, all the while knowing that within a matter of hours, Daisy would be gone from him forever.

"Do I have them down right?" Davis asked after reading the directions back to Roman.

"Yes."

Davis glanced down at his watch. "It's probably too late to get there today. We're about out of light. But I'll be there early tomorrow." His voice rose again, as the joy of his planning became obvious. "My word! I just realized during all of this time I never once thought of Gordon. He's going to be ecstatic. They were eloping, you know!"

Roman's arm unconsciously tightened around Daisy's shoulders. So, it was Gordon Mallory. He couldn't find the will to comment.

"Mr. Justice, you'll never know what this call has meant to me," Davis said.

And you'll never know what this call cost me. "Yes, sir. I can imagine."

"May I speak to Holly one more time?" Davis asked. "I want to tell her I'm coming."

Roman handed Daisy the phone. "Here," he said quietly. "And hang in there, baby. You've come this far. Don't quit on yourself now."

She took the phone from his hand and lifted it to her ear.

"Hello."

"Holly, I'm sorry about before," Davis said quickly. "I was so excited that I didn't think about how you must feel."

She exhaled slowly, accepting the truth of her fate. Within days, Roman would no longer be a part of her life.

"I can understand that," she said.

"Good! I just want to let you know that I'm coming after you first thing tomorrow."

Panic hit again as she looked up at Roman. "But that's not possible," she said quickly. "There's still too much snow."

Davis laughed. "That won't stop me from getting to you. I'm

coming by helicopter. By this time tomorrow, you'll be safe and sound back in your own home, and this will be nothing more than a bad dream.''

Daisy couldn't comment. Her heart was breaking. What she'd endured had been all nightmare. With Roman, she'd had a very real glimpse of heaven on earth. Leaving him seemed impossible to consider.

"Oh," Davis added. "I'm on my way to the hospital now to tell Gordon face-to-face. I can't wait to see his expression when I tell him his future wife is still alive."

Daisy wanted to scream. This was the real nightmare. "I don't remember promising to marry anyone," she said quickly. "Please, Mr. Benton, I don't want to—"

Davis interrupted. "I know. I know. I just meant that Gordon should know. In no way would I shove him down your throat. Please don't be afraid. I can't bear to think you'll be afraid to come back to your own home."

Daisy sighed. Obviously, this was something that had to be faced.

"Just as long as you understand."

"Of course, of course," Davis said quickly. "Now, you rest easy tonight. I'll see you tomorrow."

"Yes," she said. "Tomorrow." She started to hang up when she heard him shouting. "Yes? Was there something else?" she asked.

Davis knew his voice was shaking, but he wouldn't let another moment of his life pass without telling her what was on his mind.

"Holly."

"Yes?"

"I love you, sweetheart. Very, very much."

When the line went dead in her ear, Daisy handed the phone to Roman. She took one look at the expression on his face, then turned and walked away.

Gordon's afternoon had been long. He'd gone over the events of the past couple of weeks so many times in his mind that he'd given himself a headache. Once he'd looked up in time to see a uniformed officer pass by his door. He broke out in a sweat, certain that Billy must have talked. When the officer passed without so much as a glance his way, his relief gave way to a hysterical fit of the giggles.

Guilt. That's all that was wrong with him. Just a case of the guilts. Everything would work out. It had to. He'd planned too diligently and done without for far too long to give it all up now. That money was his. All he had to do was find it.

He was halfway through his supper when he heard Davis Benton's voice out in the hall. He laid down his fork, preparing himself for a proper attitude of grief. What he got was indigestion instead.

Davis all but ran into the room. His face was wreathed in smiles, and there was a bounce to his step that didn't make sense.

Gordon frowned. What the hell was going on? This was no proper attitude for a man who'd just lost a daughter.

"Mr. Benton. It was good of you to come," Gordon said.

Davis laughed and clapped his hands. "This just couldn't wait," he said. "She's alive!"

Gordon froze. It couldn't be. He couldn't be talking about Holly. He'd seen her sucked out of that plane with that bag hanging around her neck like a deadweight. Even if she had survived the drop, there was no way she could have survived that blizzard.

"This isn't funny," Gordon said.

"No," Davis crowed. "It's a miracle, that's what!"

Gordon's voice cracked. "How do you know? Maybe it's a mistake!"

"No! No! No mistake! I talked to her on the phone." He turned in a circle, unable to contain his joy. "I heard her voice. Dear God, I heard her voice!"

Gordon jerked, sending the tray on his table to the floor in a crash of tin and plastic. Moments later, a nurse came running, followed by another.

Davis hugged one and patted the other one on the back. "Sorry about the mess. It's all my fault," he said, laughing at no one in particular.

They began cleaning up spilled food while Davis moved to one side, unaware that Gordon's quiet had nothing to do with shock and everything to do with pure, unadulterated fear. Gordon was convinced that any moment, that officer he'd seen earlier in the day was going to come into the room and place him under arrest. He kept trying to remember the name of that lawyer he'd played poker with back in Vegas, but his mind was blank. What he didn't understand was why Davis was so damned happy with him. If the situation had been reversed, he would have had murder on his mind. Then he stifled a laugh. The irony of what he just thought was not lost on him. Murder. That's what had gotten him into trouble in the first place.

Finally, the nurses were gone, and Gordon caught himself holding his breath, waiting for the proverbial ax to fall.

"Look, Mr. Benton, I never intended—"

Davis interrupted. "All this time, we thought she was dead. It wasn't ever said, but it's what we thought."

Gordon nodded. That much was right.

A slight frown dampened Davis's enthusiasm. "There is a small problem." And then the frown disappeared. "But nothing that time won't help, I'm sure."

Gordon flinched. Here it comes.

"She's suffering from amnesia. She didn't recognize me."

For the first time since Davis Benton had entered his room, Gordon knew a moment of true joy. Hallelujah, he thought. My luck hasn't all turned bad.

"Not even me?"

Davis frowned. "I'm sorry, but no. Not even you."

Gordon dropped back onto the pillow and closed his eyes.

There is a God.

Davis read Gordon's behavior as despair. He couldn't have been more wrong.

"Don't worry, son," Davis said. "When we get her home—you know, back in her familiar surroundings—she'll be her old self in no time, I'm sure. But for now, you must realize her position. We're all strangers to her. We must restrain from pressuring her in any way. Her emotional state is very fragile."

Gordon's relief was so great that he felt like crying. A reprieve. It wasn't much, but it was enough to go on.

Davis left soon afterward, convinced of Gordon's love for his daughter. He'd seen the tears in Mallory's eyes himself. For the first time in days, Davis went to bed with his heart full of hope, while Gordon spent a sleepless night in hell, trying to console himself with the fact that if Holly was alive, then his money must be somewhere nearby.

Roman tossed another log on the fire just as Daisy came out of the bathroom. She was wearing another one of his sweatshirts, and from the looks of her, nothing else. The ends of her hair were damp from her bath, and her face was scrubbed clean. She could have passed for a teenager until he looked in her eyes. They held a look as old as time.

Roman wanted to hold her, but he kept remembering that she'd promised herself to another man. He set the fire screen in place and then looked away, kicking at a small piece of bark that had fallen onto the hearth.

Daisy took a deep breath, and then the words spilled out of her, like blood from a wound.

"I'm afraid of tomorrow."

He looked up, then nodded. So was he.

Her face crumpled as a sob tore up her throat. Doubling her fists and thumping viciously at the sides of her legs, she began to pace.

"I hate this. I hate everything about it. I thought I wanted to remember, but I was wrong. I don't want to remember anything but you." She collapsed on the sofa and buried her face in her hands.

Roman couldn't stand back any longer. He knelt before her and then took her hands away from her face.

"Look at me!" he demanded.

She turned her face away, unable to face what he might have to say.

Roman ached, for her and for himself, but several hours earlier, he'd accepted a truth about himself. If he had it to do over again, he wouldn't change one minute of their time together.

He cupped the side of her face, his voice softening.

"Look at me, baby."

She did, because he asked—because she didn't have it in her to deny him anything.

"Did you ever stop to think that when you see your father, your fears might go away?"

"But they won't," she sobbed, and threw her arms around his neck. "I know they won't."

Roman groaned and pulled her close. "You don't know that for sure."

"Oh, Roman, you don't understand. I keep thinking back to when I first saw you. I was so scared. I wanted to run away, but there was nowhere to go. And you were so angry with me and so distrustful." When he would have interrupted, she shook her head, refusing to give him the right. "No, don't argue," she said softly. "It's the truth, and rightly so. But something happened to me that I didn't expect. I fell in love with you, and when we made love, it sealed that fact in my heart. I am afraid to let you out of my sight. I am afraid if I never see you again that I will die from this pain."

Roman's heart had been aching ever since he'd talked to Royal, but when he heard what she said, it felt as if he were coming apart at the seams. It hurt to draw breath. It was killing him to be touching her now and still know she belonged to someone else. In spite of his pain, he had to be strong for her. She didn't belong to him anymore. Hell, if he would be honest with himself, she'd never really belonged to him, except in his dreams. He grabbed her by the arms, shaking her to get her attention.

"Damn it, woman, you didn't die before. You're not going to die now," he said roughly.

"But, Roman, in a way, that's not true. I did die. I mean Holly died. You gave Daisy life, and she's all I know."

He lifted her fingers to his lips, gently kissing the palm of each hand. Her scrapes were almost healed. They'd been the last visible reminders of her accident. Soon she would be gone, just like the scars from her fall. It took every ounce of strength he had not to rage at the injustice of fate.

Daisy leaned forward. Her lips grazed the edge of his mouth, then centered on the curve of his lips.

"Roman, please don't let me go. Fight for me, damn it. Tomorrow, tell Davis Benton that I matter to you." Then her voice shattered, like splintering glass. "Or am I fooling myself? Am I the only one who cares this much?"

Anger darkened the blue in Roman's eyes to a thunderous shade of gray.

"Don't even go there," he said shortly. "I care." Then he took a deep breath. He was about to cross a line, but she'd bared her soul. The least he could give her was what was left of his heart. "I care." His voice softened. "But I made love to Daisy. Holly is marrying another man."

Daisy started to cry in earnest. "I'm not! I won't! And I wish tomorrow would never come."

He crawled onto the sofa beside her, then wrapped his arms around her, burying his face in the curve of her neck.

Daisy dug her fingers into his hair and pulled, forcing him to look her straight in the eyes.

"Today isn't over. Today I'm still Daisy. Make love to me, Roman, before it's too late."

Everything inside of him said no, but for once, his heart wouldn't listen. He inhaled sharply, breathing in the scent of her, then rolled, pinning her beneath him.

"This is only going to make the goodbye worse."

She shook her head. "Nothing is worse than goodbye."

There wasn't enough fight left in him to argue. And God help him, he wanted this, more than she could know.

Chapter 9

Roman's mind was telling him no, but his heart was shouting yes. He lifted Daisy from the couch and started walking toward the stairs that led to the loft. When he paused, she looked up. Before they went any further, he had to ask.

"No regrets?"

Blinded by tears, she shook her head. "Don't ask me that," she said. "Just take me to bed. At least for tonight, make this nightmare go away."

He could no more have refused her than he could have stopped breathing. He went up the steps, holding her close to his heart and wondering if she could hear it breaking. By the time he laid her down on the bed, his vision was blurred from unshed tears. For a moment, neither moved—neither breathed. They were lost in the pain on the other one's face.

Daisy reached for the hem of her shirt, and Roman moved.

"No, baby, let me," he said softly, and pulled it over her head, leaving her bare to his sight.

Daisy held up her arms. "Come lie with me, Roman. Make love to me now so that I never forget."

Her words tore at him in a way he could no longer ignore. Hit with the unfairness of it all, his pain turned to anger. He tore off his clothes and then moved on top of her, as if staking a claim. His words were clipped and low, his body shaking with unchecked passion. He grabbed her arms and pinned them above her head, branding her mouth with his, tasting the salt of her tears and taking away her breath.

"Don't you ever forget!" he said harshly. "You *were* mine. Even if it wasn't right. Even if it wasn't fair to those who knew you first. Even then...don't you *ever* forget!"

Daisy tore free from his grasp and wrapped her arms around his neck, pulling him closer, urging him with every ounce of her being to take her.

"Then give me something to remember you by."

Without foreplay, without warning, Roman slid between her legs and thrust, wanting to bury himself within her, wishing he could stay there forever.

Daisy arched to meet him, giving back as much as she took, and still it wasn't enough. She kept trying to concentrate on the scent of her man, on the way he held her close and the feel of his breath upon her face. But soon everything turned from thought to feeling as her body began to burn.

Time had no meaning. Focus shifted to the sound of flesh upon flesh, of quick gasps and harsh grunts, of soft, meaningless cries and deep groans of sweet joy.

Daisy left the earth first, taking flight on a hard, desperate plunge. Out of control, her body bucked beneath him, taking the last ounces of pleasure from the best of the pain.

Locked in the ebb of her climax, Roman gave up the fight and let go, spilling deep into the woman beneath him. One spasm after another, he shuddered, then groaned, holding back nothing, giving her all that he was. All that he would ever be. And when it was over, rolled her up in his arms and held her while she cried.

Roman hadn't slept a wink. Long after they'd made love for the last time, he lay quietly on the bed in the dark with Daisy still in his arms, watching the contours of her face becoming more and more apparent with each passing hour. The tracks of her tears were still on her face when the day began to dawn.

There was a phrase that kept going through Roman's mind. Something about morning coming softly. He wanted to curse. This morning wasn't coming softly. It was ripping through the darkness, taking away the last vestiges of hope.

And while dawn was meant to signify new beginnings, for them it was the beginning of the end. Roman had walled himself off from all feelings, concentrating instead on what was to come.

A helicopter that would invade their solitude.

A father in search of a daughter.

A return to a past that Daisy couldn't—or wouldn't—let herself remember.

He kept trying to work the duffel bag full of money into the facts as he knew them, but no matter how many ways he considered them, nothing made much sense.

A child of wealth, as Holly Benton obviously was, had no need to steal, yet she was in possession of a king's ransom. As an investigator, he knew to never overlook the obvious, and that would also include the other passengers who'd been on that plane. Whatever the pilot had or had not known about the situation was now moot. He was dead and buried. That left the Mallory brothers. What was it Royal had said? Real estate? They dealt in real estate? Eloping with a million dollars, give or take a few thousand, wasn't standard procedure. Had the Mallorys been up to no good? And did Holly know, or was she somehow an innocent party to whatever had gone down? He frowned. Everything was supposition until she remembered.

Daisy stirred in his arms, and he tightened his hold, unwilling to turn loose of their last moments together. But then she opened her eyes and looked up at him without speaking. In the silence, he felt the pain of her withdrawal. The accusation was still on her face: if you loved me, you wouldn't let me go.

He cupped her cheek with the palm of his hand, silently pleading for understanding. It wasn't up to him to choose. Until she remembered everything from her past, they had no chance at a future.

She went limp in his arms and buried her face against his chest.

"Oh, God, Roman. It's here."

It took everything he had not to make love to her again. "What's here?"

"The morning."

There was such devastation in her voice, and he knew just how she felt. But delaying the inevitable was futile.

"I know, and I think we should be getting up. It would be better if you were dressed when your father arrives."

She groaned and clung even tighter. "It might be better for him, but not necessarily for me."

Roman gave her one last, long embrace and then crawled out of bed, giving her the space to do the same. He began pulling on his jeans.

"I'll make some breakfast."

"I don't want to eat," Daisy said. "I will throw up if I try."

His expression softened. "Then coffee. You can at least have some coffee."

She rolled to the side of the bed, then sat on the edge, staring down at the floor.

"Remember the night when I crawled out from under this bed?"

As he reached for his boots, he saw his hands were shaking. He sighed. That night was a lifetime ago. He dropped down on the side of the bed and began pulling them on.

"Yes, I remember," he said.

"I felt certain I was going to die." A small smile broke the somberness of her face, never quite reaching her eyes. "But I didn't, did I?"

He shook his head, letting her ramble, waiting for her to make her point.

"That's what you've been trying to tell me all along, wasn't it?" she said.

"What do you mean?" Roman asked.

"It's the uncertainty about all of this that scares me the worst. You, I know. You, I love. I don't remember loving Davis Benton, but maybe I did, and I know I have to give this meeting a fair chance."

"Good girl."

"But there's something I want you to do for me in return."

"Name it," Roman said.

"Hang on to that money for me. There's something inside of me that's afraid to let it be known it's in my possession. Call it instinct, call it lack of guts, call it anything you choose. But for now, I don't think anyone should know I have it."

He frowned. "I don't like it. I think you should show your father—"

"No!" Her vehemence was impossible to ignore. "Don't you understand? Until I remember everything, I don't know who to trust. The only person I know and trust is you." She stood, holding the sheet in front of her like a limp and wrinkled shield. "Will you help me?"

Against his better judgment, he agreed. "I'll help you, and you know it. But if I don't hear from you within a few days, I'll make my own decisions about the damned stuff."

She nodded. "Fair enough."

He finished dressing and stalked downstairs, telling himself he was probably getting into something way over his head. But there was no denying that Daisy didn't know whom to trust. And there was every possibility that someone had committed a crime to get that money. Until they knew for sure where it came from, he would keep her secret safe.

They stood together on the porch, watching as the helicopter descended from the sky. A good portion of the snowfall had already turned to runoff, leaving the ground beyond the cabin a mixture of mud, slush and snow. Daisy leaned closer against Roman's shoulder, then reached for his hand. Threading his fingers through hers, he squeezed gently, just to let her know he was there.

"Holly, they're here."

Startled, she looked up at him. "Why call me that now?"

It hurt to say it, but a truth was a truth. "Because that's who you are and who you have to be."

"And if I don't want to?"

He shook his head.

A short, stocky man emerged from the chopper. Ducking the downdraft of the blades, he started toward the cabin at a lope.

Something clicked inside of her. Although she didn't recognize him, there was a familiarity within her that eased part of the tension she was feeling.

"Easy, baby," Roman said softly. "It's going to be all right."

She looked up at Roman and shook her head. "Not from where I'm standing."

"I'm right here beside you," he said.

"For how long?" she muttered, and looked back at the man coming toward them. "You're sending me away, remember?"

Roman groaned beneath his breath. "I'm not sending you anywhere. You're going home. There's a difference."

Daisy wouldn't budge. Her chin jutted mutinously. "I'm standing on the only home I know."

"Damn it, don't make this any harder than it already is."

Her eyes flashed. "Then don't let them take me—"

Davis Benton heard the last part of what she was saying and interrupted before she could finish.

"Holly-berry, I won't take you anywhere you don't want to go."

She froze. Somewhere in the back of her mind, she could hear herself laughing at the name. She gasped as her belly drew itself into a knot, then stared long and hard into the stranger's face.

"Davis Benton?" she asked.

This was harder than Davis had expected. Knowing that the very sight of him brought fear to his own daughter's face was devastating. But he'd fought longer wars than this and won. Holly was worth whatever it took to get her back.

"Yes, dear, I'm Davis Benton. I'm your father."

Up until now, she'd refused to think of herself by that name, but now there was no denying it.

So, I truly am Holly Benton. She stepped forward and held out her hand.

Awkwardly, Davis grasped it, wanting to pull her to him, but settling for a brief handshake, instead.

"And you, sir. You would be Roman Justice?" Davis asked.

Roman nodded.

Davis's smile was wide and open. There was no mistaking his gratitude and joy.

"You've given me back a reason to live. How can I ever thank you?"

Roman glanced down. Daisy—he amended the thought—Holly was silent, too silent. There was a distant expression on her face, as if she'd removed herself from the both of them to preserve her sanity. He looked back at Davis. There was no mistaking the seriousness of the tone of his voice.

"By taking good care of your daughter."

"That's a promise," Davis said, then glanced at what Holly was wearing. The clothes were outdated and a little bit large. He glanced back at Roman.

"The least you can do is let me reimburse you for the use of your wife's clothing."

Roman's expression never wavered. "I'm not married, and I told you before, the only reward I want is Holly's safety."

Davis looked from Holly, to the man beside her and then back again. He glanced down. They were holding hands. In itself, that meant nothing. It was simply a gesture of reassurance for a woman who was afraid to let go. And then he looked at the expression on his daughter's face. Not once in the time she'd been dating Gordon had she looked at him like she was looking at the man beside her. A piece of anger turned loose in his mind. Had this man taken advantage of her when she was most vulnerable?

Roman could almost hear what was going through Davis Benton's mind, and it was the last straw in a day that had barely started.

"Benton."

Roman had Davis's attention. There was more than warning in his voice.

"What?" Davis asked.

"Don't even go there," Roman said softly.

Davis flushed. "I don't know what you—"

"You know exactly what I mean," Roman said. "Get that look off your face. Get that thought out of your mind."

Holly had been puzzled as to what was going on, and then suddenly grasped what was *not* being said. Anger spilled out of her in a rush.

"Mr. Benton, if you have something to say to me, then say it," she cried. "But don't start laying blame at anyone's feet." And then she laughed bitterly. "I realize I can't speak for Holly Benton, but I can certainly speak for Daisy, and she's a grown woman. She doesn't need anyone's permission to do anything she chooses."

When she called him "Mr. Benton," Davis began to worry. This woman looked like his Holly, but she was certainly more forceful than Holly had been.

"If it will make you more comfortable, I will call you Daisy. And you're right. No twenty-seven-year-old woman needs her father's permission to do anything."

Holly relaxed, absorbing the tiny bit of news that she was only twenty-seven. It felt as if she'd lived a lifetime after what she'd been through last week.

"You call me what you choose, but you will not judge me. I won't accept it."

"Fair enough," Davis said, exhaling slowly. That was close.

He gave Roman a closer look. Whatever had gone on between them, his daughter was obviously ready to defend her right to do it.

"Mr. Justice, are you certain we can't give you a lift? From the air, it's quite obvious that the roads are still impassable."

Roman shook his head. "No."

Davis glanced at his daughter. "Is there anything you want to take with you?"

She glanced at Roman. Only him. When Roman's gaze darkened, she looked away and answered. "No, I guess not."

"Then we'd better be going," Davis said. "I chartered a plane to take us back to Las Vegas." He waved his hand toward the snow and mountains. "The sooner I get back to warm air and sunshine, the happier I'll be."

Holly tensed. This was it. She turned to Roman, begging him with one last look to stop this madness before it was too late.

"Holly."

Hope surged. He wasn't going to let her go after all. She took a step toward him, but the look on his face stopped her intent.

"What?" she asked.

"Find the truth, and the truth will set you free." Then he lifted his hand to her face, brushing a flyaway strand of hair from her eyes. "I'll be in touch."

She suddenly panicked. "I don't know how to reach you!"

Roman pivoted. "Wait a second. I'll be right back." He disappeared into the cabin, leaving the pair alone on the porch.

Davis fidgeted, knowing quite well it would be prudent to wait before he mentioned the rest of what he had to say, but prudence was not one of his strong suits.

"Your fiancé is in the hospital, anxiously waiting for your return. I'll take you to visit him before we fly home to Vegas."

Holly stiffened. "I don't have a fiancé," she said shortly.

Davis persisted. "But of course you do! You were eloping when the plane went down. Didn't Justice tell you?"

Her chin jutted mutinously. "Yes, actually, he did. And I'll tell

you, just like I told him. I don't believe it. I don't feel it in here."
She put her hand over her heart, but Davis ignored it, and her.

"You just don't remember, that's all. In time, it will all come
back to you. You'll see."

She kept thinking of the money. Something was wrong with
this story; she just knew it.

She glared at him, muttering to herself as much as to him.
"Don't treat me like I'm simple. I didn't have a ring, so I wasn't
engaged. How long had I known him?"

Davis looked startled. "Oh, uh, about three or four months, I
believe."

"Was I an impulsive woman?"

He shook his head. "No, actually, you're pretty grounded in
everything you do."

"Was I the kind of woman who would elope with a man I
hardly knew?"

She was backing him into a corner, and he knew it. "Actually,
I was a little surprised, but he said you were—"

Holly pounced. "Oh! Then we're operating on the word of a
man who thought I was dead."

Davis frowned. Put like that, it sounded suspect. And then he
discarded the idea.

"Holly, dear, you're just distraught, and I can understand why.
Please believe me when I tell you that you're under no pressure
from me or anyone else to do anything you don't want to do. Just
come home. Give us a chance to prove we're right."

"I have little option," she said, and then turned to look as
Roman came out the door.

"Here," he said, and handed her one of his business cards.
"Call me any time, day or night. I check my messages regularly.
I will get back to you as soon as possible, okay?"

Holly clutched the card tightly in her fist and, for the first time
since the helicopter had landed, felt a small sense of relief. At
least now she didn't feel as if she was losing him for good. Even

though she was leaving him behind, he'd given her a way to reconnect.

Ignoring Davis Benton's presence, she threw her arms around Roman's neck.

"Thank you for everything."

Roman hugged her fiercely, knowing that when he let go, Davis would take her away.

"Like I said, I'll be in touch," he whispered.

To Roman's surprise and her father's dismay, she kissed him soundly before tearing herself away.

Davis took her by the arm and began leading her to the waiting chopper. She kept looking back, as if expecting some sort of reprieve.

And even after they were airborne and flying away, her gaze stayed fixed upon the man on the porch. It did her heart good to know that the entire time she was watching, he hadn't moved a step away from watching her go.

Holly exited the hospital elevator with a rebellious glare. Davis took her by the arm and began escorting her down the hall.

"Just for the record, this is entirely against my wishes," she said.

In spite of the fact they kept moving toward Gordon's room, Davis seemed sincerely apologetic.

"But what if it triggers a memory?" he asked. "Don't you want to remember?"

More than you can know. But she didn't say why. Until she could explain the money to herself, she wasn't about to mention it to anyone else.

"This is it," Davis said, and stepped aside, motioning for her to enter first.

At that moment, Holly wished Roman were at her side, not this man who called himself her father. She took a deep breath, bracing herself for the confrontation, and walked through the doorway.

* * *

Gordon was dozing. Roused by a touch on his arm, he heard someone calling his name and opened his eyes. The last person he expected to see standing beside him was Holly Benton. And the still, almost judgmental, expression on her face came close to stopping his heart. Afraid to move, he held his breath, terrified of what she might say.

Aware that things weren't going as he'd envisioned between the pair, Davis began the conversation.

"I know just how you feel," Davis said. "When I saw her, I was speechless, too. Aren't we blessed?"

Gordon nodded, trying to smile and hoping it didn't look as sick as he felt.

"My God," he muttered, looking back at Holly again and knowing he had to say something appropriate. "Holly...my darling, this is a miracle."

Holly didn't speak. She kept staring and staring into Gordon Mallory's face, and the longer she looked, the less she trusted him. He had yet to meet her gaze straight on, and he didn't seem glad to see her; he seemed scared. Why would her appearance cause him this type of concern? Her eyes narrowed thoughtfully as she took careful note of his injuries. He looked pretty good, considering the fact that he'd survived a plane crash.

Gordon was worse than nervous. That cold look on her face, as well as her silence, was unnerving. He cast a nervous glance at Davis, wishing them both to hell with no way back.

"What's wrong with her?" he asked. "Has her speech been affected by the accident, too?"

Holly answered on her own behalf. "There's nothing wrong with my speech, or my mind," she said. "The fact that I can't remember either of you does, in no way, mean I've lost the rest of my faculties. I'm sure you can understand how unsettling this is for me. I'm thrust into the midst of strangers who expect me to take their word for everything, which in fact, I cannot."

"Of course, of course," Davis said quickly. "No one expects you to—"

Holly interrupted, her patience worn well past the pretense of manners.

"I'm sorry, sir," she said. "But that's the problem. *You* do expect things from me I'm not willing to give, and I'm sorry if it hurts to hear that. I've promised to go back with you to Las Vegas, but I will in no way honor a promise I don't remember making. I have no intentions of marrying this man—ever." Holly turned to Gordon, fixing him with a cool green stare. "I'm sure you understand my position," she said shortly. "And while I wish you a speedy recovery, I have no intentions of trying to resume any sort of relationship."

Ire flooded Gordon's being. The infernal little bitch. How do I know she isn't pulling this amnesia stunt to get out of revealing the whereabouts of my money?

Davis took his daughter by the arm. "Holly, dear, I can see that coming here was a mistake after all. This could have waited until we all got home and in more comfortable surroundings."

She gave her father a startled look. "What do you mean, 'we all get home'?"

Davis looked a bit nervous as he explained. "Why, I've invited Gordon and his brother, Billy, to convalesce at the estate."

Holly felt as if the walls were closing in around her. Roman, damn you, why did you let them take me away? Then she remembered his card and felt in her pocket, making sure it was still safely intact. It was there. He was only a phone call away. She exhaled slowly.

"That shouldn't be a problem. The west wing is always reserved for guests. We..."

Stunned by what she'd just said, both men couldn't help but stare at her.

Holly shrugged. "That keeps happening to me. I don't know what I'm going to say until it pops out. Roman says that's normal and that one day I'll remember everything."

Davis was elated. What had just happened confirmed what the doctor who'd examined her had also said. He had to restrain himself from hugging her. This was such a positive sign and one he'd been praying for since he'd learned she was alive.

As for Gordon, he could only stare in horror. For him, it was another nail in his coffin. The more time passed, the less were his chances of escaping justice. Between Billy's revival and Holly's resurrection, he was another step closer to ruin.

Chapter 10

The temperature was in the high eighties when Roman pulled into the parking garage below the complex in which his office was located. He got out of his car, then stood beside it, giving the area a thorough sweep before he popped the trunk. The weight of the duffel bag he slung over his shoulder was nothing compared to the weight of responsibility he felt in having it in his possession. He headed for the elevator with his hand resting on the gun beneath his jacket.

The ride up to the fourteenth floor was swift, but for him, none too soon. Last night, before he'd left the cabin, he dumped the money in the middle of the living-room floor and started to count. When he passed the five-hundred-thousand mark, he began to sweat. When the count had risen to over nine hundred thousand, he'd gone into shock. By the time he had finished, the count was so close to a million dollars, the few thousand it was off hardly mattered. And he'd promised to baby-sit the damned stuff until further notice.

Within a few short minutes, it would be safe and sound behind lock and key.

His secretary looked up as he entered the office, surprised to see him.

"Mr. Justice! I didn't expect you in today."

"Afternoon, Elizabeth. And you still haven't seen me, okay?"

She smiled. "Yes, sir. I understand. If you don't mind my asking, when *am* I going to see you?"

Roman returned the smile. "Day after tomorrow. I'm going out to the ranch in the morning. Got to see a little lady about a cat. At last report, it was flea-bit and severely off limits."

Elizabeth's smile broadened. Her boss's fondness for his four-year-old niece was a well-known fact. She would have been stunned to know that another woman had gotten under his skin, as well, but in a different sort of way. She went back to her work as Roman entered his office, shutting the door behind him.

Roman paused inside, adjusting to the culture shock of civilization. This ultra modern high-rise was a far cry from the simplicity of the Colorado cabin he'd left behind. There was a stack of faxes on his machine and a small mountain of messages on his desk. A couple of packages had come in the mail that had yet to be opened, and a picture hanging on the wall over his desk was slightly askew.

But his focus was on the locked door across the room that led to a large walk-in closet. Inside were the classified files he kept regarding all of his cases, as well as a genuine reissue of an old Wells Fargo safe. More than once, he'd considered getting rid of the monstrosity. Now he was glad he had it.

In a few quick strides, he was inside the closet and down on his knees, working the combination. When the last tumblers clicked, he opened it, tossing the duffel bag inside. Only after the safe was shut, and the door locked behind him, did he breathe a quiet sigh of relief.

He dropped into the chair behind his desk and then swiveled toward the bank of windows, staring blankly out across the Dallas skyline. The view was lost upon him. He kept remembering the hurt on Holly's face and the fear in her voice.

Don't let me go. You are my world. Don't let me go.

He jumped up from the chair as if he'd been catapulted and stalked to the windows. The traffic on the streets below seemed to be moving in fits and starts, just like the beat of his heart. Guilt was a kicker. He closed his eyes and took a slow, deep breath. Damn this situation to hell and back.

Moments later, he found himself back in the chair with the phone in his hand.

"Elizabeth, get me the home phone number of Davis Benton in Las Vegas, Nevada."

"*The* Davis Benton?"

"Yeah. *The* Davis Benton. And if the damned thing's unlisted, you know what to do."

"Yes, sir," she said curtly.

A few minutes later, she rang him back. "Mr. Justice, I have the number for you. Shall I make the call?"

"No. I'm going to make the call from home."

"Yes, sir. I'll bring it right in."

"No need. I'm on my way out. I'll pick it up."

When he hung up, his pulse was racing.

A short while later, he pulled into his driveway and parked, glancing up at the front door of his house. Just for a moment, he let himself imagine what it would be like to know that Holly would be inside, waiting for him to come home. He felt in his pocket for the phone number Elizabeth had given him, then got out of the car and hurried up the walk to his house.

Even though the decor was definitely masculine, the burgundy upholstery with dark blue accents, as well as the jade vase on the mantel, retained a measure of casual elegance. Heading for the phone, he paid no attention to the gleaming hardwood floors and glistening windows, or the perfectly arranged throw pillows on the overstuffed sofa. And if he had looked, he would have thought little about it. Those were services provided by his cleaning lady, not by the love of his life.

He punched in the numbers and then caught himself counting the rings and holding his breath.

"Benton residence."

Roman frowned. It wasn't Holly's voice, although considering Benton's life-style, he hadn't really expected it to be.

"May I speak to Holly Benton, please? Roman Justice calling."

"Miss Benton isn't taking calls. Would you care to leave a message?"

"She'll take mine," Roman said.

"I'm sorry, sir, but Mr. Benton has left strict orders that Miss Benton isn't to be disturbed."

Roman's eyes narrowed angrily. The tone of his voice softened, but what he said could never have been misconstrued as compliance.

"Then you tell *Mr.* Benton that I called, okay? And you also tell Mr. Benton that I will call again tomorrow evening, at which time I expect to be put directly through to Holly or know the reason why. Got that?"

The maid hesitated, but just enough to let Roman know he'd gotten under her skin.

"Yes, sir, I will tell Mr. Benton you called."

"And who are you going to say called for Holly?" Roman asked.

"Mr. Justice?"

"That's right. I just wanted to make sure you were paying attention. You have yourself a nice day."

He hung up in her ear, then headed toward the front door. He had to unload the camping equipment and then let Royal know he was back.

Holly stood at her bedroom windows, gazing out across the carefully landscaped grounds. She couldn't help but compare them to the wild beauty of the Colorado mountains. Here, everything was laid out in geometric patterns. Dark greens became the backdrop for the early-blooming flowers, while variegated greenery had been interspersed among shrubs and bushes that had yet to yield their blooms. A complex irrigation system seemed to operate on some sort of timer. She'd noticed it coming on and going off at various times of the day and wondered how much money it took to keep a place like this in operation. Somehow, the luxury of it all seemed a terrible waste, considering the fact that, except for staff, she and her father were the only two people in residence. Then she frowned, amending that to four, counting Gordon and Billy Mallory, who were to arrive tomorrow by special plane.

Her shoulders slumped as she turned away from the windows to stare at the room in which she stood. It was decorated in shades of blue. A thick off-white carpeting covered the floor of the entire room. An elegant four-poster bed was obviously the focal point of the furnishings, with a matching dresser and armoire sitting on either side of it.

It was a woman's room—all whites and laces, accented with china and crystal figurines. There were a few pictures on the walls, none of which seemed remotely personal in nature. No family photos. No school mementos. Just understated elegance. Holly frowned. It was very, very beautiful, and she felt as if she were in jail.

As she looked around the room, it dawned on her that she'd seen it before—back at the cabin—during one of her fleeting moments of lucidity. She sighed. If this wasn't proof of her identity, then nothing would be. Just because she didn't remember it all certainly didn't mean it wasn't so.

But she was lonely here. The staff tiptoed around her as if she had the plague. No one seemed willing to talk to her, and she wondered if this was normal behavior or if her father had given them orders not to bother her with questions she obviously couldn't answer.

She dropped into a nearby chair. The term *heavy heart* had new meaning for her, because that's exactly how hers felt. A phone sat on the table, only inches away from her hand. She thought of Roman and wondered if he'd gone home, or if he was still in the cabin, waiting for the weather to clear.

Downstairs, she heard a telephone ringing and stared at the one beside her, wondering why it didn't ring in here, as well. Then it dawned on her that this was probably a private line. Testing the theory, she picked it up. The dial tone sounded in her ear. The urge to call Roman was almost overwhelming—to reconnect with someone she knew and loved.

Instead, she set the receiver back on the cradle and stood abruptly. Daydreaming would get her nowhere. She wanted this nightmare over, and the only way it could happen was to remember why it started. Davis Benton had brought her back to her roots. Maybe there was something here that would jar her memory.

The room around her beckoned by the very fact that nothing looked familiar. She kicked off her shoes and headed for the closet to change into something more comfortable than the dress she was wearing. A few minutes later, wearing shorts and a T-shirt, she began by going through the drawers in her dresser and praying for a miracle.

Billy Mallory was confused. He'd been so certain they were going to die that he'd expected to wake up in heaven...or hell, whichever the case might be. He hadn't been prepared for the pain, or the around-the-clock circus of needles, monitors and nurses, prodding, poking and talking about him as if he weren't even there. Just because he chose to keep his mouth shut didn't mean his brain was dead. The way he looked at it, he and Gordon were already in more trouble than they could say grace over. There was no use adding to the pot by spilling his guts in a drug-induced stupor. Choosing sleep over worry, he closed his eyes, willing the flow of painkillers in his system to take him away to that place where sound doesn't go.

"Hey. Billy boy, it's me, Gordy."

Billy opened his eyes. When he tried to speak, his tongue felt too thick for his mouth.

Gordon reached for a nearby cup and spooned up a chip of ice. "Here you go, buddy. Let's have ourselves a little ice."

Billy took the ice, grateful that someone understood his problem without his having to ask. The cold felt good on his tongue, and right now, the moisture it generated tasted better than his favorite cold beer.

"Umm," he mumbled, indicating his appreciation.

Gordon grinned and patted his brother on the leg. "You just rest. I'll talk. You listen."

Billy blinked an okay, anxious to know what had been going on while he'd been unconscious. But that was before he heard what Gordon had to say.

Gordon leaned close, whispering in Billy's ear. "Holly Benton is alive. Her father has taken her back to Vegas, and tomorrow morning, we're flying there, as well."

Billy's eyes bugged as a nearby monitor suddenly beeped.

"No, no, you're reading this all wrong," Gordon said. "You don't know the best part. She has amnesia. Not only does she not remember what happened to her, she also doesn't remember her old man, or even her own name. We're in the clear. And—" he almost giggled "—here's the best part. Benton invited us to recuperate at the estate because I told him Holly and I had been eloping."

Billy groaned and managed to mumble, "What about the crash? What are they saying?"

Gordon glanced over his shoulder, making certain they were still alone, and then continued. "As far as everyone is concerned, we don't know what happened other than the plane suddenly lost pressure. You were supposedly up front talking to the captain and that's why you were in the copilot's seat. And I conveniently blacked out, so I don't have to answer any awkward questions."

Gordon chuckled, more to himself than to Billy. "It's about as perfect as it gets." Then his smile slipped. "Except for that spoiled brat of a female. I'd lay odds she's still got that money and is playing it cagey, probably planning to keep it all for herself.''

Billy grabbed at Gordon's arm. "No...not Vegas. Get away. We need to get away.''

Gordon frowned. "Don't be foolish. I'm not going anywhere until I've got my hands on that money. And don't give me any grief about this, because this mess is all your fault. Just be glad you're my brother. Otherwise, I'd be inclined to break your fool neck.''

Holly was down on her knees and digging through a closet when someone knocked on her door.

"Come in," she called.

Davis entered with a smile on his face. It didn't stay there long. "My stars, girl! What on earth are you doing?''

She rocked back on her heels and gave him a long, studied look.

"Looking for Holly Benton.''

Startled, Davis was at a momentary loss for words. Finally, he found the gumption to speak. "I'm sorry, but I don't—''

She pulled a stack of letters from a box and then sat down without looking up.

"This is my room, right?''

"Yes.''

"So...everything in here would be mine, right?''

"I suppose so. I haven't been any farther than the door in years.''

She glanced up. "Why not?''

The question startled him, and the longer he thought about it, the more he realized he didn't have a good answer.

"I don't know," he finally said. "I just haven't.''

"Weren't we friends?''

Davis dropped down beside her, then reached out and brushed the side of her face with the back of his hand.

"Oh yes, Holly-berry, we're friends. And you are loved. Even if you don't remember that, please don't doubt it."

An odd sort of comfort settled within her. She nodded, then managed a smile.

"Just asking."

Ignoring the fact that he was still wearing a very expensive suit, Davis sat down beside her, curious as to what she was reading.

"What do you have there?" he asked, pointing at the letters in her hand.

"I don't know," she said. "Looks like they are from someone named Shirley."

Davis laughed. "Your college roommate, Shirley Ponselle. You two were inseparable during those years."

Holly smiled. "Are we still friends?"

"I suppose, but it's been years since you two communicated other than by letters. She's an archaeologist and on a dig somewhere in South America."

"Wow, an archaeologist. I'm impressed!" And then she thought. "What do I do?"

"What do you mean?" Davis asked.

"I mean, I graduated, didn't I?"

"Yes, with honors," he said proudly.

"What was my degree? What do I do for a living?"

Davis looked a bit uncomfortable, but he managed to answer. "You have a degree in literature."

Holly's mouth dropped. "Really! Do I teach?"

He shook his head. "No, dear, you don't actually work in an official capacity. But you stay very busy, acting as hostess on my behalf and standing in for me at various functions when I'm unable to attend."

She frowned. "I have a degree in literature and I don't do anything but go to parties and spend money?"

Put like that, it sounded worse than it was, but Davis was unable to lie. "You make it sound worse than—"

She snorted beneath her breath. "A dilettante is a dilettante, no matter how you word it. No wonder you thought I was going to elope with that toad."

Now it was Davis's turn to look startled. "Gordon Mallory is no toad. He's a well-established businessman."

She stuffed the letters back in the box without reading them and got to her feet. From where she was standing, her father suddenly looked like a little old man and not the commanding figure he practiced to project.

"Whatever. I still say you're way off the mark with this eloping."

"Why?" Davis argued. "Just tell me why. You don't remember me. You don't remember living here. Why do you think you would remember Gordon?"

Holly offered him her hand, grunting as he pulled himself up. Then she picked a piece of fuzz off the hem of his jacket.

"It's hard to explain," she said. "Although it's true I don't exactly remember you, there are times when you say and do things that I know I've heard before."

Davis looked pleased. He hadn't realized she'd experienced any sort of progress.

"But that's wonderful," he said. "If one thing comes to you, then others will follow."

"That's what Roman said." Then her mood turned pensive, and she looked away.

Davis saw the look in her eyes. He knew how reluctant she'd been to leave the man. His first instinct had been to take her and run back to Vegas, but now that he'd had time to think, it would seem that the Justice man hadn't done her harm. In fact, it was entirely due to Roman Justice that he had his Holly back. And then he remembered why he'd come.

"He called today."

"Who called?" she asked.

"Roman Justice."

Disappointment filled her voice. "Oh, no! Why didn't somebody tell me? I was here."

"Because I left orders for you not to be disturbed."

Anger overwhelmed her, and it took everything in her not to shout.

"Without asking me first?"

"I'm sorry," Davis said. "I didn't think about him calling. I just thought about the people who might call that you wouldn't remember. I was trying to protect you. Not deceive you."

"Don't do that again," she said. "I want to talk to him. I have to talk to him. He's very important to me. Do you understand?"

Davis sighed. "I wish you could hear yourself. You are all but raving about a man you hardly know."

"I know enough," she said shortly.

"He said he would call again tomorrow night."

Holly relaxed, but only a little. The idea that she was being controlled in any way didn't sit well.

Davis knew when to push and when to step back, and right now, retreating would be wise.

"I suppose we'd better change for dinner," he said, and started out of the room. "We have about a half an hour."

She looked down at her bare feet and the shorts and shirt she was wearing. Roman wouldn't care what she wore to eat in. Then she smiled to herself. In fact, he liked her best when she wore nothing at all. And he would call tomorrow. It was enough for now.

"Okay," she said, and then a thought came out of nowhere. "Oh, Mr. Benton..."

He interrupted her. "Please. If you can't call me Dad, like you used to, at least call me Davis."

At that moment, Holly truly felt sorry for what he must be going through.

"I'm sorry...Dad."

The smile on Davis's face was startling in intensity. "Thank you," he said softly.

"You're welcome."

"What was it you wanted to tell me?" he asked.

"Oh, that's right," she said. "About Roman. I want you to leave him alone."

"But I had no intentions of—"

"You know how you are," Holly said. "Every time a stranger comes on the horizon, you call that stupid service of yours and have them investigated and you—"

Both of them stopped, their faces mirroring the surprise they were feeling.

"Oh, my," Davis said softly. "Oh, my."

Holly sighed. "That's the way it happens. Just when I think I can't find my way out of a paper bag, along comes this neat pair of scissors and snips away a little bit more of that stuff clogging up my brain."

"Okay," Davis said.

She looked up. "Okay what?"

"Okay. No investigation. If you vouch for the man, then that's good enough for me."

For the first time since she'd walked through the front door of this house, it felt right to be here.

"Thank you...Dad."

Davis retraced his steps long enough to hug her, and then left before she could object.

Even after he was gone, she still wore the smile on her face, and knew, somehow, it was going to be all right.

It was just after 3:00 a.m. when a siren broke the silence of the neighborhood in which Roman lived. Although the sound was common, it invaded his sleep and became part of his dream.

Holly was standing naked in the middle of a snowy field and crying tears that kept turning to ice. As soon as a tear would solidify, it would slide off of her face and onto the ground at her feet.

Roman called out her name, but she didn't seem to hear. And then it began to snow and he started to run, fearing that she would freeze to death before he could reach her. But it wasn't snowflakes that came out of the sky. It was hundred-dollar bills. They fell to earth, scattering with the wind wailing down the draw.

"Holly! Come to me! Hurry, hurry!"

Instead, she held up her arms, as if warding off the money falling down around her head, and before he could reach her, she disappeared before his eyes.

When he reached the spot where she'd been standing, all he could hear was the echo of her voice crying, "Money, money everywhere and not a cent to spend."

He woke up with a jerk to find himself drenched in sweat and wrapped in a tangle of bedclothes.

"My God," he muttered, and rolled out of bed.

Sweat was running down the middle of his back, and his heart was hammering as if he'd been running for miles. He thought back to the dream and groaned. He *had* been running, trying to get to Holly.

"This is crazy," he said, and headed for the bathroom.

Moments later, he was standing beneath the shower head and washing away the sweat, as well as what was left of the dream. By the time he came out, the only thing left from the episode was a lingering reluctance to go back to bed. Instead, he headed for the kitchen for something cold to drink, welcoming the feel of the cool air against his bare body as he moved from room to room.

He opened the refrigerator and got a cold can of pop, rubbing it against his forehead for a few seconds before popping the top. The metal was smooth and chill against his skin, cooling the fever of the dream.

Roman.

Although the sound was only an echo in his mind, he instinctively shuddered, as if a ghost had just passed by. He was hearing her voice because he'd been dreaming of her. That's all. She wasn't in danger. There couldn't be anything wrong because she was with her father. But the feeling wouldn't go away.

Don't let them take me.

He spun, this time actually searching the shadows for form and substance. Goose bumps broke out on his forearms, but he turned away, disgusted with himself and what he viewed as a weakness.

He popped the top of the can, listening to the carbonated hiss as the seal broke, then draining it in one continuous gulp before tossing the can in the trash. The sound of metal against metal broke the silence with an abruptness that made him blink.

Make love to me, Roman. I don't want to forget.

His heart was aching as he turned away. Forget? Only if he died. Right or wrong, when they'd made love, he'd staked a claim on a woman he wasn't willing to lose. What scared him to death was loving her now before she remembered her past. Then he sighed. But he'd known that from the start. It was a risk he'd been willing to take then. The least he could do was trust in her now and wait and see. And...he'd call her again tomorrow.

He glanced at the clock. It was already tomorrow. Too early to call anyone, even Royal, and too late to go back to sleep.

His belly growled, and he thought of the supper he hadn't wanted last night. There wasn't any food in the house, but somewhere out there was an all-night restaurant that had a steak with his name on it.

He reached for his pants.

Chapter 11

It was just after 10:00 a.m. when Roman got to the ranch. The worst was behind him, and knowing that he would be talking to Holly this evening had him in a better mood.

He parked and reached for the sack on the seat beside him just as the front door opened. Madeline Michelle Justice teetered out on the porch, wearing a bright green T-shirt that hung down to her ankles, with a pair of red high-heeled shoes peeking out from beneath the hem. There was a moth-eaten feather boa around her neck and trailing the ground behind her, as well as a lady's straw hat that had completely blocked all vision from her left eye.

He got out of the car with a grin on his face.

"Hello, madam, I don't believe we've met. My name is Mr. Justice, and who might you be?"

Maddie giggled, then slid into the make-believe with all the skill a four-year-old can muster.

"I am Miss Piggy and I'm waiting for my Kermie to take me to town."

Before he could answer, Royal appeared in the doorway, grabbing at his daughter's arm just before she toppled off the side of the porch.

"Watch it, piglet, that first step's a doozie," he said, and aimed her back to the house.

"Piggy, Daddy! Not piglet...piggy. Miss Piggy," Maddie said, and clip-clopped her way inside.

Roman laughed out loud as Royal rolled his eyes.

"I never did learn what made women tick, and God gives me a daughter," he muttered, waving Roman inside. "Come on in. Coffee's on the stove. I have one more call to make, and then I want to hear all about your trip."

Roman shut the door behind him as Royal disappeared into the den. Still in her Muppet phase, Maddie moved down the hall toward her room, leaving a trail of feathers behind her.

As Roman stood, listening to the ordinary business of Royal's life, he was struck by the emptiness of his own. Unlike the orderliness of his own home, Royal's house looked lived-in. There was a pair of old boots by the door, and Maddie's pajamas and her precious blankie were slung over the arm of a chair. He picked up the blanket and then lifted it to his face, inhaling the faint but lingering little-girl smell. It was a mixture of talcum powder and soap, with something sweet thrown in. There was a sticky place down on one corner. If he was of a mind to guess, he'd say it was syrup, probably left over from her breakfast.

A longing for something like this of his own hit him hard, leaving him empty and aching and thinking of Holly. He set the sack on a nearby table and headed for the kitchen. He was going after coffee, but what he needed was his head examined. He'd fallen in love with a rich man's daughter who couldn't remember her own name. Added to that, he was in possession of enough unclaimed money to start a small war, and that summed up the mess he was in.

He was standing at the window with a coffee cup in his hand when Royal came in the room.

"Sorry about that," Royal said. "I've been trying to connect with that man for a week."

Roman turned and then shrugged. "No big deal. I wasn't going anywhere." He took a slow sip of the hot brew, savoring the kick of caffeine.

Royal's eyebrows arched. "You mean you're in Dallas and still haven't gone back to work?"

"Something like that," Roman said.

Royal grinned. "So, taking time off was good after all. Don't you hate it when I'm right?"

The thought of Holly hit Roman belly high. It was all he could do not to groan from the pain that came with it, but Royal was too busy congratulating himself to notice.

"You obviously didn't get to fish, but at least you got some rest," Royal said, and then glanced over his shoulder to make sure Maddie wasn't eavesdropping on their conversation. "I can tell you, if that had been me, I would have slept the clock around before I ever got out of bed. Between my daughter and the ranch, I can't remember the last time I overslept."

"Didn't sleep all that much," Roman said.

Royal frowned. "Why not?"

"I kept waiting for the woman on the sofa to snore."

Royal's mouth dropped open. Before he could speak, Maddie burst into the room, running barefoot and wearing blue jeans and a T-shirt that was inside out. Miss Piggy had obviously been laid to rest.

"Uncle Roman! Uncle Roman!"

He scooped her off the floor and into his arms, grinning as she threw her arms around his neck and plastered his face with kisses.

"I've been wondering where you were," Roman said. "Some strange lady met me at the door."

Maddie giggled. "That was me."

"No!" he gasped, pretending great surprise.

She giggled again, and began tracing the dark arch of his eyebrows with the tip of her finger, giggling even harder when he made them wiggle beneath her touch.

"Uncle Roman?"

He nuzzled the side of her neck, stealing kisses on a ticklish spot beneath her right ear.

"What, Little Bit?"

"You knew it was me, didn't you?"

"Knew who was you?" he asked, pretending to be puzzled by her remark.

She threw her arms into the air in a gesture of surprise.

"Miss Piggy! I was Miss Piggy!"

"No!"

"Yes, yes, I was!" Then she looked at Royal. "Daddy, isn't it funny? I fooled Uncle Roman."

"Yeah, it's real funny," her father said, as always marveling at the remarkable change that one small female could make in Roman Justice's demeanor.

Roman set Maddie down and then took her by the hand. "Come on, kid. We've got to see a cat about some fleas."

Royal frowned. "Hey, Roman. About the woman on—"

"Not now," Roman said. "Maddie and I have something important to do."

Royal followed them into the living room, grumbling all the way.

"Dang it, Roman, you can't just drop a bombshell like that on me and then expect me to ignore it."

Roman picked up the sack he'd brought and started out the door.

"First things first," he said. "If you need us, we'll be at the barn."

Royal thrust a hand through his hair in frustration. "What's at the barn?"

Roman turned. "A flea-bit cat."

Royal's face turned red. "Now, look here. Don't resurrect a mess that's already been ironed out."

Roman held up the sack. "No mess. Just flea powder and a cute little pink collar."

Royal groaned. "Damn it, Roman. I won't have a cat in the house."

"I didn't say anything about bringing it in the house," Roman said. "We're just getting rid of the fleas so she can play with it. Nothing wrong with that, is there?"

Royal was caught and he knew it. His eyes narrowed, and it was all he could do not to punch his brother square in the nose. Add to that, his daughter was clinging to Roman's hand like a cocklebur with a look on her face he couldn't bring himself to ignore.

"Fine, then," Royal muttered.

Roman grinned. "Come on, Maddie. Let's go find us a kitty."

She was so excited she tore free of Roman's grasp and bolted for the barn, her bare feet churning up the dust as she ran.

Royal stuffed his hands in his pockets. "Before you completely spoil my child, you ought to get one of your own."

"Been thinking about it," Roman said, and then went to catch up with his niece.

For the second time in the space of five minutes, Roman had stunned Royal into speechlessness. All he could do was gape as Roman disappeared into the barn. Snowbound with snoring women? Having children? What the hell had Roman been doing at the cabin anyway?

It was ninety degrees and climbing when the private jet Davis Benton had chartered touched down in Las Vegas. Gordon and Billy Mallory were about to embark upon the next phase of their lives. It was one that would either make them or break them. Billy was scared half out of his mind. Gordon was riding an adrenaline high. Within the hour, they would be housed beneath the same roof as a woman he'd intended to kill. They'd fled Las Vegas because of a murder he hadn't planned to commit. Now here they were, in essence, returning in style to the scene of the crime. Gordon had come to the conclusion that he was invincible. Somehow he would discover the whereabouts of his money before Holly regained her memory. And thanks to Benton's misplaced generosity, Billy was going to have the best of care while Gordon rectified the mistakes his little brother had made. It was a perfect plan. Nothing could possibly go wrong.

Medical personnel were on hand as they touched down, obviously waiting for their arrival. Before Gordon had time to disembark, they were on board, readying Billy for transport to the Benton estate. There, a special room and private nursing had been set up for his around-the-clock care. Gordon had been released from the hospital with the understanding that he would see his personal physician as a follow-up for his healing ribs. Gordon had willingly agreed. At that point, Gordon would have agreed to anything.

As they started to lift Billy from the stretcher onto the waiting gurney, Gordon laid a hand on Billy's arm.

"Take it easy, little brother. No one's going to hurt you. I promise."

Weary from the trip, as well as arguing with a brother who had visions of grandeur that would probably get them both killed, Billy closed his eyes, gritting his teeth against the pain of being moved. The problem with Gordon was, he dreamed big but thought small. Billy was too injured to fight the inevitability of the ax he expected to fall. He had nightmares about sleeping under Holly Benton's roof, of waking up to find her standing over his bed and pointing an accusing finger in his face. But as always, Gordon hadn't listened to him. Gordon was the big brother and, therefore, the one who must always be in charge. And like the follower he was, Billy hadn't enough gumption to strike out on his own. Instead, he continued to follow in Gordon's footsteps, no matter how deep the mud in which they walked.

Davis glanced out the library window as the ambulance pulled up to the estate.

"They're here," he said, and dashed out of the room before Holly had a chance to react.

Frowning, she followed her father out of the room. The closer she got to the front door, the slower her steps became. She couldn't get past the notion that she was moving toward danger.

Damn you, Roman Justice. I don't want to do this alone.

But she kept walking, well aware that if he were standing by her side, he would expect her to make these last steps alone. *I'm not welcoming anybody,* she thought. *I'm only finding my way to the truth.*

Up ahead, she heard voices in the foyer. She recognized her father's, probably directing traffic—and then some people spouted jargon that branded them as medical personnel. But it was the loud, jovial male voice that made her pause in midstep. A memory of something dark, something awful, tugged at the back of her mind. The urge to turn and run was strong. Then she reminded herself that she was home, that nothing could hurt her here. And still she stood out of sight, listening and trying to remember.

"I say, Davis, this is wonderfully kind of you," Gordon said. "Billy's had a rough flight and is looking forward to rest, aren't you, Billy?"

Billy nodded, then pointed toward a small bag that a maid was carrying away.

"Those are my things."

Gordon laughed. "She's only taking them to your room," he explained. "Besides, you won't be needing them for a while."

Down the hall, Holly suddenly felt the floor beginning to tilt. The words she'd just heard had triggered an unpleasant memory.

Where you're going, you won't be needing them.

She reached toward a nearby wall for support as her legs threatened to give way. Swallowing several times in nervous succession, she closed her eyes and took slow, calming breaths, trying to rid herself of the terror that had swamped her. But as hard as she tried, she couldn't get past it. Somewhere before, she'd heard that same voice, saying nearly the same thing to her. But it hadn't been said as lightly as it had been just now. When she'd heard it, there had been a real and tangible threat behind every single syllable.

She could hear them! They were coming closer now, and every instinct she had told her not to let them see her fear. In the midst of her panic, Roman's words came back to her so strong, it was as if he were standing beside her, saying them again for the first time.

The truth will set you free.

She took a slow, calming breath and straightened her shoulders. When the men came around the corner, she was ready and waiting.

Davis knew Holly had been unhappy about the arrival of the Mallory brothers and was pleased she had come to greet them.

"Holly, darling, there you are! We're in the process of getting everyone settled."

"I heard," she said, and then turned her full attention to the man at her father's side.

The smile on Gordon's face slipped, but only a little. Play the part, he reminded himself. Play the part.

"Holly! Darling!"

Before she could react, Gordon had embraced her.

"The last time I saw you, it was so awkward. Me lying flat on my back in the hospital, and your dear little face so full of fear."

Holly withdrew from his touch as if she'd accidentally walked into something foul.

Gordon's face flushed with anger, but he refrained from comment, pretending he hadn't seen a thing.

"Well, now," he said heartily. "I'd better see Billy settled in before we make any plans."

Holly gave her father an angry glance. She'd warned him about pushing her into something that didn't feel right. If he thought she was going to knuckle under, rather than make a fuss, he had another think coming.

"We have no plans to make," she said shortly.

This time, Gordon made no effort to hide his displeasure. He looked at Davis, as if waiting for him to smooth things over. But Davis had already seen Holly's mood for himself, and wisely, decided to make himself scarce.

"I'll just show them the way to Billy's room," Davis said quickly. "Lunch will be in thirty minutes. See you then."

He walked away, leaving Gordon and Holly alone in the hall to sort out their own affairs.

Forced to deal with the issue himself, Gordon turned his attention to Holly.

"It seems we've been left on our own. That was thoughtful. Your father knows we would have plenty of things to discuss."

Holly's expression never wavered. "He's mistaken. There is no 'we' and there's nothing to discuss."

Gordon wanted to shake her. He wanted to put his hands around her tiny white throat and squeeze until she admitted what she'd done with his money. But that was too premature. That might come later...if his other plans didn't work out.

"Holly, darling, you just don't remember. We meant everything to each other...you mean everything to me!"

Again, Holly recoiled as if she'd been slapped.

Gordon flushed and reached for her arm. "Damn it, you're not being fair."

She stepped out of his reach. "No, Mr. Mallory, you're the one who's not being fair. We have nothing to discuss, because I have no memory of you, or of us."

"We were on our way to Nassau! We were going to be married!"

She frowned. "So I've been told."

"Then how can you be so cruel as to ignore my feelings? Don't you know how much your withdrawal has hurt me?"

Now Holly was certain her instincts about him had been right. Hurt him? Didn't he know how much fear and confusion she'd been dealing with?

"You miss the point, Mr. Mallory. I can't ignore something I never knew existed. And if you cared for me as much as you claimed, you wouldn't be pushing me. Now, please excuse me. As my father said, lunch will be served shortly. I'm sure we'll see you then.''

She walked away, leaving Gordon alone in the hall with his thoughts. And while they were far from kind, it wasn't what bothered him most. It was that cool, assessing look in her eyes, as if she'd just taken his measure and found him lacking.

Royal was in the kitchen, finishing the dishes from their noontime meal. He glanced out the window, as always, checking to see where his daughter had gone, although with Roman still here, she wouldn't go far. He could hear the creak of the porch swing, and an occasional murmur of voices. That meant they were on the back porch, probably still playing with that damned kitten, although he had to admit that since Roman had given it a bath and a good dusting of flea powder, it was sort of cute. And Maddie was beside herself with delight. It had been all he could do to coax her inside long enough to eat lunch before she'd begged to go back outside.

He gave the last pan a good rinse and set it aside to drain before drying his hands. He still didn't have any satisfactory answers from Roman about what had gone on at the cabin, but he would have before the day was out or know the reason why.

''What's going on?'' he asked, as he stepped out on the porch.

Roman pointed. Maddie was dragging a piece of string behind her, while the kitten scrambled after it, trying to pounce.

''Frisky little beggar,'' Royal said, and sat down on the steps.

Roman nodded.

Royal sighed and gave his brother a studied look, then glanced up at the sky. The air was muggy. Far off on the horizon, a line of thunderheads was building.

''Probably rain before morning,'' he said.

Roman squinted up at the sky. ''Probably.''

Royal shifted gears. "At least we won't have to worry about this rain turning to snow."

The mere mention of snow made Roman think of Holly, which wasn't difficult since she'd rarely been off his mind. He glanced down and then quickly raised his feet as the kitten came racing toward him. It scampered beneath the swing, with Maddie not far behind.

As she started to run past, Roman scooped her off of her feet and into his arms.

"But, Uncle Roman, Flea-bit is going to get away!" she cried, struggling to get down.

"No, she won't," Roman said. "See, there she comes now. Why don't you sit here with me awhile. Flea-bit needs to rest. She's only a baby, remember?"

Maddie nodded. "But I could hold her."

"No, honey, it's too hot to hold her. She'll be cooler if you just let her be for a while."

Maddie sighed, but she knew better than to argue. While she sometimes talked her daddy into a compromise, when her uncle Roman put his foot down, it stayed put.

"Okay," she said, and leaned back in his arms.

Roman winked at Royal and then set the swing to rocking—not a lot—just enough of a gentle to and fro that lulled Maddie into a much needed sleep. The kitten was down at his feet, less willing to give up the play, but it, too, soon succumbed to the lazy afternoon heat.

Royal leaned back against the porch post, watching the ease with which Roman had put his daughter to sleep.

"Thanks," Royal said. "She needed that."

Roman looked down at the sleeping child in his arms—at the dark, flyaway hair and lashes so thick they made shadows on her plump cheeks.

"It was my pleasure," Roman said softly, and smiled.

Instead of breaking the mood by taking Maddie inside, Royal

stayed put, aware that Roman could hardly bolt and run with Maddie asleep in his arms.

"Roman."

Roman looked up. Here it comes, he thought.

"What happened at the cabin?"

Roman sighed. As much as he wanted to keep Holly to himself, there were too many extenuating factors to ignore.

"There was a woman at the cabin when I got there."

Royal stiffened. "What happened? Did she break in? Was anything missing?"

Roman shook his head. "No, no, nothing like that."

"Then talk, damn it. I never did like guessing games."

"She'd been injured. There were scratches all over her and blood on her clothes. Had a hell of a knot on her head." He thought back to the look on her face when she'd seen him pointing the gun at her head. "And she was scared to death."

"Man," Royal muttered. "Car wreck?"

Roman shook his head. "Nope. Parachute."

"What?"

"Remember me asking you to find out if a plane had gone down anywhere in the area?"

"Yeah."

"Turns out she'd been a passenger on that plane. Only someone strapped a parachute on her and dumped her out a short while before it crashed."

"Good lord! Why?"

"We don't know."

"What do you mean, you don't know? Didn't she tell you anything?" Royal asked.

Roman shook his head. "She couldn't. She has amnesia. Right now, she's operating on instinct."

"What happened to her? Where is she at?" Royal asked.

"Back in Las Vegas, with her father."

Royal's eyes widened with sudden understanding.

"Are you telling me that you found Davis Benton's daughter? The one everyone thought was dead?"

"Yes."

Royal stared at his brother for a long, silent moment, and when he finally spoke, there was conviction in his voice.

"You fell in love with her, didn't you?"

Roman didn't answer, but he didn't have to. Royal could see it in his eyes.

"My God! I didn't think there was a woman alive, other than my daughter, who could bring Roman Justice to his knees."

"Shut up, Royal. There's nothing funny about any of this."

And then Royal remembered she'd been eloping with one of the men on the plane.

"Oh, hell, the fiancé."

Roman looked away.

"Damn, I'm sorry, Roman. I suppose when she regains her memory, they'll—"

Everything he'd been worrying about suddenly came to a head. "I'm going after her," Roman said.

Royal looked startled. "But I thought you said—"

"I know what I said," Roman muttered. "And I know what I told her when I sent her away. I told her it was for her own good, and that she needed to remember everything before she could make a decision about something this important."

Royal frowned. "Are you saying that she fell in love with you, too?"

"Yes. And I sent her back to someone else without a fight."

"So, what are you going to do first?"

"Put Maddie to bed and then catch the next plane to Las Vegas."

Chapter 12

It was fifteen minutes after 10:00 p.m. For Holly, the day had passed in snail-paced increments with everything moving toward a single, important conclusion—waiting for Roman's call.

She'd endured the entire day, including meals, with Gordon Mallory hovering over her every move, and every minute spent in his company made her increasingly nervous. If he looked at her, she found herself looking away. If he spoke, the very sound of his voice grated. And if he so much as reached in her direction, she had an instinctive urge to pull back. Whatever had been between them before hadn't been good, no matter what she'd been told. Just because she couldn't remember didn't make her stupid. Subconsciously, she knew she must be protecting herself.

Eventually, Holly had made her excuses and escaped to her room. And now, she was waiting. She'd had a bath. She'd washed her hair. She'd done her nails. She'd even suffered a small spurt of feeling sorry for herself and cried. None of which had produced the desired result. No phone call. No Roman.

She kept telling herself that, in his line of work, anything could have happened. He might have been called out on an important case. And she had to admit that he also might have changed his mind. While her heart wouldn't let her believe that he was an out-of-sight, out-of-mind kind of man, there was no escaping the fact that she'd known him less than a week.

Put in that perspective, the feelings she had for him could have seemed ludicrous. No one falls in love within a period of days, never mind falling into bed with a stranger. But she had done both and would do it again in a heartbeat.

She glanced at the clock, then rolled over on her bed and closed her eyes, making a bet with herself. It was twenty-two minutes after ten. He will call before eleven. It was a silly game, but it was a way to get through the next thirty-some minutes without going crazy.

Seconds later, she heard the faint, but unmistakable sound of the front doorbell. It seemed very late to be receiving visitors, but without any memory of her father's habits, she had no way of knowing if this was out of character for the household.

She reached for the blue silk robe draped over the end of the bed as she got up. It wasn't as if she would be expected to appear, but just in case...

Moments later, she heard voices, and much louder than they should have been. Curious, she opened the door and stepped out into the hall. And in that moment, she heard the familiar sound of a beloved voice.

Sweet music to her ears! Roman was here!

Forgetting that she was in her nightclothes, she bolted for the stairs.

Davis Benton was in a state of disbelief. Roman Justice had appeared on his doorstep and all but pushed his way inside. Angry with being disturbed, he had half a mind to call the police.

"Look, Mr. Justice, at any other time, I would be more than happy to receive you as a guest, but this is ridiculous. Do you know what time it is?"

"Couldn't get an earlier flight," Roman said, setting his bag on the floor at his feet. "And I'm not going to bed until I see Holly."

"Go to a hotel, get some sleep, come back tomorrow," Davis said. "She's already in bed."

Like Holly, Gordon Mallory had become curious and was half-way down the stairs when he heard Holly's name being mentioned.

"What's going on out here?" he demanded.

Davis turned. "Gordon, I'm sorry you were disturbed. Go back to bed. I'll deal with this."

But it was more than curiosity that made Gordon stay where he was. The stranger was looking at him in a judgmental manner, and like a herd bull sensing his territory was about to be invaded, he took the man's measure—and instant offense.

Although the man seemed ordinary enough, in Gordon's opinion, his style of dress left plenty to be desired. His clothing was entirely Western. Although he was wearing slacks, his white, long-sleeved shirt and Western-style sport coat seemed a bit too much. Added to that were black boots and a wide-brimmed gray Stetson. And then his attention moved from what the stranger was wearing to the man himself, and Gordon found himself wanting to bolt. *He knows!* But he took a deep breath, reminding himself there was no way he could know. No one but Holly knew and she couldn't—

A sudden burst of panic made his belly knot. Dear God, what if this had all been a ruse? What if Holly didn't have amnesia? What if they had planned this all along just to get him and Billy in a vulnerable position? What if...? He shuddered and grabbed hold of the railing for support. *Get a grip,* he reminded himself. *Don't quit when you're still in the game.*

Roman's attention was completely focused on the man on the stairs. *This is the man she was going to marry?* Granted, by present-day standards, the man was good-looking enough. A thick head of brown, wavy hair, large eyes and a trim physique. But there was something about him—a weakness about the chin and a reluctance to meet one's gaze straight on—that made Roman doubt. His eyes narrowed, his face becoming blank. Right now, Mallory was wearing a smug expression, but Roman couldn't help wondering how Gordon would have looked if he'd come in with the bag of money.

And then he heard Holly's voice and forgot about everything except her.

"Roman! You came!"

Davis turned and then groaned beneath his breath as Holly came flying down the stairs. From the look on his daughter's face, this mess was just beginning.

When she called out his name, Roman knew he'd been right to come. This woman was worth the fight and then some. He walked past Davis and headed toward the stairs.

Unprepared for Holly's sudden appearance, Gordon saw her run past him before he could stop her. When she threw herself into the stranger's arms, his stomach began to knot. This was worse than he'd thought. This man was obviously more than a stranger to Holly, and he was a threat to Gordon's plan. Now what should he do?

Holly leaped from the bottom step into Roman's arms.

"I thought you were going to call," she said, and threw her arms around his neck as he lifted her off the floor. Completely oblivious to the fact that she had an audience, she began hugging him, over and over.

Once he had her in his arms, every knot in Roman's body began to unwind. "I came to tell you that you were right," he said, and kissed the side of her cheek.

"Right about what?" Holly said.

"I shouldn't have let you go the way I did."

Her spirit soared. "So, are you saying—?"

Roman silenced her with a look, and then turned, still holding her in an embrace. His voice was strong and unwavering, his gaze clear and focused as he stared Davis Benton straight in the face.

"I came to tell your father something, too."

But Davis was in no mood for revelations. This type of behavior was unseemly, and completely out of character for the way he believed a daughter of his should behave.

"Now, see here, Holly," Davis cried. "This is extremely inconsiderate behavior in front of your fiancé. Have you no shame?"

"I keep telling you," she said. "I don't have a fiancé. I was never engaged. I was not eloping with that man, I just know it."

Roman's arms were around Holly, but his gaze never left Davis's face. "When you came to get her, she begged me not to let her go. I've been sorry ever since. I made a mistake. I came to fix it. Plain and simple."

Davis was floored. "Look here, Justice. Caveman tactics went out with woolly mammoths. People in our class don't behave in such a bohemian manner."

Anger settled deep in Roman's heart as his expression stilled. His voice was low and steady, but there was no mistaking his meaning.

"I don't come from class. I come from Texas. Down there, we fight for what's right, and right now, I'm the only familiar thing in your daughter's life." Then he looked at Gordon, waiting for him to argue.

Gordon was speechless. The truth be known, that damned Texan could have her. All he wanted was his money. But it was painfully obvious that all eyes were suddenly on him, waiting to see what he had to say about this. And to keep himself on the good side of safe, he knew he had to at least make a fuss. So he came down the stairs, hoping for the right tone of shock in his voice.

"Holly, darling, how can you do this? After all we meant to each other?"

Roman didn't give her time to answer. "You know something,

Mallory, I'm beginning to believe Holly was right about you all along."

A fresh spurt of panic shot straight to Gordon's heart.

"Right about what?" he muttered.

"That you two were not about to get married after all. If this situation was reversed, and some man had just interrupted my world and tried to take my woman out from under my nose, I would have punched his face. Then I would have taken said woman—and myself—into a room and locked the door. And I would have made damned sure I had changed her sweet mind before I let her back out."

Gordon began to sputter. "All men aren't like you. Some of us are sensitive."

Holly wanted to laugh at what Gordon just said, and she looked at him, her voice rich with indignation.

"You, sensitive? Really, Gordon. I saw you run over a dog without even looking back. To you, *sensitive* is a four-letter—"

When she stopped in midsentence, it dawned on them what had happened. Once again, a truth had come out when she least expected.

"Well," Holly said. "I believe I've done it again."

Gordon pivoted and stalked upstairs without looking back. Davis threw up his hands and gave his daughter a long, hard look.

"I hope you know what you're doing," Davis said.

"I told you, Daddy. Trust me."

"You're flying by the seat of your pants," he muttered.

Roman felt it was time to finish what he'd come to say.

"Please, Mr. Benton, hear me out."

Davis shifted his glare from Holly to the man who held her.

"What more could you possibly have to say that you haven't already said?" he asked.

"I mean no disrespect, but your daughter is too important to me to just give her up without a fight. I've never backed down from anything in my life, and I'm not about to start now." Then Roman took a deep breath and looked at Holly. "But I take noth-

ing for granted until she remembers who she is. I can't lay claim
to a woman who doesn't remember her own existence. However...making her wait this out on her own wasn't fair."

Holly's heart began to pound, and her eyes began to burn. "So
what you're saying is you came because you feel sorry for me?
I don't need sympathy. There's too much in this house already.
What I need is some faith. I need someone...anyone...to believe
what I do know!"

"And what would that be?" Davis asked.

Holly wanted to scream, but she stifled the urge, speaking instead in shaky and uneven tones.

"That I might not remember being Davis Benton's daughter,
but I know who I am. I would *not* marry a man like Gordon
Mallory." Then she pinned Roman with a piercing stare. "Unlike
you, I don't have to wait for revelations and rainbows to know
what's in my heart. However, I'm glad you're here."

Roman took a deep breath. "So am I."

She closed her eyes and leaned against his strength, gladly
sharing the burden of her load.

Davis Benton hadn't become rich by being weak or indecisive,
and he appreciated strength, both of body and character, in others,
as well. He hated to admit it, but the man intrigued him in a way
Mallory did not.

Davis glanced at Holly and then shrugged. "As she reminded
me earlier, it's not up to me. This is Holly's decision. But I would
ask you to give her some space. Don't pressure her into any
decisions she's not ready to make."

Roman nodded. "Fair enough," he said, and held out his hand.
Davis shook it.

Holly hugged her father, and then started to pick up Roman's
bag.

"Holly, darling, what on earth are you doing?" Davis asked.

"Roman is staying here, of course."

"But—"

The smile on her face turned to ice. "Since you invited the

Mallorys—people I don't even remember—I'm sure you won't mind Roman being here. At this point, he is the *only* person I do know.''

Davis turned red with embarrassment. He had bullied her into accepting the Mallory brothers' presence. Put like that, he had no option but to accept with grace.

"Of course," he said quickly. "I was just thinking of the propriety of the situation."

"I fail to see the connection," she said. "I'm not in love with Gordon."

"But you were," Davis spluttered.

She shook her head. "It was Gordon who put that thought in your head. You told me you were surprised we were eloping. Why are you so dead set on believing a man you hardly knew?"

Davis threw up his hands. "I'm going to bed. Mr. Justice, I wish you a good night's sleep." He started up the stairs, muttering more to himself than to Roman, "And you're probably the only one who's going to get it."

Gordon was worried. Not only had that damned Texan just yanked his reason for being in the Benton mansion out from under his nose, but he'd been unable to regain favored status and he knew it.

Instead of going to bed, he headed for Billy's room. He didn't consider the fact that Billy was probably asleep, or that he needed his rest. There was a kink in the plan that he'd made. Billy needed to know—just in case.

He burst into the room, slamming the door shut behind him. Billy woke with a jerk and then groaned from the motion. Blinking sleepily, he looked up.

"Gordon? What's going on? What time is it, anyway?"

Gordon began to pace. "It's time to worry," he said. "That's what time it is."

Billy yawned. "I've been trying to tell you that for days."

Gordon frowned. "Shut up," he muttered. "I'm trying to think."

"That's what keeps getting us into trouble," Billy said. "Look, why don't we just move out tomorrow? We can get a place of our own and as soon as I'm able to travel, we could—"

"Get a place with what?" Gordon growled. "Thanks to you, we don't have any money."

"And thanks to you, I'm an accessory to a murder. Carl Julian is dead because of us," Billy muttered. "Besides, what about the ten thousand we left in the bank?"

Gordon ignored the reference to the money in the bank. Ten thousand was peanuts compared to the million he'd lost.

"Shut up. Shut up. I don't want to hear Carl Julian's name mentioned again."

"You could try getting a job," Billy said.

Gordon laughed, but it was a heartless sound, completely devoid of mirth.

"Doing what? I know how to run a scam, pick locks and cover my tracks. The openings for good con artists are few. I dare say my chances for employment would be better flipping burgers at a fast-food restaurant."

"At least it would be honest," Billy said.

Gordon's eyes widened in disbelief. "Since when have you grown a conscience?"

"Since I saw you cut a man's throat."

Gordon blanched. Even he had succumbed to a moment of weakness afterward. But it had happened so fast. One minute they were on their way to financial security, and the next moment Carl Julian had caught them in the act. Even after Julian had promised not to tell, Gordon had reacted without thought, cutting off Julian's pleas with the man's own letter opener. It had been easier than he might have thought, and they'd escaped without further detection. At least they had until Holly Benton had overheard their argument on the plane.

Gordon combed his hands through his hair in a gesture of frustration.

"Here's what we're going to do. I've still got a few friends here in the city. All I need is something to make Holly talk." When he saw the look on Billy's face, he quickly added, "Nothing that will hurt her. Just something to make her spill her guts."

Billy glared. "You mess with her again, and I'll tell everything I know. I'd rather go to jail than go to hell later on."

Shock spread on Gordon's face. "Since when did you get religion?"

"Since I woke up from the crash and found myself alive."

Gordon was stunned. He'd never heard his brother speak with such conviction. Now he was faced with the choice of doing what he wanted and leaving Billy behind when he ran, or changing his plans again. But he couldn't get past the lessons of his childhood. Take care of your little brother. Don't let Billy get hurt. Watch out for Billy wherever you go.

He glared. "Damn it, Billy, you're making this harder than it has to be."

But Billy wouldn't budge, and Gordon was forced to restructure his plans again.

"I'm going to bed," Gordon said. "You try and get some sleep. We'll talk tomorrow." He left, slamming the door behind him.

But for Billy, sleep was slow in coming. Doom was hovering on the horizon, and he didn't know how to stop it.

Roman woke to the smell of warm bread and creamery butter. He opened his eyes just as Holly was setting a breakfast tray on a nearby table. Her hair was piled high on her head, and the loose strands were still damp, obviously from a morning shower. The robe she was wearing was the one she'd had on when he'd arrived—sheer blue silk, with a matching gown beneath. It had taken every ounce of his willpower to leave her at the door to her room last night, but he'd done it. Now she was back, bringing temptation with her. There wasn't a Justice alive who'd ever been accused of passing up a good thing. He saw no reason to ruin the family's good name by starting now.

"Good morning, baby," he said softly, and then patted the bed. "Come here to me."

She did without hesitation, settling down beside him as if she'd done it a thousand times in the past.

"I can't believe you're here," she said softly, touching his arm, his bare chest, then smoothing back the hair on his forehead. "I kept telling myself this has happened too fast, that you would get home, take a deep breath and realize you'd made a mistake."

Roman frowned. "The only mistake I made was in letting you leave alone. I had nightmares." His frown deepened. "I haven't had nightmares in years, at least not since..." He stopped. That was a part of his life he'd never shared, not with anyone.

Holly waited, letting him decide how far this conversation needed to go.

Roman sat up in bed, pulling her close within the shelter of his arm. When she cuddled close, he settled her head beneath his chin and sighed. It was time to let go of a few ghosts of his own.

"I don't have a real good track record with women."

Again, she remained silent, giving him the freedom to pick and choose his words.

"My mother died when I was small. That left Dad to raise us three boys by himself. Considering the hell we gave him, he did a good job." He closed his eyes, remembering as a child the lonely, empty years of yearning for the gentleness of a mother's touch. "I decided at a pretty young age that I was too tough to cry. I don't know whether my older brothers drilled that into me with their constant heckling, or if it was my way of hardening my heart against any more pain."

Holly hurt for him. She had vague memories of her own empty years without a mother, of yearning to be held and rocked and fussed over, as only a woman can do.

"I'm sorry, sweetheart," she said softly.

He smiled and then stroked her hair, letting his thoughts drift. "I thought I could handle anything life dished out. After all, I'd already lost a parent, what more was there to lose except my own life?" Then he took a deep breath.

"That just shows how innocent and naive I still was. My senior year in high school, a new girl moved into town. Her daddy was the new head football coach at school, and her mother was my English teacher. Her name was Connie. For the next two years, we made plans. We dreamed dreams. We were inseparable. We were in love."

Holly held her breath, afraid to hear what came next, and at the same time, knowing it had to be said.

"She drowned the summer between my freshman and sophomore years at college. I stood on the shore of the lake, watching her as she skied past." He shook his head. "She was laughing and waving at me, so pretty and so full of life. Less than a minute later, a speedboat came out of nowhere and hit her. We couldn't get to her in time to save her. I watched her live, and I watched her die. After that, I just...well, I just quit."

Tears were running down Holly's cheeks. "Oh, Roman, it's a miracle that you even gave us a chance, isn't it?"

Roman looked down at Holly, at the tears on her face, at the love in her eyes, and knew a great sense of belonging.

"Naw, it wasn't a miracle," he said, trying to tease away the tears. "It was those damned daisy panties."

She laughed on a sob.

Roman cupped her face with the palms of his hands and then wiped away all traces of her sadness.

"I didn't tell you that for sympathy, baby," he said softly. "But I want you to understand that I do not—have not—given love lightly. Right now, there is a peace in my heart that hasn't been there in years, and I have you to thank. I've loved and lost two very different women in my life. I'm not looking forward to losing another."

"But you won't lose me. You can't! I love you, remember?"

"I remember a hell of a lot more than you do," he said shortly.

She looked away. "That's not fair," she muttered.

His expression hardened, and there was a warning in his eyes that she couldn't mistake. "You're right. It's not fair. None of this is fair. And telling you about my past when you're still lost from your own may seem selfish. But you need to know something about me right now, before it's too late. When it comes to love, I won't fight fair...but by God, I will fight."

Holly tilted her face for the kiss she saw coming. Just before his mouth touched hers, she whispered, "Then that's all I need to know."

Minutes later, when they had come up for air, Roman whispered against her cheek.

"Holly...baby?"

"Hmm?"

"Is the door locked?"

Drugged by the strength of his kisses, her eyelids fluttered sleepily.

"I don't know, why?"

"I'm going to make love to you. Didn't know whether you wanted an audience or not."

She turned the lock before he could change his mind.

There was an uneasy quiet during lunch that day. The only person unaffected by the silence was Roman, and that was partly due to the satisfying blush he'd put on Holly's cheeks and to the fact that he had metaphorically laid his cards on the table.

And while it was impossible to miss the dark, anxious looks Gordon Mallory kept slinging around the table, Roman couldn't help thinking it had nothing to do with losing Holly and everything to do with a bagful of money. The problem was, how to prove it. Since his investigator's license did not extend to the state of Nevada, he had a little networking to do.

A few hours later, Roman exited the court of records with a satisfied smile on his face. For a man who was supposed to be dealing in real estate, Gordon Mallory was sadly lacking in proof. There wasn't a single piece of property in the city—or the state—that was registered in either Mallory's name. Not only that, but neither one had ever been licensed to sell real estate.

There was another interesting fact that he'd turned up during his afternoon search. The Mallorys no longer had a Las Vegas residence. Just prior to the flight to Nassau, they'd moved out of their apartment and discontinued their utility services.

Roman could look at that two ways. Either Gordon had been planning on moving into the Benton estate after their marriage, or he'd never planned to come back from the Bahamas at all. With a million unclaimed dollars on board the ill-fated flight, Roman was leaning toward the last theory.

But these were still suppositions. There was still the matter of the money. If it hadn't been ill-gotten gains, someone would have reported it missing by now. Both Gordon and Billy should have been shouting to the heavens that it was gone.

In Roman's eyes, their guilt was confirmed by the simple fact that they hadn't said a word.

And he was honest enough with himself to admit that the possibility still existed that Holly had, in some way, been part of the scheme, but every instinct he had denied it.

For one thing, she had no motive. It was obvious that Davis Benton would give her anything she asked for, so she would have no need to steal money, except maybe for the thrill, and he ruled that out. She wasn't that kind of a person. That left the Mallorys as the prime suspects, but proving their guilt would be the kicker.

Chapter 13

Roman returned to the mansion just as they were about to sit down to dinner. Holly had been anxiously watching the driveway. When she saw the cab pulling up to the house, she breathed a sigh of relief. She'd been dreading sitting down to dinner with Gordon and her father casting mournful looks in her direction, as if it were all her fault she didn't remember her past.

As Roman walked in the door, Holly took him by the arm, pulling him toward the dining room.

"Where have you been? I thought you weren't going to get here in time to eat with us."

Roman grinned. "Hey, baby, I missed you, too, but give me time to hang my hat, will you?"

She rolled her eyes. "Sorry. In my other life...which I can't remember...I must have been a bit of a compulsive fanatic."

He bit the lobe of her ear and then whispered against her cheek, "If that has any bearing on the way you make love, I'm all for it."

Holly's face was still pink as she entered the dining room and took a seat to her father's right.

"What kept you?" Davis asked.

She picked up her napkin and then spread it across her lap.

"Roman just arrived. He'll be right in."

Davis frowned and then gestured to a maid who was standing by with a tureen of soup, waiting to serve.

"No, don't serve it yet," he said. "We're not all here."

Gordon cast Holly a nervous glance and then laid his own napkin in his lap. He reached for her hand.

"Holly, my dear, how have you been? I see almost nothing of you during the day. Were you resting?"

She moved before he could touch her. "No."

He cast her a soulful look. "I can see that I assumed too much when I thought we'd at least be able to talk. If you'd let me, I'm sure we could work things out between us."

"When nothing is there, there's nothing to work out," she said bluntly.

Gordon flushed. "You've changed. You never used to be this cold. It's that man. He's brainwashed you, that's what."

After what I endured, I'm lucky I still have a brain. And then Roman came in and sat down beside her, saving her from having to respond.

Roman glanced at Davis and nodded.

"Sorry I'm late. You shouldn't have waited. Daddy always said if you can't get to the table on time, then don't complain about what you have to eat."

Davis laughed before he thought, and then motioned for the soup to be served.

"I think I would like your father. What does he do?"

A shadow crossed Roman's face, but he didn't hesitate to answer.

"He was a rancher all of his life. Died in a plane crash a little over a year ago. My oldest brother, Royal, now runs the family ranch."

Both Holly and her father looked startled. She had known he was dead, but not how he'd died.

"I'm sorry," Davis said.

"Was he flying commercial or private?"

Roman's mood darkened. "Private. Another of my brothers is a pilot. They were in the crash together. Ryder survived. Dad didn't." And then he shook off the feeling. "Ryder owns his own charter service out of Mississippi."

Davis nodded. "That's a long way from Texas. How did he wind up there?"

"He married Casey Ruban, one of Mississippi's finest," Roman said, and then winked at Holly.

Davis's spoon clinked against the bowl, a social faux pas that he rarely made. But the name startled him. Any businessman worth his salt knew that name.

"Any kin to Delaney Ruban?" Davis asked.

"His granddaughter."

"Oh," Davis said, eyeing Roman with renewed respect.

"I'm sorry to say I don't know the name. Is she anyone special?" Gordon asked.

"My brother thinks so," Roman said.

Gordon flushed. He'd like nothing better than to put his fist in that man's smug mouth, but the truth was, the man intimidated him. He was too physical...too animal. Give him a cultured crook any day of the week. At least he could speak their language.

"She inherited a megaconglomerate from her grandfather," Davis said. "Everyone expected her to fail at it, and instead, she's run it with an iron hand, just like the old man did before her."

Gordon couldn't help staring at Roman. He was far removed from the type of men he normally associated with and he couldn't quite figure him out.

"So one of your brothers is a rancher, another a pilot. What do you do?" Gordon asked.

"I'm a private investigator. I got my license about a year after I quit the military."

Gordon choked on a spoonful of soup. It took several moments and a glass of water before he caught his breath.

Perfect! This was just about perfect! A professional snoop had been added to the mess he was in.

"Sorry," he said, dabbing at his mouth with his napkin. "I choked."

Roman gave him a curious stare. "It happens."

"So, you're a private investigator," Davis said. "Who do you work for?"

Roman never cracked a smile. "Me."

Davis glanced at Holly, who seemed terribly focused on her soup bowl. This was so unlike the loquacious daughter he'd known before the accident. Like Gordon, he, too, wondered if she'd been brainwashed. It wouldn't be the first time a man had tried to get at Davis's money through his daughter.

"It takes a while to start up your own business," Davis said, expecting to hear a mouthful of excuses as to why it had yet to happen.

Roman frowned, thinking back to the first few months he'd gone into business.

"I suppose," he said. "But we were running in the black before the first year was out."

Davis's eyebrows arched. "My goodness."

Gordon had had enough of soup and of Roman Justice. It was time to put the man in his place.

"Don't you find that sort of work mundane?" Gordon asked.

Roman looked up, and if Gordon had known him better, would have been nervous about the look that came on his face.

"And what kind of work are you referring to?" Roman drawled.

"You know, cheating husbands, wayward wives, delinquent fathers and the like. It all seems so tawdry."

Roman's voice softened, but the glitter in his eyes was getting colder by the minute.

"I don't handle domestic disputes," he said.

Gordon sneered. "Then what do you *handle?*"

"Mostly corporate work relating to fraud, embezzlement and

industrial thievery. Sometimes, if the injured parties hire me, I work in conjunction with the authorities on a pending criminal case.''

Gordon's cocky attitude faded. This man worked in the big leagues, and the knowledge made him nervous. Stealing a million dollars was big; murdering to get it was about as big as it got. He glanced at Holly and then down at his plate. Damn, damn, damn her devious little hide. What the hell had she done with his money?

Davis eyed Roman with renewed respect. He knew all too well what fees that sort of work demanded. So, maybe Holly's instincts weren't so far wrong after all. And maybe he *was* a man to be trusted, but just in case... He glanced at Holly, remembering that he'd promised her no background investigation, but it wouldn't hurt to make a couple of calls.

Just then the maid came in with the main course.

''Ah,'' Davis said. ''Prime rib, my favorite.''

Holly smiled. ''And lobster, and venison, and...'' She caught herself. ''Oh! I'm doing it again!''

Davis all but clapped his hands with delight. ''Wonderful! Isn't this wonderful, Gordon? Billy is on the road to recovery. And my precious Holly, who we thought was lost to us forever, is getting well before our eyes!''

Roman looked at her and winked. ''And the more time passes, the easier the memories will come.''

Gordon tried to smile, but his belly was too full of panic to manage more than a weak grin. He had to do something to delay the inevitable. His mind was in a whirl as he forked a bit of the meat. Think, Gordon, think! You beat Carl Julian at his own game. You can do this, too.

He chewed thoughtfully, his eyes on his plate, but his mind on the business at hand. Suddenly, something occurred to him. He looked up.

''Holly, dear, I've been thinking about how frightened you must have been when you fell out of the plane, and how brave

you were to find your way to shelter.'' He beamed at her, knowing he was on the right track. ''Did you have to walk far after
your parachute landed?''

She didn't bother to hide her surprise. In all the time she'd
been home, this was the first time Gordon had showed any interest
in the actual events that had happened to her.

''I don't know. Probably,'' she said. ''I had no way of judging
distance.''

He looked suitably concerned. ''I say, Justice, where is your
cabin located as opposed to where Holly landed?''

Roman's mind was on something else. Something Gordon just
said was bothering him, but he couldn't figure out what it was.
It took him a moment or two to answer.

''Probably a good two or three miles downhill, although that's
just a guess. I saw no need to retrace her steps to check her story.
And even if I had wanted to, the snow prevented us from doing
anything about it.''

But Gordon wouldn't let go.

''Must be nice to have your own cabin. I might look into something like that as an investment.'' Then he added. ''I'm in real
estate, you know. Is it far from Denver?''

Now Roman knew he was lying about something. Mallory had
no ties to the real-estate business.

''A couple of hours southwest, as the crow flies.''

Gordon nodded, then proceeded to butter a piece of bread, letting the conversation drop. This was getting him nowhere. The
man was too cagey, and he couldn't press the issue or they'd
begin to wonder why he cared. However, he'd figured another
way to eliminate a possibility. All he had to do was call in a few
favors from some people he knew. After that, he'd know which
way to proceed.

Roman sat without eating, still trying to work through what it
was that kept niggling at him. *How frightened you must have been
when you fell out of—*

Roman looked up, fixing Gordon with a calculated stare. All

along, everyone had been assuming that Holly jumped from the plane. After all, she was wearing a parachute, which indicated planning on someone's part. But just now, Gordon said, "When you fell..." Those were two entirely different means of leaving a plane.

"Say, Gordon, exactly why did the plane go down?" Roman asked.

Startled, Gordon looked up. "Why, um, I was coming from the cockpit when I heard—"

Davis frowned. "I thought you told me you didn't know what happened," he said. "You said there was an explosion and then you blacked out, remember?"

Gordon blanched. Caught. Caught in his own lies. "Of course," he said quickly. "I was about to say, when I heard an explosion. I'm sorry to say I don't know anything else."

"Then why did you say Holly fell out?" Roman asked. "She was wearing a parachute, which indicates some sort of planning. And it's my understanding that no one else had one on. Why would she fall out if she'd been planning to jump?"

In the act of taking a bite of her food, Holly heard that same voice from her past.

Here. Put this on and be quiet. He'll hear us.

Staring at Gordon, she laid down her fork.

"Yes, Gordon. Why *was* I wearing a parachute? Why would you say I fell?"

Tiny beads of sweat began popping out on Gordon's forehead and above his upper lip. He shrugged and tried to smile.

"I'm sorry if I misled anyone," he said quickly. "It was just a figure of speech. As I said, I was in the cockpit with the pilot just prior to the incident, so I have no way of knowing why Holly was wearing a chute. I guess I just assumed she fell out during the explosion."

He was too nervous, and both Holly and Roman knew it. But why he would lie was beyond them. It was a small plane. They'd been on the same flight. Unless it had to do with the money in some way, this made no sense.

"Enough talk about that horrible event," Davis ordered, and the conversation moved to another topic. "On a different note, I saw in the paper that the police are still investigating Julian's murder."

"Who's Julian?" Holly asked.

Davis quickly apologized. "I'm sorry. I keep forgetting, sweetheart. Carl Julian was the manager of a downtown casino. He was murdered in his office a day or so before your accident."

"Did I know him?" she asked.

Gordon spoke quickly, too quickly for Roman's peace of mind. "No! No, you didn't."

"But that's not so," Davis said. "She did know Julian. They chaired a fund-raiser together last year. A charity event for a local homeless shelter, I think."

Gordon hoped he didn't look as aghast as he felt. Everywhere he turned, his life was becoming more and more immersed in the Benton web.

"Sorry, Holly, I didn't realize. I suppose that was before we met."

"How awful for his family," she said.

"He doesn't have any," Gordon added, and then realized he'd given away too much knowledge about a subject he wasn't supposed to know anything about.

"That's true," Davis said. "He wasn't married. But he was a decent enough man. I heard the police had exhausted all of their leads."

Good, Gordon thought. At least one thing was still in his favor.

No one else at the table noticed the faux pas except Roman. He made a mental note of it, but let it slide without comment. Somewhere within all of this mess was the answer to the mystery surrounding the money. The sooner he found it, the better off everyone would be.

* * *

It was just after midnight when Holly heard footsteps in the hall outside her bedroom door. She'd been in bed for hours and trying without success to sleep. Every time she closed her eyes, her mind filled with images she couldn't identify. While she supposed it was flashes of her memory trying to return, instead of elation, she felt nothing but frustration. If her body was bound and determined to flood her mind with bits and pieces of her past, the least it could do was furnish subtitles to match.

The footsteps continued, and she thought nothing of them until they stopped just outside her door. She rolled over in bed and sat up, watching in sudden horror as the doorknob began to turn.

"Who's there?" she called, and the moment she spoke, whoever it was quickly hurried away.

The safety of her bedroom had suddenly become more of a jail than a refuge, and she got out of bed in a panic. Without grabbing a robe, she ran toward the door. Holding her breath, she eased it open just enough to make sure the hallway was empty. That was all she needed to know. She headed toward Roman's room, telling herself that as soon as she got there she'd be safe.

The same moment she burst into the room, Roman rolled over. He was out of bed and at her side within seconds.

"What's wrong?"

Holly couldn't quit shivering, although now that the moment had passed, she kept telling herself she'd made a big deal out of nothing.

"Someone was outside my room," she said. "When I called out, they ran away, as if I'd surprised them by not being asleep."

Roman shoved her toward his bed and then grabbed his pants, yanking them on in a rush.

"Stay here," he said. "Lock the door behind me when I'm gone and don't let anybody but me back in here."

His behavior startled her. "But, Roman, maybe I was just—"

He grabbed her by the shoulders. "Someone's missing a million dollars, remember? As you pointed out, people have been killed for a whole lot less. You stay here and do what I say. I'll be back.''

Now she *was* afraid. She'd let herself believe that the money was somehow going to explain itself and then disappear. And when Roman suddenly pulled out a gun and started toward the door, she grabbed him.

''Roman, I couldn't bear it if anything happened to you.''

''Nothing's going to happen to me,'' he said shortly. ''But I can't say the same thing for whoever the hell scared you. Lock the door behind me.''

She did as she was told, then scurried to his bed, crawling beneath the covers and into the spot where he'd been lying, taking comfort in the fact that the mattress still held the heat from his body.

Roman slipped into his old military mode, moving without noise and listening and looking for anything out of place. He knew that what she heard might have been nothing. But then again, there was too much at stake to ignore the least sign of danger.

He paused outside each door, listening for sounds of life. He had no way of knowing who occupied which rooms, or how many were empty. But it was after midnight. If someone was still up, they were going to have to explain why to his satisfaction.

Just as he was about to start downstairs, he noticed a faint light beneath the door at the end of the hall. Whoever occupied that room was about to receive a visitor. Without knocking to announce himself, he pushed it open, recognizing Gordon, but not the man in the bed.

When Gordon saw the gun in Roman's hands, he gasped. ''What's the meaning of this?''

Roman stepped inside and closed the door, then walked toward the bed without taking his eyes off of Gordon. When he reached the foot of the bed, he looked down. This must be the brother.

''I asked you a question,'' Gordon cried. ''You have no right to come in here like this. Can't you see my brother is in fragile condition?''

Roman fixed Gordon with a cold, unwavering look. ''Where were you about five minutes ago?''

Even by lamplight, Roman saw him flush.

''I was right here,'' Gordon cried. ''I've been here ever since we retired.''

Unintentionally, Billy Mallory gave away his brother's lie. Roman saw the surprise, then something that looked like concern, spreading across Billy's face.

Roman turned to the brother. ''Is that right?''

Only then did Billy look away, but not soon enough to hide what he'd been thinking.

Gordon stood abruptly. ''Don't question my brother as if he was on trial.''

''Somebody tried to enter Holly's room. It scared the hell out of her, and I'm making certain it doesn't happen again...not even unintentionally.''

The warning was there. All Gordon had to do was grasp it. And grasp it he did. At this point, he knew he'd do anything to get this man...and that gun...out of their room.

''I'm sorry I snapped,'' Gordon said, trying to smile. Then he pointed at Billy. ''You can understand my concern.''

Roman's voice fell to just above a whisper. ''And you can understand mine. You know, for a man who was supposed to marry, you show damned little concern for the bride-to-be. That leads me to doubt your story. And when that happens, there's usually a reason behind the lie. I don't like to be lied to. And I don't like people threatening my woman.''

He took another step forward until he and Gordon were face-to-face. As his voice became quieter, the threat behind it became more real.

''And I'm sure you can understand *my* concern.''

Without giving Gordon time to answer, Roman turned his back

on both Mallorys and stalked out of the room, shutting the door behind him with a very distinct thud.

Billy felt as if he might throw up. "Who the hell was that?"

Gordon's anger was about to erupt. "That, brother dear, was Roman Justice, the man who pulled dear Holly out of the snow and saved her sweet behind."

"I thought you said he was a nobody," Billy cried. "Nobodys don't carry guns. That was a Luger, for God's sake."

"So I was wrong," Gordon said.

Billy groaned. "Why does that not surprise me?"

"Shut up!" Gordon hissed. "I've got everything under control."

"That's what Captain Kirk said just before they blasted his butt into some far-off galaxy."

Gordon spun. "What?"

Billy rolled his eyes. "Never mind. It was just a figure of speech."

"This is no time to be fooling around," Gordon said.

Billy glared. "Then try to remember that the next time you pass Holly's door. You promised me you'd leave her alone."

"I wasn't going to hurt her," Gordon muttered, taking a syringe from his pocket. "It's supposed to loosen inhibitions. I figured it might loosen her tongue, as well."

Billy snorted beneath his breath. "You weren't going to hurt her, huh? That's rich. It's probably what Julian thought right before you slit his throat."

Gordon blanched, and then a dark, angry red spread up his face and neck.

"I told you not to mention his name again," Gordon said. "Someone could hear you."

"They'll hear a whole lot more than Carl Julian's name if you don't leave Holly alone," Billy said.

"I am, I will and I don't intend to discuss her with you again," Gordon growled. "The way you act, anyone would think you were the one who'd been dating her."

Billy was too quiet. When Gordon turned to look, he saw the truth on his face. For the first time since the entire fiasco began to unwind, now he understood why.

"You're in love with her."

Billy didn't respond, but he also didn't deny. Gordon wanted to slap him, but it would have done no good. The damage was already done.

"You little fool! You ruined everything for us because of a woman who doesn't even know you're alive."

"That remains to be seen," Billy said. "One of these days, she'll regain her memory. When she does, she will at least remember that I didn't want her dead."

Gordon pivoted angrily and stalked out of the room. He was so blinded by rage he didn't even notice the dark shadow of a man standing at the far end of the hall.

But Roman saw everything, including the anger Gordon had taken with him. A muscle jerked in his jaw. It was the only thing that gave away his emotion. He kept trying to think of a reason to get Holly out from under this roof without causing a scene. Because as long as Gordon Mallory was here, he knew she was in danger.

Two days later, and right in the middle of a busy intersection in downtown Las Vegas, Roman's cellular phone began to ring. He pulled into a parking space and then answered.

"Hello."

His secretary's familiar voice came over the line all too clear.

"Thank goodness," Elizabeth said. "I've been trying to get you for more than an hour. The darned call wouldn't go through."

Roman frowned. She wouldn't have called if there hadn't been trouble. He slumped down in the seat, trying to stretch his long legs. It was no use. Holly's car was too damned small to stretch anything but imagination.

"What's up?"

"The police just left, and Royal's been calling and leaving

messages here since early this morning. Someone broke into the cabin and messed it up. Royal said a ranger discovered it after driving by and noticing the front door was ajar.''

Roman frowned. "Damn. I locked it when I left—I know I did.''

"Yes, the door had been kicked in," she said.

Roman sighed. "That's too bad, although I don't know how we could have prevented it. Do they have any leads?''

"No, but that's not everything," she said. Then she took a deep breath. "The police were here this morning because someone also broke into your house last night. According to what they told me, it seems to be in a similar condition as the cabin had been. They said it looked as if someone was looking for something, because there was a lot of valuable property that they completely ignored.''

Roman sat up. "That's no coincidence," he said shortly.

"After Royal talked to them about the incident at the cabin, the police are inclined to agree with you. The detective asked me if you were working on any case that might cause such a reaction. I told them you hadn't taken on any new ones, and that as far as I knew, there was nothing pending that would indicate such behavior.'' She hesitated. "Was I wrong?''

"No, Elizabeth, you weren't wrong. At least not about the cases. However, I'm working on something here in an unofficial capacity that does.''

"Oh! Well, should I call the police and—''

"No. I'll do it myself," he said, then he thought of the money he'd locked in the safe. "The office...was it untouched?''

He heard her gasp. "Why, yes, but is there a chance that—''

"Yes.''

"Oh, dear. What should I do?" she asked.

"Call Texas Securities, tell them I want around-the-clock guards on my office, and I want it to continue until they hear from me.''

"Yes sir," she said, making fast and furious notes.

"Oh, and Elizabeth…"

"Yes, sir?"

"Under no circumstances are you to go to the parking garage alone. Better yet, just close the office until I return."

"But your calls—"

Roman's eyes darkened. "Your safety is worth more than new business. If they're serious, they'll call back."

"Yes, sir. I'll get on this right away."

"Good, and give the authorities this number. If they have any more questions, they can ask me."

He disconnected, and then stared out through the windshield. But he didn't see the constant stream of pedestrian tourists. All he could think was that someone was looking for the money. Suddenly, the trip he'd been about to make to the newspaper archive seemed less important than getting back to Holly. Someone was getting desperate, and she could easily be their next target.

Chapter 14

Holly was coming out of the library with a book when Julia, the downstairs maid, called out to her.

"Miss Benton, your hairdresser is on the phone. Do you want to cancel your standing, or should I tell him you'll call him back?"

The question took her aback. Again, she was faced with how much of her life was lost. Somewhere within the city was a hairdresser who knew more about her than she knew about herself. And when the maid spoke again, Holly realized she must look as troubled as she felt.

"Miss Benton, why don't I tell him you'll call back?" Julia asked.

Holly nodded, mouthing a thank-you. Moments later, the maid was gone, leaving Holly alone in the hall and holding a book she no longer cared to read. She laid it on a nearby table and started toward the patio, thinking that sunshine and fresh air might lift her spirits.

As she was passing the ornate mirror in the formal dining room, she caught a glimpse of herself. There, framed in gilt and visible within the pristine reflection, she knew a moment of recognition and stopped. Her heart began to pound, and there was a long moment of anticipation as she looked down at her feet, at the white leather sandals she was wearing, and had the distinct memory of trying them on before she'd bought them.

"Oh God, oh God," she whispered, then closed her eyes and turned. When she opened them, she was facing the mirror and staring at the woman within.

For a long silent moment, she stared, analyzing the dark, shoulder-length hair, the wide, sea green eyes, as well as the woman's trembling lips. She stood without moving, waiting for that fleeting bit of recognition to expand. It never came.

Finally, she turned away, unaware that she was shaking. And that was how Roman found her. Standing in the middle of the room and wearing a look of defeat.

"Holly...baby...what's wrong?"

She walked into his arms.

"Oh, Roman, I thought..." She sighed and hid her face against his chest, relishing the feel of the soft white linen and the hard, steady rhythm of his heart.

"You thought what?"

"I thought I was going to remember."

His grip tightened. "You will."

"It was so close." She pointed to the mirror. "I saw my reflection, and for a fraction of a second, I almost knew the woman in there."

Roman had been wondering what excuse he would use to get her out of the house. Now he had it.

"You know what? I think you need to get away for a while. Let's take a drive. We'll pick up something later. Maybe have a picnic."

She sighed. "I'll go, but only if you promise I don't ever have to come back."

A wry grin tilted a corner of his mouth as he dug his hand

through the back of her hair and pulled her to within inches of his lips.

"No promises," he whispered.

Tears came swiftly, but she blinked them away. "I know, I know, and no regrets."

"Where's your father?" he asked.

"I don't know, probably in his study. I heard him say something earlier about making some calls."

"Go change into something comfortable. I'll tell him we're leaving."

Now he had her attention. "Where are we going?"

He leaned down and whispered in her ear. "You'll see. Just hustle. I have this sudden and terrible need to get you naked."

Her eyes widened, and a small smile broke across her face. "An offer I can't refuse," she said, and took the stairs two at a time.

Roman watched her go, telling himself he was playing with fire. Day after day, he kept opening his heart to a woman who might one day give it back.

Ah, God, I've lived life on the edge before, but never to this extent.

All the way to Davis's study, he was wrestling with his conscience and trying to decide how much to tell her father about what was happening. By the time he got there, his decision had been made. Basically, he could tell him nothing without revealing the fact that she'd bailed out of a plane with a million dollars in her possession. The door to the study was open. He paused on the threshold.

"Mr. Benton?"

Davis was deep in a financial report and answered without looking up.

"Hmm?"

"I'm taking Holly out for a drive."

Now Roman had his attention. Davis dropped the report and

looked up. There was a frown on his face, and Roman could already see the objection coming.

"She needs to get away for a bit. The pressure she's under is getting to her."

Davis stood. Anger was thick in his voice. "I do not pressure my daughter, and I'd rather you didn't take her off the premises."

"Mr. Benton, just because something bad happened to her once doesn't mean it will happen again. You can't keep her locked up. She won't get well until she regains a normal life." Then his voice hardened. "Don't forget what I do for a living...and I'm good at what I do."

Davis's shoulders slumped. "I overreacted. I'm sorry. But you have to remember that I thought I'd lost her. When you called and told me she was still alive, I felt as if I'd been given a miracle."

Roman turned to leave. "I understand. But it doesn't change what she's going through now."

"I know, and I'll try harder to give her space."

"That's good," Roman said. "If we're going to be late, we'll call."

"Fine," Davis said. "Have a good time."

Davis picked up his report and sat down, but Roman hadn't finished.

"Mr. Benton..."

"Please, call me Davis."

"Davis, then. Where is Gordon Mallory?"

Benton shrugged. "I don't know. He said something at breakfast about going to his apartment to get some more clothes for himself and for Billy. Why?"

"Just curious," Roman said, and left.

Now his interest was piqued. What apartment? According to the Las Vegas city billing records, Gordon Mallory no longer had one. He headed up the stairs to get Holly, but as he reached the landing, made a quick decision and went to Billy Mallory's room, instead.

He knocked. A private nurse he'd seen in the halls came to the door.

"Yes?"

"Is he asleep?" Roman asked.

"No, but he's—"

"I won't stay long. I was looking for Gordon and thought maybe he knew where I could find him."

She glanced over her shoulder. "I don't know," she said, still hesitating. She'd had orders straight from Gordon Mallory himself to keep people out. Still, it seemed cruel, keeping the young man all alone like this. In her opinion, a good frame of mind helped a body heal, so what could this hurt?

"All right, but only for a moment," she said.

"Thanks," Roman said. "Why don't you take the opportunity to take a break? I promise I won't leave until you get back."

She smiled. "Why, thank you. That's very kind. I did need to make a call."

"Take your time," Roman said. "I'll be here."

"Mr. Mallory, you have a visitor," she said. "Since it's nearly time to take your medicine, I'll go down to the kitchen to get it, rather than have staff bring it up. Would you like me to bring you a snack?"

Billy shook his head. "I'm not hungry," he said, wondering who his visitor could possibly be.

The nurse smiled. "I'll be right back."

She walked out the door as Roman walked in, and Billy had an urge to call her back. But he didn't. The worst thing he could do was give way to panic. As far as the world knew, there was no reason on earth why he should dread seeing anyone from this household. Right now, only he and Gordon were aware of their duplicity, and he wanted to keep it that way.

Roman stopped at the foot of the bed and nodded. "Mallory."

"Mr. Justice...isn't it?"

Roman nodded. "We didn't exactly get introduced last time we met."

"True," Billy said. "I saw more of that Luger than I did of you."

Roman refused to be intimidated by the remark. "Like I said before, I take a threat to Holly as personal."

Billy shifted his position on the bed, grunting painfully as aching bones and muscles objected.

"That's fine by me. I would never fault you for that," he said.

Roman frowned. That was a remark that Gordon should have made. He stared thoughtfully at the young man, judging him to be in his early twenties. He was smaller than Gordon, a bit fairer in hair and complexion than Gordon. One might say he was a faded version of the original. But Roman reminded himself that this man had been a passenger on the plane. He had to know more than he was saying.

"I assume you're healing," Roman said.

"Yes, but far too slowly for my peace of mind. If I had my way, I would be out of this bed and on my way to the Bahamas." And then he realized that he might have sounded a bit desperate and added. "I was looking forward to beaches and babes, if you know what I mean."

"If it was meant to happen, then it will happen," Roman said.

Billy's frown deepened. That was a rather cryptic remark.

"Did I hear you asking the nurse about Gordon?"

Roman nodded. "Where is he?"

"After waving a gun in his face the other night, I can hardly believe you want him for a tennis partner. Why do you ask?"

"Had some questions I wanted to ask him," Roman said. "Maybe you can help me, instead."

Panic returned twofold. Calm down, Billy reminded himself. All I have to do is play dumb. Gordon does it so well, surely I can handle a couple of lies on my own.

"I'll try," he said. "Although I don't remember much about the crash. In fact, I expected to die." He laughed harshly. "Imagine my surprise when I woke up in the hospital instead."

Roman didn't respond, but it occurred to him that, for someone who should have been thanking God that he was still in one piece and breathing, the man was rather bitter.

"So, what do you want to know?" Billy asked.

Roman strolled over to the window, giving the man a chance to relax. When he turned, his question caught Billy off guard.

"Everyone says that Gordon and Holly were eloping."

Billy's heart skipped a beat. He could tell by the tone of the man's voice that he doubted the story.

"Yeah, that's right," Billy said.

Roman kept baiting the trap, waiting for the man to give himself away. "That's odd."

"What's odd?" Billy asked.

Roman walked back to the end of the bed, pinning him with a hard, unflinching stare.

"You know the old saying—'Two's company, three's a crowd.' If they were eloping, then why were you there?"

Billy choked, and it felt as if all the air went out of his lungs at once. *Damn, damn, damn you, Gordon. I knew we shouldn't have come here. This man is too curious and he's asking questions no one else has thought to ask.*

"Every groom has to have a best man," he said, trying for a smile. "I'm Gordon's best friend, therefore the best man, right?"

"Oh, then you're saying that they were making a party out of eloping."

Billy relaxed. "Yeah, that's it. It was going to be a real party."

Roman shook his head. "Only three of you? Who was going to stand in for Holly? I find it strange that Gordon would insist on taking a witness, but Holly would not."

The smile stayed on Billy's face, but that's as far as it got. Panic continued to spread throughout his system.

"Don't ask me, ask them," he finally said. "I was just going along for the ride."

"Yeah, that's right. Babes and beaches, you said." Then before Billy could regroup, Roman fired another question that left Billy stuttering to answer.

"I'll bet you'll be glad to get up and about and get back to your own home, your own things. Do you live far from here?"

He was saved from having to answer as Holly appeared in the doorway and waved at Roman.

"There you are," she said. "I've been looking for you. I'm ready to go."

Roman held out his hand. "Come say hello," he urged.

She hesitated, and then entered. She knew this was Billy Mallory's room, but up to now had not paid him a visit.

"Mr. Mallory, I hope you're feeling better."

It was hard for Billy to breathe normally. Of course, he knew about Holly's amnesia, but the total lack of recognition on her face was disconcerting. In a way, it lessened his perception of his own identity.

"I'm doing fine."

He kept staring at her, taking careful note of everything about her, from the old Levi's she was wearing, to the tank top and tennis shoes. She was nothing like the stylish and perfectly manicured woman he'd been used to seeing, but he thought he liked this Holly better.

Suddenly embarrassed, she glanced at Roman. "I guess I'll wait for you downstairs."

She started to leave when Billy called out her name.

"Holly! Wait!"

She turned. "Yes?"

"I'm very glad you are all right."

His sincerity was obvious, and because it was unexpected, it touched her deeply.

"Why, thank you," she said, and then impulsively, walked to his bedside. "I know this must be strange to you, but were we good friends?"

He sighed. "Not as good as I would have liked, but yes, I'd say we were friendly acquaintances."

Holly nodded. "I thought so."

Her answer surprised him. "Why?" Billy asked.

"I'm not uncomfortable around you."

Billy smiled. "That's good. I would hate to think I made you afraid."

Dump her out if she doesn't change her mind.

A pervasive chill suddenly swept through her body. "I need to go now," she said, and bolted from the room.

Roman's eyes narrowed. Something had spooked her. He glanced down at Mallory. Billy's expression said it all. I'll be damned, Roman thought. The man's in love with her.

"Tell Gordon I was asking about him," Roman said.

Billy blinked, as if coming out of a trance, and then nodded. "I'll be sure and do that," he said.

"Here's your nurse," Roman said as the woman entered the room. "Wouldn't want to outstay my welcome."

As Roman left, Billy had the distinct impression that his and his brother's days were numbered. Roman Justice was no man's fool. Their story about the reason for the flight and explanation of the events leading up to the crash were weak, and he obviously knew it.

Billy rolled onto his side, testing his strength and mobility. A sickening pain hit instantly, and he fell back with a groan.

"Please, Mr. Mallory," the nurse cautioned. "You must not move."

Move, hell. Thanks to Gordon, I need to be able to run, and soon. I have a feeling our time is running out.

They drove west from Las Vegas, passing casino after casino until there was nothing to see except desert and the mountains in the distance. The closer they got to the foothills, the more relaxed Holly became.

"Roman."

"Yeah?"

"I'm so glad you thought of this. Thank you. I should have done it days ago."

Roman gripped the steering wheel a little tighter. She was so happy, and what he had to tell her was going to ruin the mood.

"You're welcome, baby."

She leaned back in the seat, completely relaxed and enjoying the lulling motion of the ride.

"When you left this morning, I expected you to be gone most of the day. Coming back was a nice surprise." Then it dawned on her that he had come back. She'd never asked why.

"Roman?"

He grinned as she scooted closer to him. "Now what?"

"I was so wrapped up in my problems I never did ask why you'd come back. You hadn't been gone an hour. Did you forget something?"

"No, I didn't forget anything."

There was something about the tone of his voice that alerted her to a problem. She sat up.

"Then why?"

He took a deep breath. There was no easy way to say what had to be said.

"I got a call from my secretary. The police had come to my office looking for me."

All the blood drained from her face as she straightened with a jerk. Clutching her hands in her lap, she was unable to look at him and afraid of what he was going to say.

"This has something to do with me, doesn't it?"

He pulled over to the side of the road and then stopped.

"Holly, look at me."

She turned and then waited.

"Someone broke into the cabin."

Her heart skipped a beat.

"They didn't take anything, just tore it up." He paused, then added. "As if they were looking for something."

She swallowed nervously.

"And last night, someone broke into my house back in Dallas and did the same thing."

She covered her face with her hands. "Oh God, oh God. It's the money."

He sighed. There was no use lying to her. "Probably."

"Probably? There's no *probably* about it. It's my fault this is happening to you. I asked you to hide that money for me. You tried to talk me out of it, but no! I wouldn't listen. And now your home and your property have been vandalized, and it's all my fault."

He took her by the hand and pulled her into his arms.

"Hush, baby, it's okay. It comes with the territory of my job."

She pulled back, unwilling to let him bear the burden of her mistake.

"But this is my fault, and it's not all right. What are we going to do?"

He traced the shape of her face with the tip of his finger and then grinned.

"I know what I want to do."

She grimaced. "Oh, Roman, be serious."

He bent his head until their lips were only inches apart.

"You want me to get serious? Here? In broad daylight? Where everyone can see?"

"You know what I mean," she said.

"Well, I might, then again, I might not. Are you saying you want to trade spit and hugs, or just talk about Gordon and Billy Mallory?" He grinned. "Personally, I'd a whole lot rather love you, but I'm a man of the nineties. I'm willing to let a female be boss."

She grinned, which was exactly what he'd been aiming for. "Trade spit and hugs! Where on earth did you ever come up with a phrase like that?"

"My daddy. That was his standard warning to all of us boys before we went out on a date. Boys, don't be tradin' nothin' but spit and hugs with your girl. You go any further than that, and you'll be changin' diapers before your time."

She laughed aloud. "He must have been quite a character. I wish I could have met him."

"I do, too," he said softly.

She looked at Roman. "Can we worry about the money later?"

A slow grin spread across his face. "You bet, baby. We've got all night and all day tomorrow to worry about that damned stuff."

"Good," she said. "Then let's go back to plan A. What was it you said earlier? Something about getting me naked?"

Roman threw back his head and laughed. Then he laughed some more. He couldn't remember the last time he'd felt this lighthearted, or this much in love.

"That's close enough," he said, and started the car. For today, he was willing to pretend that everything in their world was perfectly in place.

The Wild Horse Hotel and Casino was just off the highway and about a quarter of a mile from the foothills of a nearby mountain, although it wasn't the scenery that pulled in the customers. It was the luck of the draw...the game of chance...the opportunity to become rich from a throw of the dice. Even out here in the middle of nowhere, the place was packed.

Roman walked up to the desk with Holly beside him. It was all he could do to keep her still until they had checked in.

"You act as if you've never seen a casino before," he teased.

She grinned. "I'm sure I have, but for the life of me I can't remember where." Her eyes were alight with interest as she looked around. "However, I think I like them."

He leaned down and kissed her square on the mouth. "Looks like I picked a hell of a place to talk you into getting naked. I may have to tie you to the bed to keep you away from those one-armed bandits."

His reference to the slot machines was amusing, but not as funny as the notion that she'd rather gamble than make love to him.

She turned and slipped her arms around his neck, then whispered. "You can tie me to the bed any time you want, cowboy."

His eyes glittered dangerously, but there was a go-to-hell grin on his face as he turned to the man behind the desk.

"We'll be needing a room," he said shortly. "Nonsmoking, king-size, for as long as it takes."

The clerk's mouth dropped. He took one look at the couple and reached for a key. Within ten minutes, they were in a room.

Roman locked the door and then tossed his hat on a nearby table.

Holly arched an eyebrow. "Is this going to be kinky?" she asked.

Roman grinned. "Why do you ask?"

"Well, you told me to wear something comfortable, so I was wondering...what, exactly, were you planning to do with me...besides tie me to the bed?"

He shook his head, and there was a distinct gleam in his eyes as he started toward her.

"Holly, baby, you are a caution and that's a fact. But I don't think I'll be needing that rope. I haven't had any trouble getting you in bed, and I'm not expecting any now."

Her heart was beginning to race. All she could think about was lying in his arms and coming undone.

"No trouble, I promise," she said softly, and pulled the skimpy tank top over her head.

"And no regrets," he said, tossing his shirt across the back of a chair, and reached for her.

Bare to the waist and aching to feel his weight on her body, she trembled beneath his touch.

"Ah, Roman, make love to me now."

Caught up in the heat of the moment, they discarded clothing, leaving it where it fell. The need between them was strong, the urgency mutual. She grasped his shoulders, pulling him with her. He followed willingly, pinning her to the bed with his weight.

Somewhere down below, the gamblers still played, sometimes

staking their future in hot pursuit of a fast fortune. But there was no risk involved in what Roman and Holly were about to do. They'd been this way before. They'd danced this dance. They'd played this game. And all they had to do was bet on each other. He didn't have to be a gambling man to love his lady. She was a sure thing, all the way.

Holly looked up, imprinting every facet of him into her mind, wanting to remember this moment, to savor this feeling of certainty and of belonging for all time.

Roman felt himself falling, down into those eyes, past her soul and into infinity—and knew a moment of sheer terror. He loved this woman beyond anything he'd ever known before, but the mystery still surrounding her was escalating to the point of danger.

Lying beside her, he braced himself up on one elbow, and began tracing the shape of her face with the tip of his finger, measuring every feature by touch, as well as sight. Her eyelids were fluttering, trying to stay open, yet mesmerized by the slow, sensuous stroke of his hand. A muscle jerked at the side of his jaw. His voice was low and rough with emotion.

"Mine."

Her eyes flew open.

"Daisy...Holly...whatever you call yourself today or tomorrow, you're forever mine."

Swift tears filmed her vision. Her voice was shaking as she answered. "I wasn't about to argue the point."

His eyes narrowed, following the darkness of his thoughts.

"Right now, you don't remember enough to argue. It's afterward that I'm talking about. I don't know who you loved before, and I don't care. It's now and tomorrow that has to matter. You're mine now."

She laid a hand on the side of his face, settling the darkness back where it belonged—in the past.

"And I'll be yours tomorrow, and every other tomorrow that God gives me. I swear."

He tunneled his fingers through the back of her hair and then pulled her close. Her breath was soft on his face as he opened his mouth. When their lips met, he stifled a groan and let himself go, losing sight of time and reason in sweet Holly's arms.

Chapter 15

Holly lay still within the warmth of Roman's embrace, savoring the aftermath of his love. He had quite a way about him that she couldn't deny. He'd taken her high and let her down easy, and in spite of the time that had passed, was still trembling from the onslaught.

Footsteps passed their door, some hurried, others dragging. It was easy to tell who had won at the tables tonight and who'd lost. Holly pitied them for believing that money brought happiness. She'd obviously been born to money, and look what had happened to her. Added to that, there was a bag full of money that had nearly gotten her killed. Now the break-in at Roman's home, as well as the cabin. She was afraid. How was this ever going to end?

Roman stroked the length of her back, from the base of her skull to the curve of her backside, up and down, over and over, just like the way they'd made love. And even though passion had been satiated, he wasn't ready to let go of the motion. She was in his blood, in his heart, in his mind. And something else had happened during their drive out here. He had come to a decision she might not like. There was no time left to wait for her memory to return. He had to make something happen before something happened to them.

"Roman, what are we going to do?"

He paused in midstroke, with the palm of his hand splayed in the middle of her back. So the interlude was over. It was back to reality. He gave her a quick but gentle squeeze and then leaned back so that he could see her face.

"I have an idea, but it will involve how skilled you are at telling a lie."

She rose up, a startled look on her face.

"Lie? About what?"

"Remembering."

She frowned. "I don't understand."

"I know, baby," he said softly. "But when the time comes, you will."

She hid her face against his shoulder.

"I am afraid—for you, and for myself."

"Don't be," he whispered, and then pressed his lips against the crown of her head. "Trust me?"

She sighed. "Yes."

"Then let me worry about the details, okay?"

"Okay."

"That's settled, then," he said, and glanced at the time. "It will be dark before we get back to the city. I told your father that we'd call if we were going to be late."

"I'll do it," she said.

Ignoring her nudity, she rolled over to the side of the bed and picked up the phone, punching in the numbers without thought.

Roman watched her, waiting to see how long it took her before she realized what she'd just done.

"This is Holly. Let me speak to my father." She waited. Moments later, Davis picked up the phone. "Dad, it's me. We'll be late getting back, so don't wait dinner. We'll get something on the way."

Roman watched as she listened to her father's response. A few moments later, she told him goodbye, then hung up.

"That's that," she said, and then leaned back against him, reluctant to give up the body-to-body connection.

Roman ran a hand down the length of her arm, then pulled a stray strand of hair away from her cheek.

"Hey, you," he said, and tugged at her hair until she turned to look at him.

She grinned. "What?"

"What's your home phone number?"

The grin slipped. "Why, it's, uh..." She frowned. "I don't..." Then it dawned. "I did it again, didn't I?"

He nodded.

She thrust her fingers through her hair, combing it away from her face. "When I don't concentrate, I remember, but only the little things...the things that don't matter. Why can't I remember jumping out of a plane? Or why I had all that money? My God, Roman, this is crazy."

"No, baby. In a way, it makes a whole lot of sense. You aren't remembering that stuff because you don't want to. The more traumatic the event, the deeper your subconscious will bury it. It's simply a self-defense mechanism your body uses to protect itself."

She thumped the bed with her fist and then got out of bed, reaching for her clothes and pulling them on with angry motions. Roman hurt for her. He could only imagine how she felt, but within a couple of days, it should all be over. And the moment he thought it, his belly drew tight. He didn't want everything to be over. Not the love. Dear God, for his own peace of mind, let it go on forever.

Distracted and suddenly moody, he got out of bed and reached for his jeans, then began pulling them on. As he was dressing, he spied a small bit of color partially hidden beneath the fallen covers. When he bent down to get it, his mood quickly lightened. When he straightened, he was wearing a cocky grin.

"Uh, Holly?"

She had her tank top in one hand and a sock in the other. "What?" she asked, still looking about the room for her other sock.

He waved the lingerie above his head. "Forget something?"

She looked up. Her panties were dangling from his fingers.

"Oh, great. I'm not wearing my underwear!" She yanked it out of his hand and began unzipping her jeans. "Now I have to start all over."

There was a gleam in his eyes as he grabbed her hand, slowing her intent.

"Only if you insist," he drawled, and then slowly pulled the tab the rest of the way down.

Disgust left her, and in its place came a quick urge to be with him again.

"Are you sure?" she asked breathlessly.

He guided her hand to his zipper and the hard bulge behind it. "What do you think?"

Her voice was soft with longing. "That you're Superman?"

He shook his head and then smiled a slow, easy smile. "No, baby," he said softly. "Just a man." A man in love. But he didn't say it. He'd already said more than he should have. Besides, there was more than one way to say *I love you.*

After finding out that Roman had been in Billy's room, Gordon was livid. The urge to break something, preferably Roman's damned neck, was overwhelming. But it wouldn't give him what he wanted, so he let the urge slide.

Gordon was shaking with anger. "Why did you even talk to him?"

Billy glared. "You said to behave normally. You said not to raise suspicion. What did you want me to do, have him thrown out on his ear for paying a visit?"

Gordon picked up a pillow and threw it across the room.

Billy frowned. That only added to the decision he'd already made.

"I want to leave."

Gordon spun around, his face flushed with frustration and rage. "Then start walking."

Billy started to beg. "Please, Gordon. Let's get out. We've got some money, we can get more, but not if we're locked up in jail."

Gordon stalked to his bed, pointing a finger in his face. "We wouldn't have to get more money if you hadn't given mine away."

"You were going to kill her."

Gordon threw his hands up in the air. "So what were you thinking? That you would just give her the money as a going-away present?"

Voices sounded outside the door, and then faded as they moved away. Gordon lowered his voice.

"You wanted to save her so you put her in a parachute and let her jump. Okay, I can understand that." Then he started to shake, and a froth of spittle began forming at the corner of his mouth. "But why in the name of all that's holy did you give her the money, too? Tell me? Why did you do it?"

Billy's gaze never wavered. "It was blood money, Gordon. You killed for it. I wanted no part of that, just like I want no part of you now. Just help get me out of this place, then you can do whatever your heart desires."

"My heart desires vengeance," he grumbled. "She has something that belongs to me, and I think Justice is in on it. I had that cabin searched, as well as his place in Dallas. They came up empty, but that doesn't mean a thing. There are other options."

Billy paled. "Like what?"

"When I get everything worked out, I'll let you know."

"My God, Gordon, you've lost all reason. Did you know that?"

Gordon shook his head. "No, little brother. All I've lost is a million dollars." He turned on his heel and stalked out of the room.

Billy closed his eyes and swallowed past the knot in his throat. "You're wrong, Gordon. That's not all you're losing. You're about to lose a brother, as well."

Morning was little more than a promise on the horizon when Roman picked up his cellular phone and headed for the door. After the events of the past few days, leaving Holly alone was no longer an option, but he was going no farther than outside the house. The patio overlooking the tennis courts was spacious. He had some calls to make, and he didn't want them overheard.

He walked down the hall to her bedroom door, then looked inside, making sure she was still asleep. When he saw her lying there, it was all he could do to stay put.

The temptation was strong to crawl in beside her and kiss her awake. He wanted to thrust his hands through that spill of dark hair on her pillow, to feel the swell of her breasts beneath his palms, to watch her eyelids fluttering as he entered her body. But now was not the time. With one last look around the room, he stepped out, closing the door behind him before heading for the stairs.

Downstairs, the staff was up and beginning their day, although they paid no attention to his presence as he passed. When he stepped out onto the patio, he took a deep breath and then closed his eyes, inhaling the morning day and comparing it to a new day back home.

Here, the air was brisk and drier, making the scents it carried more distinct. Spring in Texas usually brought thunderstorms, which gave free rein to the lush growth of anything green. In turn, the air would be filled with a damp, sweet aroma of everything that was in bloom. There was a beauty about this area that couldn't be denied, but he was a Texan born and bred, and it would forever be the place where his heart felt at rest.

At the thought, his eyes narrowed against a familiar spurt of old pain. Would Holly come with him one day? Or would he leave her behind when he left?

And then he shook off the mood and began to walk, moving farther away from the house with every step. Right now, he couldn't think about his future until he was certain that Holly's would be safe. While his entire plan hinged upon his brothers' cooperation, he was in no doubt they would come to his aid. It was the Justice way.

Pausing beneath the overhanging branches of a nearby tree, he glanced back at the house once more before punching in a quick series of numbers.

Ryder Justice picked up the phone on the second ring.

"Justice Air."

Roman relaxed. "Ryder, it's me, Roman. I need a favor."

Ryder didn't even bother to think before answering. After what Roman had done last year to help save Casey's life, he would have walked on fire if asked.

"Name it," he said.

"Are you free to fly to the ranch tomorrow?"

"No, but I will be after I make a few calls. What do you need?"

"If it wasn't important, I wouldn't ask," he said briefly.

"Hell, little brother, I knew that," Ryder said. "Just tell me what you want me to do."

"I need you to fly out to the ranch, then bring Royal out here to Las Vegas."

Ryder grinned. "Las Vegas. What are you doing out there?"

"Sort of guarding a woman named Holly."

Ryder's grin spread. "Holly, huh? Is she a tall, leggy blonde?"

"No. She's a half-pint brunette."

Ryder chuckled. "Too bad. She's way off your course, right?"

"I wouldn't exactly say that."

Ryder stopped in the middle of a laugh. That wasn't the remark he'd expected to hear. If some woman could actually catch Roman's interest, then Ryder was curious, too.

"So, this...what did you say her name was?"

"It's Holly Benton, but I used to call her Daisy."

"Do I need to know why?"

"No."

Now Ryder was interested. "So you have a client named Holly, who's really Daisy, or vice versa, and you're guarding her sort of, but not really. Is that about it?"

Roman shifted the phone to his other hand and began to pace.

"Ryder, do me another favor, and shut up and listen, okay?"

Ryder chuckled. "Okay. Let 'er rip, although it's beyond me why you need to see Royal. Won't I do?"

"It isn't Royal I need to see, it's what he'll be bringing with him."

"And that would be?"

"A duffel bag."

"A duffel bag? You can't just go buy one out there?"

"Not one like this," Roman muttered. "For once in your life, I need you to listen."

It began to dawn on Ryder that his brother was serious.

"Sorry. I'm listening."

"After you and Royal get to Vegas, I need you to bring the duffel bag to the Benton estate on LaJolla Avenue. It's up in the hills. I'll leave word at the gate to let you in."

"You've got it," Ryder said. Then he paused. "Say, Roman, what's in this duffel bag, anyway?"

"A million dollars, give or take a few thousand."

Ryder took a deep breath and then swallowed twice in rapid succession.

"I'm not even going to ask."

"Good. See you tomorrow around noon."

"We'll be there. I'll see if I can talk Casey into taking the day off. She can stay with Maddie while we're gone," Ryder said, and disconnected.

Roman sighed in satisfaction. One down. One to go. He glanced toward the east and at the sunrise in progress. The vast cloudless sky was streaked with pink and gold. He looked at his watch. It would be after seven at the ranch. Maddie was a sleepy-head, so Royal would probably still be in the house. There was no use delaying the inevitable.

He made the call, again relieved to hear his eldest brother's voice on the other end of the line.

"Hello?"

"Royal, it's me, Roman."

"Where are you?" he growled. "I expected you to at least call after the break-in at the cabin."

"Didn't Elizabeth tell you we talked?"

Royal grabbed at a bowl of cereal and milk, just before Maddie pulled it off the side of the table.

"Yes, she told me. Madeline Michelle, you sit! I'll carry the cereal."

Roman grinned. As always, life with Maddie was never dull.

"Tell my favorite niece I said hello."

"Not until after she's through eating or I'll never get a bite in her mouth."

Roman laughed. "Fair enough." Then he got back to business. "About why I called. I need you to do me a favor."

"And that would be?"

"Do you remember a couple of years ago when I gave you the combination to that big safe in my office?"

Royal frowned. "Yes."

"Do you still have it?"

"Somewhere," Royal said. "Why?"

"Get a pen and paper. I'm going to give it to you again."

Royal took down the numbers. "Okay, got 'em," he muttered. "Now what?"

"I need you to go to my office. There will be an armed guard from Texas Securities on the premises. I'll call them ahead of time and clear you. There is a duffel bag in my safe. I want you to take it to the ranch. In the morning, Ryder will come and get you and fly you and the bag out here to Las Vegas."

Royal started backing up. "Las Vegas? I'm a parent, little brother. I can't just walk off and leave Maddie at a—"

"Casey is coming with Ryder. She'll stay with Maddie until you two get back."

Royal sighed. "Fine. So, I get this bag. We bring it to Vegas. Then what?"

"Ryder will tell you when he gets there. And the less said about the bag, the better. Put it somewhere where Maddie can't find it. I don't want her using the contents to cut out paper dolls."

Royal grinned. "What's in the damned thing, anyway?"

"A million dollars."

Royal cursed before he thought, then rolled his eyes when Maddie looked up with interest. This was great. Miss is-it-Maddie-or-is-it-Memorex? probably wouldn't forget a word of what she just heard. He turned his back on his daughter, lowering his voice so that only Roman could hear.

"Is it legal?" he asked.

Roman grinned. "I'm not sure. I'll find that out after you get here."

"Oh, fine," Royal muttered.

"Will you do it?" Roman asked.

Royal sighed. "Hell, yes," he grumbled. "You knew I would when you called."

"Thanks," Roman said. "See you tomorrow around noon."

Royal snorted beneath his breath. "I can hardly wait. What's for dinner?"

Roman's grin widened. "I'm not sure, but it may be crow."

Royal hung up in his ear.

All the way back to the house, Roman kept thinking of Holly and how she was going to play in the hand he'd just dealt. If he knew his lady like he thought he did, she was going to shine like a new penny. The secrets and lies within these walls were about to end.

* * *

It was just after lunch when a cab pulled up to the front door of the Benton estate. Billy was downstairs in his wheelchair, and had been watching for it for some time. His nurse came hurrying from the powder room, clutching at her purse and giving her hair a last-minute pat.

"I see our cab has arrived."

"Whose cab?" Holly asked.

Billy turned, unaware that she was there, and then sighed. He'd planned on leaving without anyone's noticing, but in a way, he was glad. It hurt to think that he would never see her again, but it was for the best. There never had been anything between them except what existed in his mind. To her, he was nothing but Gordon's younger brother.

"It's mine," Billy said, eyeing the white gauzy dress she was wearing and admiring the way it floated around her ankles, then clinging in all the right places. "Doctor's appointment."

Holly frowned. "I'm sure we could have had a doctor come here. Are you certain you're up to this?"

Billy managed a smile. Just like Holly. Always thinking of everyone but herself.

"Oh, yes. This was inevitable."

She thought nothing of his remark. Of course it would have been inevitable that one day he would be up and out of the bed. She had no idea he was referring to the split he was making with Gordon.

"Well, then," she said. "I hope your checkup is good, and you'll soon be able to join us at the table for meals."

His expression stilled as he let himself look at her one last time.

"Thank you, Holly Benton."

She smiled. "Why, you're welcome, but whatever for? I didn't do anything but wish you well."

"Yes, actually you did," he said softly. "One day you'll remember, but for now, let's just say that you were always kind to me. I won't forget it."

She laughed. "My goodness, you're only going to the doctor, not the moon. See you later," she said, and then waved them off as the cab drove away.

She thought nothing of their exit until a couple of hours later when Gordon stormed into the library.

"What the hell have you done with Billy?" he cried.

Roman was sitting at her side, and when Gordon burst into the room, he instinctively stood, putting himself between the man and Holly.

"Back off," he said shortly.

Still anxious, Gordon did as he'd been told. "I'm sorry, but Billy's not in his room."

"Oh, today was his doctor's appointment," Holly said. "He and the nurse left around—" She glanced at her watch. "My goodness, it was hours ago. I hadn't realized it had been so long. It's nearly five. They must have been delayed."

Gordon paled. Billy didn't have a doctor's appointment. In fact, they hadn't even connected with the doctor they'd been advised to see after Billy had been moved from Denver. Instead, the only medical personnel his brother had seen since their arrival was the nurse Benton had provided and a physician's assistant who'd come by a couple of times in the beginning. And while he knew it was possible that Billy had done so on his own and hadn't seen fit to mention it, he sincerely doubted it. Billy just wasn't the take-charge type.

He stuffed his hands in his pockets and then yanked them out, unintentionally scattering a handful of small change across the floor. Instantly, he was on his knees, gathering it up as if the coins were solid gold.

Roman frowned. There was more to this than a brother's concern. This man was about to come unglued, but why? Because they were a little bit late? He didn't think so.

"Why don't you give the doctor's office a call? I'm sure they can clear all this up for you," Holly said.

Gordon got to his feet. "Right," he said, and dropped the coins back in his pocket as he bolted from the room.

Holly frowned. "That was strange."

Roman stepped out into the hall, watching to see where Gordon had gone. A short while later, he saw a cab pull up, and then watched Gordon make a run for the door. Something was up, but what? As an investigator, he knew the best way to find out. Go see for himself.

"Get your purse, Holly. We're going for a ride."

"Maybe I'd better change," she said, brushing at a nonexistent speck on the front of her skirt.

He grabbed her hand. "No time. And never mind about that purse, either."

Holly didn't stop to ask why. She could tell by the way Roman was moving that time was precious. Within moments of Gordon's exit, they were in her car and heading down the driveway, following the yellow cab that was disappearing down the street.

"What's wrong?" she asked.

"I don't know," Roman said. "But Gordon is in a panic about something, and I think it has to do with his brother. After everything that's happened in the last few days, I'd rather know than guess."

She nodded, then grabbed her seat belt and buckled herself in as he turned a corner, tires squalling.

Gordon was alternating between fury and fear. He kept telling himself that Billy *was* at some doctor's office, but his gut instincts were telling him different. He didn't want to believe that he had actually acted upon his threat.

A short while later, his cab pulled up at the bus stop. Leaving orders for the driver to wait, he bolted inside, staring at faces all the way into the ticket counter, hoping and praying he'd see his brother in one of them. But it wasn't to be. And after a brief inquiry, he learned that no one named Mallory had purchased a ticket today.

That left the airport. He glanced at his watch. It was getting late. He took a deep breath, telling himself to calm down. Maybe he'd just jumped the gun. Maybe Billy was back at the Benton estate already and wondering where he had gone. There was one sure way to find out. He headed for the phone.

As always, a maid answered. Gordon wasted no time on explanations, he just blurted out what he wanted to know.

"This is Gordon Mallory. Is my brother back from the doctor?"

"Just a moment, sir. I'll check," she said.

Gordon waited impatiently, cursing beneath his breath when someone ran past him, bumping his leg with a suitcase. He glared at the man who was standing in line behind him. If he wanted to use this phone, he was going to have to wait.

"Mr. Mallory?"

Gordon spun and then gripped the receiver a little tighter. "Yes? Who's this?"

"Your brother's nurse."

Gordon went weak with relief. It was true. He had overreacted after all. He felt like laughing and crying all at the same time.

"I was just checking on Billy," he said quickly. "I'll be a little late getting back and wondered how he was doing."

She frowned. "Why, I thought you knew! He's gone, Mr. Mallory. I just came back to pack my things."

The relief in Gordon's belly tied itself in a knot. Oh, God. I was right. It took everything he had to keep the tone of his voice at a normal pitch.

"Gone? Did he say where?"

"Why, no!" She started to worry. "Oh, dear, I felt bad about this all evening, but he was so insistent, and he said that you were aware of the trip."

Gordon managed a laugh, although if she could have seen his face, she would have known how insincere it really was.

"Oh, sure," Gordon said. "We were planning to leave all

along, but I would have preferred that he wait for me. However, I should have known better. Billy has no patience, you know."

"Then it's all right that I let him go?" she asked.

"Of course," Gordon said. "I just hope he made all the proper arrangements to get help along the way."

"He certainly did," she said. "I heard him asking for wheelchairs and attendants at every stop."

"That's good," Gordon said, and then added as if it was an afterthought. "By the way, what flight did he take?"

"I don't know."

"But weren't you at the airport with him until he left?"

"Oh, no. When we left the Benton estate, we went straight to a travel agent. He made all of the arrangements with them. Of course, I was nearby, but I never overstep my bounds. Patient care and maintaining privacy are paramount in my book. I would never have eavesdropped."

"Of course not," Gordon said. "I didn't mean to imply—"

"Excuse me," she said. "But Mr. Benton is here now. Would you like to speak to him?"

Gordon panicked. The last thing he wanted Davis Benton to know was that his brother had skipped out on him.

"No, of course not," he said quickly. "Just tell him not to wait on dinner for me."

"Yes, sir, and may I say, it was a privilege to take care of your brother. He has a very kind heart."

"Thanks," Gordon said, then stood transfixed, listening to the buzz of the empty line, even after the nurse had disconnected.

His shoulders slumped. The nurse was right. Billy was too soft for the world in which Gordon lived. And while it gave him a lost, empty feeling to know that for the first time in his life he was on his own, he knew it was all for the best. Billy would just hold him back. He hung up the phone and walked away.

Half a block away, Roman watched from their car as Gordon came out of the bus station and got into the cab.

"Wonder what he was doing in there?" Holly asked.

"If he's smart, probably getting a ticket out of town," Roman muttered.

Holly looked startled. "What if he leaves before I remember everything? What if I never remember? How will we ever figure out where the money comes in?"

Roman waited a few seconds until the cab had passed them by before pulling out into the traffic behind it.

"Unless I'm wrong, he isn't going anywhere until he takes it with him." Then he added. "Besides that, remember what I told you. By this time tomorrow, it will all be over."

She sighed. "I hope you're right."

Roman glanced at her and winked. "Baby, it's time you realized I'm always right."

She rolled her eyes. "What have I let myself in for?"

Roman grinned. "If you're lucky, about seventy-five years of a real wild ride."

She laughed. "Then I hope I have the stamina of a cat," she said.

"Why a cat?" Roman asked.

"Well, they're supposed to have nine lives, and I've already used up a couple of mine. With you around for that long, I'm pretty sure I'll be needing more."

Up ahead, the cab was forced to stop for a stoplight. Roman reached for her hand as they, too, paused in traffic. There was a glint in his eyes as he lifted it to his mouth. Turning it palm up, he traced her lifeline with the tip of his tongue. He couldn't say what he was thinking. Giving life to his fears was dangerous. He kept telling himself that even when she remembered, their relationship would still be the same. But it wasn't Roman's way to lie...not even to himself. So when the light turned green, he accelerated through the intersection, channeling his focus back to Gordon Mallory.

Holly leaned back in the seat, for the time being, letting Roman do all the worrying about their future. It was after this mess was

over that had her concerned. She didn't want to wake up one
morning and become someone other than who she was now.
Daisy had fallen in love. Surely God wouldn't be so cruel as to
awaken Holly and then let Roman slip away.

Chapter 16

Gordon couldn't sleep that night, and Roman wouldn't. For the first time since coming to Davis Benton's home, Roman had seen Holly to bed and then stayed in her room. He couldn't get over the notion that Mallory was getting desperate. And desperate men had been known to do desperate things. With a million dollars at stake, anything could happen.

Breakfast was a stilted affair. Davis Benton knew something was wrong, but no one seemed eager to talk. He'd thrown enough conversational tidbits into the silence around the breakfast table to have started a dozen conversations and had yet to get one going.

Gordon was behaving strangely, and Davis had overheard the staff talking about Billy Mallory's sudden disappearance from his home. Roman was pretending to eat, but Davis was no fool. The man was spending more time observing Gordon Mallory's panic than he was chewing food. Added to that, his beloved Holly was pale and nervous. She'd dropped a spoon, as well as a fork, and at this point, had completely given up trying to eat.

Davis took a deep breath and set his coffee cup down. By God, this was his house and Holly was his daughter. These two men were all but strangers to him, and their appearance into her life had brought about drastic changes he didn't like.

"I want to know what the hell's going on."

His words shattered the silence in which they sat. Holly's cup clinked against the saucer. Gordon's heart skipped a beat, and he had a strong urge to run and never look back. Only Roman showed no reaction. Instead, he reached for a slice of toast and began buttering it as if Davis had never spoken.

"What do you mean?" Holly asked.

Davis glared. "Holly, I've known you for twenty-seven years, and you have yet, pardon the cliché, to pull the wool over my eyes. Something is going on, and I would very much like to know what it is. In fact, I think I deserve that much consideration, considering the fact that this is my house—and my table—and my patience that you are trying."

The urge to blurt out the truth about everything was strong, but now was not the time. She looked to Roman, silently begging for support, but he was spreading jelly on his buttered toast as if it had suddenly become the most important thing in his life. She wanted to scream at him. He had to know she was floundering. Why hadn't he come to her aid?

And then Gordon began to stammer and stutter, and glanced at Roman and then relaxed. Roman had known all along that, if for no other reason than guilt alone, Gordon would not be able to stay silent.

"I'm terribly sorry," Gordon said quickly. "I had no idea that my concerns were so obvious. It's just that I was thinking about my brother." He gave Davis a nervous smile and kept talking, almost without taking a breath. "We've been planning to leave, and soon. We couldn't presume upon your kind hospitality forever, but Billy got impatient and left yesterday without me. I will, of course, be following shortly, but there are a couple of things I still have to attend to."

Davis leaned back in his chair, listening without bothering to comment. He'd sat in on too many boardroom meetings not to know fast-talk when he heard it, but this made no sense. Other than the fact that Roman Justice has stepped into the picture and Gordon had been moved out, there was no reason for the man to be nervous. Angry maybe. Nervous, no.

"I see," Davis said. "So, where did he go?"

Gordon's face paled, and then a few moments later, flushed a high color of red.

"Uh, we've got a... There's a place we always went to.... It used to belong to—"

A maid came into the room, interrupting Gordon and unintentionally saving him from having to proceed.

"I'm sorry, Mr. Benton, but there's an emergency phone call for Mr. Justice," she said.

Roman stood. "Excuse me," he said, and left.

Gordon stood, taking the opportunity to escape Davis's third-degree. "And I'm afraid I must be excused, as well. I've got several calls to make. I'll be in my room if anyone needs me."

Holly watched both men exit and knew that her father deserved more than he was getting. When they were finally alone, she leaned forward.

"Dad, I know you're not stupid. And yes, something *is* going on, but I'm not sure what. All I can say is, Roman assures me that it will be over by tonight. I trust him. Will you trust me?"

Davis made himself relax. "I don't like this one bit," he muttered.

Holly reached for his hand. "Look at this from my point of view. I not only don't like it, but it scares me to death."

Davis frowned. "What do you mean, scares you? You're safe here. You have nothing to be afraid of."

She shook her head. "No, that's not true. In fact, Roman and I are convinced that there's something I should be remembering...something that had to do with the crash."

"I don't understand," he said.

"Neither do I." Then she, too, stood to leave. "Just make sure you're home for lunch, okay?"

Davis's frown deepened. "After what you just said, and the way everyone was behaving, I have no intention of setting foot out of this house. I'm not trusting your safety to anyone else until I know what's going on."

"It's your decision," she said. "But please know that if you need to, you could trust Roman Justice with your life. Believe me, I know. I already have."

She walked away, leaving her father to make what he chose out of the remark.

Gordon made it to his room without further incident, but the moment he got inside, sat down on the bed and started to shake. It would seem that Billy had the right idea all along. Everything was starting to come undone. Maybe it was time to leave. He'd been so certain that by staying close to Holly Benton, he would find a way to get back his money. But he could see it just wasn't going to work. Her memory was coming back faster than the headway he'd hoped to make. And so he sat, stewing in the juices of his own mistakes and planning his next move.

The longer he sat, the calmer he became. It's *his* fault, Gordon thought. If Roman Justice hadn't appeared on the scene, everything would have worked out all right. He'd had Benton's confidence, and simply by being under the same roof as Holly, he would have been able to gain hers, as well.

He stood and looked around the room. It had served its purpose, but now it was time to retreat. Several days ago, he'd noticed a small Pullman-type bag in the back of his closet. He didn't have many belongings here. Whatever it would hold would be all that he would take. If he had to leave something behind, he could always buy more. At least he still had the ten thousand in the bank. It would be enough to get a new start.

And then something hit him, and he wondered why he hadn't

thought of it before. Billy! How had he managed to buy a plane ticket? What money he'd had on him had been lost in the crash.

"No, no, no. Please tell me no," Gordon mumbled as he reached for the phone.

A few minutes later, he slammed it down in disgust, unable to believe what he'd learned. Granted the account had been in both their names, but who would have believed the little weasel had the gumption to take advantage of him like this? Within the space of minutes, the ten-thousand-dollar nest egg Gordon thought he'd had was down to five. Billy had taken his half and run.

He yanked the bag from the closet and tossed it onto the bed, then began emptying the drawers of his belongings and dumping them inside. Something hit the side of the bag with a thump, and he frowned, wondering what it was that he'd heard. Underwear didn't thump.

As he dug through the pile, his fingers closed upon an oblong plastic box, and the moment he felt it, he remembered the drug-filled syringe. Using it on Holly that night would have been the perfect answer. She would have talked her head off and the next morning not remembered a thing. Gordon's hand clenched around the box. If she'd only been asleep, his troubles would already be over.

He dropped it to the side of the bag and continued to pack. But every time he tossed something else inside, he looked down at the box. By the time he was through, he'd convinced himself to give it one more try. Instead of leaving now, he would do it tomorrow. That would be the better plan anyway. He still had to close out his account at the bank. And there was always the chance that he'd have to travel to another location to retrieve his money. No need buying a plane ticket until he knew where he needed to go.

He laid the box on top of his clothes and then zipped the bag shut before stowing it out of sight. The fewer who knew about his plans to leave, the better. He glanced at his watch. It was just past 10:00 a.m. He grinned. Plenty of time to get to the bank and

then back here for lunch. Keeping to a regular schedule within
the family was the best way to maintain his innocence. If Holly
started remembering too much, too soon, he could always claim
that she was imagining things. After all, if he'd tried to murder
her, wouldn't he have been long gone? Innocent people didn't
have to run.

Pleased that he had all the answers worked out, he called a
cab. A short while later, he announced to Holly and her father
that he was making a quick trip to the bank and would see them
for lunch. He didn't give a thought to the fact that Roman was
nowhere in sight, nor would he have suspected himself of being
followed. He was too locked in to the fact that his cover was
impenetrable.

Roman had Holly by the hand as they came down the stairs.
"Where did your father go?"

"I don't know," she said. "He was still in the library when I
left him." She sighed. "I feel badly about keeping the truth from
him."

Roman squeezed her hand lightly for assurance. "I know, baby.
But it won't be much longer now. That phone call I had earlier
was from Royal. He and Ryder are on their way. They should be
here around eleven."

"And then what?" she asked.

"We made a plan. When they get here, all you have to do is
follow my lead."

She glanced nervously around, making sure they were alone.
"They're bringing the money?"

He nodded. "They're going to make quite an entrance." He
leaned forward, lowering his voice so that he wouldn't be overheard. "This is what I want you to do."

She listened, her eyes widening with each word that he spoke.
Only after he had finished talking did she realize she'd been holding her breath.

"Think you can do that?" Roman asked.

She nodded. "I'll do anything it takes to get this nightmare behind me."

He wrapped his arms around her and pulled her into a hug.

"That's my girl," he said softly.

"And don't you forget it," she said.

A shadow appeared in his eyes, as if an old ghost had just crossed his path.

"I don't willingly lose...or forget...what's mine."

Before she could speak, he'd captured her mouth beneath his, drugging her senses and her speech with a hard, swift kiss that stole the rest of her breath.

Her hands were shaking when he turned her loose.

"Trust me, Holly. I won't let anything happen to you."

She laid her hand against the beat of his heart. "I can do that, but it's time for you to trust me, too. There's only one thing I know for certain, and that is I would not wish to spend another day on earth without you in my life."

The expression on her face shattered his reserve. He pulled her off the last stair and into his arms.

Her heart was in her throat as he dragged her beneath the stairs and then pressed her up against the wall.

"Roman, someone will see."

"To hell with someone," he whispered, and wrapped his arms around her, then lifted her off her feet. "Right now, I have this overwhelming need to be deep inside you and am having to settle for this."

Her arms were around his neck, her feet dangling inches from the floor. She was holding on for dear life...and her love. She leaned forward, brushing the surface of his mouth with the tip of her tongue.

"Then take what you need, Roman Justice, because I couldn't refuse you if I tried."

He lowered his head. A soft, unintelligible groan slipped out from between his lips, and then he got lost in her spell. A few moments later, a sound came crashing down the hall, followed by a flurry of excited voices. With reluctance, Roman tore himself free and set her gently back down to her feet.

"Sounds like something just broke," he said, tracing the edge of her mouth with his finger. "But as long as it's not my heart, I don't give a good damn."

She grabbed his hand and lifted it to her mouth before pressing a kiss into the palm.

"If it does," Holly whispered, "it won't be because of me."

"Then I'm safe," he said. "Because you're the only one who could do it. Now, let's go find your father. I need to let him know what's going to happen."

"Are you going to tell him about the—?"

"This has been your call from the first. It's not up to me. It's up to you. Do you want to?" Roman asked.

She thought for a moment and then nodded. "I think it's time."

"Then let's do it," he said.

When they walked into the library, they found Davis Benton standing at a window overlooking his estate. His shoulders were slumped, his expression grave.

"Dad."

He turned. "I wondered where you were." He eyed Roman without commenting on the fact that they were hand in hand. "Please, have a seat," he said.

"I'll stand," Roman said as he sat Holly down.

"More secrets?" Davis asked.

Holly heard the despair in his voice. "Don't be angry with Roman, Dad. He's only done as I asked."

Davis dropped into a nearby chair. "Anger isn't what I'm feeling."

Holly leaned forward. "Please, just hear us out. We don't have much time, and it's very important."

He frowned. "What do you mean, you don't have much time?"

Roman interrupted. "Baby, let me."

Holly nodded, relieved to have someone else trying to explain something she didn't understand herself.

"Then talk," Davis said.

Roman nodded. "I've been following Gordon Mallory, almost from the first day I arrived."

Davis straightened. "What on earth for?"

"Because we don't believe he and Holly were ever going to elope."

"Then why would she have been on that plane?" Davis asked. "She called me herself only hours before takeoff to tell me she was going with him."

Wait for me. This won't take long.

Holly stiffened. She could see herself getting out of a cab and walking across the tarmac to a waiting plane.

"I had changed my mind," she said suddenly.

She had their attention.

Roman had seen that faraway look on her face before. He knew that she'd just had another flash of memory.

"What are you remembering?" he asked.

She blinked, and the image was gone. There was a stunned expression on her face. "I told the cab driver to wait. I told him I'd be right back. My God, Roman, I wasn't going to go! Then why did I get on that plane?"

He shook his head. "I don't know, but you do," he said. "When it matters, you'll tell us."

She slumped back into her seat. "Where have I heard that before?"

He touched her lightly on the shoulder. "Easy does it, Holly. We're with you all the way."

Davis leaned forward. "He's right, sweetheart. Whatever's been happening, you must know you're not alone." Then he looked up at Roman. "So why the need to follow Mallory? Other than the fact Holly can't remember why she went, what's the big mystery?"

"Say it," Holly said. "You were right. I should have told him from the start."

Davis's voice was thick with frustration. "Damn it, people! Tell me what?"

"That Holly wound up with a duffel bag full of money when she bailed out of that plane."

Davis stood. "What on earth...?"

"It's true, Dad. It was at the foot of the tree when I finally freed myself from the parachute and climbed down. And I had a vague memory of someone shoving it at me and telling me to jump."

"Good lord," he muttered, and then started to pace. "But I don't understand. Why did you feel the need to keep it a secret? It surely belonged to Gordon. Why didn't you just—?"

"I was afraid."

He shook his head. "Afraid? Why? What was there to be afraid of?" And then a thought struck him, and he looked at Roman. "How much money are we talking about?"

"Just shy of a million dollars."

Davis's legs went weak, and he dropped back into the chair he'd just vacated.

"Sweet lord."

Roman gave his case another boost. "If it had been honestly earned, don't you think Gordon would have been bemoaning the loss loud and long?"

Davis wiped a shaky hand across his face. "He and his brother have been living under this roof at my invitation. If you suspected something was wrong, why didn't you say so? Why did you let it go this long?" he asked.

Holly reached out, needing to touch him when she said it.

"Because at first, I didn't know who to trust. Not you, Dad. Not even myself."

"What?"

Roman interrupted. "When we first met, she had convinced herself that she was a criminal and had come by the money illegally. It was only after we learned her true identity that we pretty much ruled that out." He grinned wryly. "Davis Benton's daughter would have no reason to steal."

"How can you be sure it was Mallory? It could have been the pilot. Maybe it was his brother, Billy! Yes, it could be him. He's the one who's run off, remember?"

Roman shook his head. "I can't explain it, but I doubt that's the case. My guess is, Billy was an accomplice in something, but he doesn't come across as the stronger of the two."

Davis nodded. "You're right. But just thinking they are involved is one thing. Do we have any proof other than guesses?"

"I did a little checking," Roman said. "Mallory doesn't have a real-estate license in Nevada, nor has he ever had one. And just before he and Billy left town for the supposed trip to Nassau, they gave up their apartment. If they were planning on coming back, they must have been counting on you to house them."

"Which I did," Davis said with a groan. "What a mess. And what are we going to do?"

"I have a plan," Roman said. "Are you with us?"

"Anything," Davis said. "I'll do anything to make sure that Holly is safe."

"Good. Now, here's what I want you to do."

Davis listened, and when it was over, looked up at Roman with renewed respect.

"My boy, if this works, you're a genius."

Roman shook his head. "It won't be genius that traps Gordon Mallory. It will be a guilty conscience."

"Where is he now?" Davis asked.

"In his room," Roman said. "In fact, he's been spending a lot of time in there today. I'd lay odds that he's planning to leave, and soon. I followed him to a bank about an hour ago. He closed an account, in the process withdrawing a little over five thousand dollars. That's not pocket change, that's traveling money."

Davis was furious to think that he'd unwittingly housed a criminal, never mind the fact that the man had lied about his relationship with his daughter.

"For two cents, I'd like to—"

Suddenly Holly waved to her father and then put her finger to her lips, indicating silence. They listened. Someone was coming down the stairs. It could only be Gordon. They glanced at each other and without missing a beat, Davis started to laugh, as if someone had just told a joke.

Gordon walked into the library with a smile on his face. "Sounds like I'm missing all the fun," he said.

Roman shook his head. "It hasn't even begun."

Before Gordon could comment upon the odd remark, Davis stood.

"You're just in time," he told Gordon. "We were about to sit down to lunch." He took Holly by the arm and winked at her. "The first course is cold shrimp salad, Holly's favorite."

Royal pulled up to the gates of the Benton estate, rolled down the window, then leaned out, pressing the small black button on a nearby call box. Moments later, an anonymous voice came over the line.

"Yes?"

"Royal and Ryder Justice to see Davis Benton."

"Just a moment, please."

Royal glanced at Ryder and shook his head. "Hell of a way to live, locked behind all this iron."

Ryder nodded as he looked around the estate. His wife had grown up almost the same way. Not behind walls and locked gates like this one, but within a world that certain members of society looked upon as fair game. The ultra-rich had their own set of problems, and in Ryder's opinion, having the money wasn't worth what came with it.

The gates began to open, and Royal glanced over his shoulder, checking for the umpteenth time to make sure the bag was still there.

"The sooner I get rid of that thing, the better I'm going to feel," he muttered.

"You forget," Ryder said. "The trouble hasn't even started. If Roman's theory is right, all hell could break loose after we get there."

Royal's eyes darkened and his jawline firmed. "I don't pretend to know what this is all about. Just remember...we watch Roman's back."

"Goes without saying," Ryder muttered, and patted his jacket, making sure that the handgun holstered beneath it was firmly in place.

"Here goes nothing," Royal said, and took off down the driveway.

As they came around a long, winding corner, they both straightened in their seats.

"Son of a—"

"Wow! Roman's 'client' has herself quite a spread," Ryder said. "That doesn't look like a house, it looks like a castle. All it needs is a moat."

They pulled up to the front door and parked. "You get the bag, I'll get the door," Ryder said. "Hope this doesn't take long. I'm starving."

The doorbell rang in the middle of the first course. Holly's fork clattered against her plate as she glanced up at Roman. He winked at her and then continued to eat as if nothing had happened.

"Are we expecting anyone?" Davis asked.

Holly shrugged. "Don't look at me. I wouldn't know who to invite, even if the urge struck me."

The sounds of footsteps could be heard coming down the hall. The long strides and steady rhythm of their steps signified men.

"That's odd," Gordon commented. "They're coming without being announced."

Roman leaned back in his chair, his gaze fixed on Gordon's face, while everyone else was staring at the doorway.

They entered side by side, their steps in unison with equally imposing expressions on their faces. Even though Holly had been prepared for the fact that they were Roman's brothers, she was unprepared for the similarities in their looks.

Well over six feet in height, with thick, black, straight hair and piercing blue eyes, the men commanded attention. Both were wearing Levi's, shiny with starch and creases that looked sharp enough to break. Their shirts were Western cut, one white, one pale blue. The Stetsons they wore were pulled low, and she had the distinct impression that it was more to hide what they were thinking than to shade their faces.

Roman stood. "You're late." Then he added an introduction as an afterthought. "Everyone, these are my brothers, Ryder and Royal Justice."

Ryder glanced around the table and then grinned at no one in particular.

"I think it's okay, Royal. They look safe enough to eat behind."

Davis Benton started to grin. He'd be surprised if he didn't like these men as much as he liked their brother.

"We've just started," he said. "Please, take a seat."

"Not until I get rid of this blasted bag," Royal said, and plopped it in the middle of the table.

Gordon's ears began to buzz as an overwhelming weakness swept through him. If he hadn't been sitting he would have surely fallen. Wild-eyed, he grabbed the arms of his chair, ready to bolt.

That's my bag! That's my money! What the hell is going on?

Everyone's attention turned from the bag to Holly when she suddenly stood. For several long, heart-stopping moments, she continued to stare at the bag as if it were evil. And then she closed her eyes and groaned, clutching at her head as if in terrible pain.

"Holly, sweetheart! What's wrong?" Davis asked.

Roman grabbed her as she swayed on her feet.

"Holly, are you sick?" he asked, pretending great concern.

Gordon started to get up when she suddenly screamed. And even though the men had been prepared for her act, they hadn't been expecting anything as realistic as what they heard.

"You!" she cried, pointing a shaking finger in Gordon's direction. "It was you!"

Completely out of his mind, he jumped to his feet. "She's hallucinating," he cried.

"No!" Holly moaned, and began circling the table, moving toward Gordon with single-minded intent.

Roman's heart skipped a beat. This wasn't part of the plan. He motioned for Royal to block the door, just in case Gordon decided to run.

Holly started to shake. There was a terrible knowledge inside of her that wanted to come out. And it came like a flood, spilling over the dam in her mind and pouring into her consciousness in one horrific memory after another.

"You killed him," she mumbled. "And you were going to kill me."

Roman was starting to panic. She wasn't pretending. She was remembering!

"She's crazy," Gordon said, and started backing up. "When she hit her head, it messed up her mind. I didn't kill anyone and I wouldn't kill her. I loved her, remember?" He pointed at Roman. "We were going to be married until he came along."

"Shut up!" Holly screamed. "You lie! You lie! You always lied, but I was too bored with my life to pay attention to the signs. There wasn't going to be any marriage. It was just a long playday weekend. But I was coming to tell you I didn't want to go to Nassau after all. Not with you. Never with you."

The brothers stood, frozen by the unexpected tableau being enacted before their eyes. They glanced at Roman. He was holding his own. They looked back at the woman. She was coming undone.

"I heard you and Billy arguing." Tears pooled in her eyes. "Carl Julian was skimming from the casino take. You said it was the perfect crime. You said he wouldn't report a theft of money he wasn't supposed to have."

Davis couldn't believe what he was hearing. In the middle of it all, a maid came into the room to serve the next course. He gave her quick orders to call the police. Looking wild-eyed, she hurried to do as she'd been told.

"You're lying," Gordon said. "Why would I kill a man I didn't even know?"

"For that!" she cried, pointing toward the bag. "For Carl Julian's money."

Roman moved, putting himself between Holly and Mallory.

"That's enough, baby," he said quietly. "We've got him now."

"No!" she said, and pushed at Roman, trying to get past. When he continued to stand in her way, she started to weep. "He knew that I'd overheard him arguing with Billy. He dragged me onto the plane. He said he was going to kill me. He was going to dump me out of the plane after it was airborne."

Roman blanked out on everything except what she'd endured at this man's hands. Before anyone knew what was happening, he had Mallory pinned against the wall with his hands around his throat.

"You cowardly son of a bitch. For two cents, I'd—"

Royal grabbed one arm, Ryder the other. "Turn him loose, Roman! Turn him loose! Let the authorities take care of him."

Holly grabbed her head and then groaned. "Please, no more," she begged. "No more killing."

It was her soft-spoken plea that reached through Roman's rage. As it began to subside and reality began to return, he dropped his hold on Mallory as if he'd suddenly become a thing of great filth. He turned toward Holly, catching her as she began to slump toward the floor.

"It's okay, baby, it's okay. I've got you and no one's ever going to hurt you again."

Her legs were shaking, but her mind was still clear.

"Billy saved my life," she said. "He put me in the parachute. He's the one who shoved the money in my hands. If it wasn't for him, I would have died."

Roman held her closer. "Thank God one of them had a conscience," he said.

At the mention of his brother's name, Gordon broke. "Hell yes, he had a conscience," he cried. "Everything was perfect until he went weak on me." He glared at Holly, and when he would have taken a step forward, found himself staring down the barrel of Ryder's gun.

"I wouldn't be moving if I were you," Ryder drawled.

Gordon stared at the gun and the man who held it. Then he looked past Holly, to the bag that was sitting in the middle of the table. So close...and yet so very far away.

Spittle was running from the corner of his mouth as he turned. "Damn you, bitch! You ruined everything. If it hadn't been for you, Billy wouldn't have betrayed me." His face was flushed with anger, and in the distance, the first sounds of sirens could be heard. The police were on the way. "He fancied himself in love with you, you know," Gordon said, and then laughed a dark, ugly laugh. "You didn't even know he existed, and yet he betrayed me, his own brother."

Holly shrank against the wall, only to find her father at her side.

"It's all right, sweetheart. He can't hurt you anymore," Davis said.

Roman pivoted, pinning Davis with a hard look. "Get her out of here. She's seen and heard enough for one day." Then he cupped her cheek as they started past him. There was a shell-shocked look on her face that made him nervous, but his pride in her overrode whatever fears he might have for their future. "You're a hell of a woman, Holly Benton."

She behaved as if she hadn't heard him speak. When she walked out of the room without looking back, he told himself not to panic. Then, before either of his brothers could stop him, he doubled his fist and turned. The punch he threw landed squarely on Gordon Mallory's jaw.

Gordon never saw what hit him, only an oncoming darkness, as if someone had just turned out the lights.

Royal took off his hat and scratched the back of his head. Ryder holstered his gun and then grinned.

"I'd say you got your point across, little brother. Now, let's get our story straight about what we're going to tell the cops."

The sirens they'd been hearing had suddenly stopped. It was obvious that they were here. There was a cold, hard look in Roman's eyes as he headed for the door.

"You don't have to tell them anything. If they want to know what happened to the son of a bitch, I'll tell them plain and simple. He messed with my woman."

All the way up the stairs, Holly kept reminding herself that her wish had come true. Now she remembered everything, including who she was, as well as who she'd been for the past few days. It was the latter that worried her more than the rest. Daisy had done things that Holly Benton would never have considered. But, Holly reminded herself, Daisy had done something in three days that Holly hadn't been able to accomplish in twenty-seven years. She'd found herself a man and fallen in love. In the face of that fact, Holly was a complete and utter failure.

With that on her mind, she fell into bed, barely aware of her father's presence.

Chapter 17

Gordon's worst nightmare was coming true, and there was nothing he could do to stop it. His jaw was aching and his head was still fuzzy. They'd handcuffed him within moments of his regaining consciousness, and now he was standing within feet of his precious money and it might as well have been on the moon for all the good it would do him.

Rage surged as an officer began to read him his rights. If he'd been free, he would have happily put a gun to Roman Justice's head and pulled the trigger, if for no other reason than to wipe the look he was wearing clean off of his face. Yet each time he looked at the man, Gordon found himself unable to withstand Roman's cold stare.

Gordon closed his eyes and turned away, momentarily focusing on the policeman's monotone voice.

"You have the right to..."

Gordon wanted to scream. Right? He didn't have any rights! What he had were handcuffs.

"If you so choose, one will be appointed..."

Choices? If it hadn't been so ironic, that would have made him laugh. He'd been making choices for most of his life, and so far, very few of them had been right. Why break tradition and start now?

"Do you understand...?"

Gordon sighed. Hell, yes, he understood. He understood everything. Other than the fact that he was pretty much screwed, there wasn't much left to determine.

And then there was silence. He blinked, suddenly aware that everyone was watching him and waiting for some sort of answer.

"Sir!" the policeman said. "Do you understand these rights as I've read them?"

Gordon glared, first at the policeman, then at Roman.

"Yes, I understand. I understand everything."

Roman's stare never wavered. Again, it was Gordon who looked away.

"Book him," the sergeant ordered, then he turned to Roman. "Sir, as I told you before, we'll be needing complete statements from everyone."

Roman nodded. "We'll be down in a couple of hours. I want to make sure Holly is up to it."

The man nodded and left, taking the remaining officers with him.

The dining room was suddenly quiet, like the lull after a storm. Roman ran a hand through his hair, and then turned to his brothers. There was a halfhearted grin on his face, and his eyes were almost twinkling.

"Thanks for coming," he said.

Royal returned the grin. "Thanks for the invitation. I wouldn't have missed this for the world."

Ryder glanced toward the table. "Hey, Roman, where were you sitting?"

Roman pointed, then grinned when Ryder picked a shrimp from his salad and popped it in his mouth.

"Missed breakfast," he said, and then reached for another.

"Help yourself," Roman said. "I've got to check on Holly."

Roman stalked out of the room, leaving his brothers on their own. They looked at each other and shrugged.

"Looks like we're going to another wedding," Ryder said.

Royal nodded. "As long as it's not mine, it's fine by me."

Ryder picked up another shrimp. "Don't be too cocky, big brother. You know what they say. The bigger they are, the harder they fall. Besides, you're the only one left and you can't hold out forever."

Royal shook his head. "You're dead wrong, Ryder. I've already got a woman in my life, and she's just about all I can handle."

They looked at each other, then back at the table and the uneaten food.

"What do you think?" Ryder said.

"What was it Mom used to say about people starving in China?" Royal asked.

"Right," they said in unison as each reached for a fork.

Roman had been through every room downstairs that Holly would have been in. The only place left was her bedroom. He took the stairs up, two at a time, needing to see her, to hold her, to make sure she was all right. He would never have imagined that their plan to trick Gordon into revealing his guilt would also result in triggering her memory. His heart was pounding all the way to her room. For her sake, he was glad the amnesia was behind her, but now he was faced with his greatest fear. In the grand scheme of the rest of their lives, where did that leave him?

He knocked once on her door and then entered. Holly was lying on her bed with an arm thrown over her eyes and a damp washcloth in her other hand. Roman thought she was asleep.

Davis was sitting in a chair near her bed. He stood as Roman entered.

"She's fine. Just resting," Davis said, and started to shake Roman's hand and then impulsively gave him a quick hug instead.

"I don't know how I can ever ' ..nk you. Thanks to you, I have my daughter back."

Roman shook his hea ... "I wasn't anything but backup. Holly is the one who deserves the credit. She had the guts to save herself, not once, but twice. It was my good fortune that she stumbled into my cabin."

But Davis would have none of it. "If you hadn't been there, she wouldn't be here, and we both know it."

Roman glanced toward Holly. He wanted to touch her, to talk to her, but he was afraid. Afraid to see the look on her face when she opened her eyes.

Davis looked at his daughter and then at Roman. "Well, now," he said briskly. "I'm sure there are a dozen things that need to be done."

"Are you going to call a doctor for her?" Roman asked.

"Yes," Davis said. "I was waiting for you to come before I left her. I'm sure she's all right, but I'll feel better if he checks her out."

Roman added. "You might want to check on my brothers. Last time I looked, they were giving the food on the table real serious consideration. There's a pretty good chance it's not there anymore."

Davis chuckled. "After the part they played in helping Holly, they can have anything their hearts desire."

"Don't tell them that or you'll be sorry."

Davis was still laughing as he closed the door behind him.

Now there was nothing in the room but Holly and a silence Roman couldn't ignore. His smile died as he turned toward the bed. Still lying with an arm across her eyes, she remained motionless. He took a deep breath and sat down beside her.

God help me. Please let this be all right.

He touched her arm. Her skin felt cold, almost clammy. He looked at her face. There were tears on her cheeks.

"Baby, are you all right?"

She turned without removing her arm, her voice sounded weak and just above a whisper. "My head. It hurts. It hurts so bad."

He stretched out on the bed beside her and then pulled her close, cradling her against the warmth of his body.

"Hang in there, Holly. Your dad is calling a doctor. He'll be here soon."

Holly hadn't been able to stop crying. The release of so much emotion had overwhelmed her. Yet the moment she felt his touch, the tension in her body began to ease. She shifted closer to him, taking strength from his presence.

"Roman?"

He pressed a gentle kiss at the back of her neck and then smoothed the hair from her face.

"What, baby?"

"Don't leave me."

As if he could. Pain tugged at his heart.

"I won't, I promise."

She sighed.

Minutes passed. Minutes in which Roman's thoughts went through hell and back. He'd held Daisy like this plenty of times, but this was the first time he'd held Holly in his arms. He loved them both enough to die for them twice over, and Daisy would have returned the favor. But what about Holly? He still didn't know her heart.

Just when he thought she'd fallen asleep, he heard her take a deep breath. She reached for his hand, threading her fingers through his and then pulling his arm a little closer around her.

"Roman."

"Yes?"

"I love you," she said softly, and then went to sleep.

God.

He closed his eyes, swallowing past the knot in his throat. Twice he took a long, deep breath, trying to gain control of his emotions. But it wasn't to be. Holly Benton had done to Roman's heart what no other woman had been able to do. She'd given him her trust and taught him to love.

Tears burned his eyes and at the back of his throat as he buried his face in her hair, inhaling the clean, fresh scent of her shampoo and the soft, sweet smell that was hers alone. He tightened his hold as his heart went free.

"That's good to know, baby, because I love you, too."

Epilogue

Night was looming as Roman took the last turn in the road.

"Are we almost there?" Holly asked.

He grinned. "Yes, Mrs. Justice, we're almost there."

Holly closed her eyes, savoring the sound of that name on his lips.

"Good."

"I hope you're not going to be disappointed. The cabin is a little rustic for a honeymoon."

She looked up. "It isn't rustic. It's romantic. Besides, it's where we started our relationship. It seemed only fitting that we should begin our married life there, as well."

Roman nodded. For the moment, speech eluded him. He loved this woman beyond words. Sometimes, it was easier to show her than to tell her. And if his brothers did as they'd been told, she would see soon enough.

"At least we don't have to worry about snow," she said, and then glanced at him and frowned. "It doesn't snow here in July, does it?"

He cocked an eyebrow and grinned. "I think we're safe."

She smiled. "Not that the fireplace wasn't cozy, but I have a new swimsuit. I want to go swimming."

"You won't be needing that suit."

Her smile faded. "Why not? Isn't there any place to swim?"

"You can swim all you want, but you won't be needing a suit."

She blushed, but the idea intrigued her. "I've never gone naked outdoors before."

His grin widened. "Well, now, you know what they say. There's a first time for everything."

When he began to slow down, Holly leaned forward in anticipation. It was strange, but in a way, this was her first visit. Daisy had been here, but Holly had not.

As they came around a curve in the road, he braked, giving her time to look. The last rays of sunlight were beaming upon the two-story A-frame cabin. The honey-colored logs seemed to be storing the fading sun's warmth. As she looked, her eyes filled with tears, remembering the relief she'd felt as she'd stumbled out of the forest and into the clearing. A place of safety.

She glanced at Roman. He was watching her. She tried to smile and failed. Her voice was shaking as she leaned against his arm. "I'm glad we came."

He tipped her chin upward, then went to meet her, capturing her mouth with a slow, gentle kiss.

"I'm glad we came, too," he said softly. Then he glanced through the windshield toward the setting sun. "We'd better get unloaded. It's going to be dark before you know it."

"Yes. I remember."

He touched the side of her face. "Feels good, doesn't it, baby?"

"What does?"

"To remember."

She sighed. "Oh, yes. More than you will ever know."

They parked at the cabin and began to unload the car. As Holly helped carry things inside, her thoughts kept returning to the events of the past months.

Of everything that had happened, one thing kept returning to haunt her. Billy Mallory. Was he all right or was he still running from his past?

As for Gordon, the evidence against him had been overwhelming. He'd been charged with theft, murder and kidnapping with intent to commit bodily harm. Holly's testimony sealed his fate. Spending the rest of his life behind bars without parole was a better sentence than he deserved.

His only saving grace had been denying that his brother had prior knowledge of any of his crimes until after they'd been committed. Gordon had maintained Billy's innocence throughout the entire trial. When asked, Holly had been able to answer truthfully that it was Billy Mallory who'd saved her life, as well as given her the stolen money to return. In the eyes of the world, Billy was a free man. It remained to be seen if he would ever forgive himself. Wherever he was, Holly hoped he knew she was grateful.

As they carried their things into the cabin, Roman sensed Holly's mood. She'd been through more hell in the past few months than most people would endure in a lifetime. Whatever it took for her to get through it was what she would have. He'd see to that.

Finally, everything was safely inside. It was only after Roman had closed and locked the door behind him that he began to relax. As he stood within the quiet, Holly came out of the kitchen. When she saw him standing by the door, she smiled. At that point, his heart took flight. It was true. She was here. And she was his for the rest of their lives.

Holly turned in a circle, looking up at the loft and then back at the kitchen.

"Oh, Roman, I feel like I've just come home."

"Come here, you," he growled, and then went to meet her, unable to wait.

He scooped her off of her feet and into his arms, then started walking toward the stairs.

Startled, she threw her arms around his neck for support and began to laugh.

"Shouldn't we unpack first?"

"It can wait. Now close your eyes."

She did as he asked.

He kept walking up the steps to the loft, holding her close against his chest as they returned to the proverbial scene of the crime. When he got to the landing, he stopped.

"Can I look?" she asked.

"Not yet," he said, and then set her on her feet.

"Now can I look?

He grabbed her by the shoulders and turned her around until she was facing the bed.

"Holly, baby..."

She was all but dancing with excitement.

"Yes?"

"Open your eyes."

The bed was the first thing she saw, and then what was on it.

"Oh, Roman."

She tried to say more, but the words wouldn't come. Her vision began to blur, but there was no way to mistake what she was seeing.

Daisies. They were everywhere. Hundreds upon hundreds of delicate white blooms with bright yellow centers. Scattered upon the bed, around the floor and across the pillows.

Roman pulled her close, letting his chin rest at the top of her head. His voice was low and filled with emotion, but there was no mistaking his intent.

"I'm going to make love to you there. And for the rest of your life, every time you see a daisy, you're going to remember this day...and me."

She turned. With tears streaming down her face, she reached for him.

"I told you once before that I might not remember my name, but I would always remember who loved me."

He nodded, silenced by the truth of her statement.

"The daisies will fade and the years will pass, but I will never...and I mean never...forget you, Roman. Do you understand?"

Nearly blinded by his own tears, he touched her face. "More than I would ever have imagined."

He picked her up and started toward the bed. Just before he laid her down among the flowers, he pressed one last, gentle kiss upon her mouth.

"No regrets?"

His tenderness was nearly Holly's undoing. Her breath caught at the back of her throat as she whispered against his lips.

"No regrets."

He'd been right after all. She would never forget the feel of silken petals sticking to her skin, or their clean, tangy scent filling the air as they crushed beneath the weight of their bodies. She wrapped her arms around him, holding on tight as he sent her to ecstasy.

It was forever a moment to remember.

Daisies in her hair.

Roman in her heart.

* * * * *

Don't miss the exciting finale to The Justice Way *miniseries! Look for Royal's story, coming in 1999—only from Silhouette's Intimate Moments.*

SILHOUETTE·INTIMATE·MOMENTS®
commemorates its

15 years of rugged, irresistible heroes!

15 years of warm, wonderful heroines!

15 years of exciting, emotion-filled romance!

In May, June and July 1998 join the celebration as Intimate Moments brings you new stories from some of your favorite authors—authors like:

Marie Ferrarella
Maggie Shayne
Sharon Sala
Beverly Barton
Rachel Lee
Merline Lovelace
and many more!

Don't miss this special event! Look for our distinctive anniversary covers during all three celebration months. Only from Silhouette Intimate Moments, committed to bringing you the best in romance fiction, today, tomorrow—always.

Available at your favorite retail outlet.

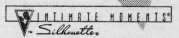

Look us up on-line at: http://www.romance.net   SIM15YR

Take 2 bestselling love stories FREE

Plus get a FREE surprise gift!

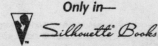

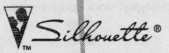

MATERNITY LEAVE

Coming September 1998

Three delightful stories about the blessings
and surprises of "Labor" Day.

TABLOID BABY by Candace Camp

She was whisked to the hospital in the nick of time....

THE NINE-MONTH KNIGHT
by Cait London

A down-on-her-luck secretary is experiencing
odd little midnight cravings....

THE PATERNITY TEST by Sherryl Woods

The stick turned blue before her
biological clock struck twelve....

*These three special women are very pregnant...and very
single, although they won't be either for too much longer,
because baby—and Daddy—are on their way!*

Available at your favorite retail outlet.